Praise for Sharon J. Mondragón

"A delightful, funny mystery populated by quirky characters and narrated by Sarah Elizabeth McCready, granddaughter of Grandma Ruth who 'doesn't go to funerals.' Grandma Ruth would never gossip, meddle, or pry, but she doesn't mind setting Sarah Elizabeth on the task of genteelly unraveling the mystery that has her oldest, dearest friend tied up in knots. A book you will want to read, then keep around to read again."

—PATRICIA SPRINKLE, author of the Thoroughly Southern
Mystery series

"Mondragón masterfully weaves a heartwarming tale of love, loss, and the enduring power of truth. With a cast of flawed but endearing characters and plenty of Southern charm, *Grandma Ruth Doesn't Go to Funerals* will stay with you long after you turn the final page."

—KATE ANGELO, best-selling author of *Hunting the Witness*

"Sharon Mondragón's stories are as charming as they are touching."

—KATIE POWNER, author of *The Wind Blows in Sleeping Grass*

"When I read Sharon Mondragón for the first time, I knew that I had found something special, a story that I wouldn't be able to forget and characters who worked their way into my heart."

—SUSIE FINKBEINER, author of *The All-American*

"The author writes with such reverence—in a way that describes a true relationship with God, Jesus, and the Holy Spirit."

—CHERI SWALWELL, founder of the Jesus in the Everyday
and author of *Adventure's Invitation*

Books by Sharon J. Mondragón

Purls and Prayers

The Unlikely Yarn of the Dragon Lady
The Tangled Tale of the Woolgathering Castoffs

Grandma Ruth Doesn't Go to Funerals

A NOVEL

Grandma Ruth Doesn't Go to Funerals

SHARON J. MONDRAGÓN

KREGEL
PUBLICATIONS

Grandma Ruth Doesn't Go to Funerals: A Novel
© 2025 by Sharon J. Mondragón

Published by Kregel Publications, a division of Kregel Inc., 2450 Oak Industrial Dr. NE, Grand Rapids, MI 49505. www.kregel.com.

The persons and events portrayed in this work are the creations of the author, and any resemblance to persons living or dead is purely coincidental.

Scripture quotations are from the ESV® Bible (The Holy Bible, English Standard Version®), © 2001 by Crossway, a publishing ministry of Good News Publishers. Used by permission. All rights reserved. The ESV text may not be quoted in any publication made available to the public by a Creative Commons license. The ESV may not be translated in whole or in part into any other language.

Funeral text excerpts taken from the Book of Common Prayer.

Library of Congress Cataloging-in-Publication Data
Names: Mondragón, Sharon J., 1957– author.
Title: Grandma Ruth doesn't go to funerals : a novel / Sharon J. Mondragón.
Other titles: Grandma Ruth does not go to funerals.
Description: First edition. | Grand Rapids, MI : Kregel Publications, 2025.
Identifiers: LCCN 2024034655 (print) | LCCN 2024034656 (ebook)
Subjects: LCGFT: Detective and mystery fiction. | Christian fiction. | Novels.
Classification: LCC PS3613.O52435 G73 2025 (print) | LCC PS3613.O52435 (ebook) | DDC 813/.6—dc23/eng/20240801
LC record available at https://lccn.loc.gov/2024034655
LC ebook record available at https://lccn.loc.gov/2024034656

ISBN 978-0-8254-4868-3, print
ISBN 978-0-8254-7433-0, epub
ISBN 978-0-8254-7432-3, Kindle

Printed in the United States of America
25 26 27 28 29 30 31 32 33 34 / 5 4 3 2 1

To Little Grandma,
whose heart was too loving,
her spirit too strong,
and her God too big
for the years she spent
confined to bed
to diminish her influence.

The steadfast love of the LORD never ceases;
his mercies never come to an end.

LAMENTATIONS 3:22

CHAPTER 1

GRANDMA RUTH DOESN'T GO TO funerals.

It's not that she gets squeamish or weak-kneed at the sight of a friend or relative laid out. She takes an avid interest in every detail of the deceased, from the tie they put on third cousin twice removed Billy Ray to how Harriet Tilson's hair turned out. Nor is it that she lacks respect for those who have gone on to glory before her. Grandma Ruth is the kind of person to whom you do *not* criticize your mother. And it's not that she prefers to stay home and watch *Jeopardy!* instead. Grandma Ruth is bedridden—has been for the past three years. Much as she would like to, Grandma Ruth isn't going anywhere.

I am Sarah Elizabeth, Grandma Ruth's favorite granddaughter. Being her favorite is a dubious honor. It means I'm her favorite to go to the store to buy birthday cards, visit her shut-in friends, and, you guessed it, attend funerals in her place.

Looking back, I realize I've been in training for funeral duty for quite a while. When I was ten, she taught me how to make macaroni and cheese from scratch to take by the home of the bereaved for the reception. By the time I was eleven, I had learned to write a tasteful and heartfelt condolence note. I attended my first funeral at twelve. (Grandma Ruth wanted to take me sooner, but Mama put her foot down and prevailed for once.) Now that I'm twenty-four, Grandma Ruth considers me not only fully qualified but socially obligated to take her place since she can't get out anymore. I don't think I've missed a single funeral in Raeburne's Ferry, Georgia, since she took to her bed.

That's why I was at Preston B. Harrington II's funeral on that un-settling January morning. I would not have gone if Grandma Ruth hadn't insisted. In fact, I tried to get out of it.

"Grandma, P. B. Harrington was a mean old buzzard. Why, one time when I was visiting, he threw a plate at his wife because his toast was the teensiest bit burnt around the edges. Mrs. Harrington just went back to the kitchen and made him another piece of toast. Now, *her* funeral you won't have to ask me twice about, but I don't want to take off work to pay my respects to the likes of P. B. Harrington."

I said this while examining the tips of my new black peep-toe high-heeled pumps. When I dragged my eyes away from my shoes to look at my grandmother, I wished I hadn't said anything at all.

Her voice was quiet, but her blue eyes snapped, crackled, and popped.

"Sarah Elizabeth McCready, this funeral *is* for Mrs. Harrington. She loved him, you know, and he wasn't always a plate thrower. Don't go telling that story around either," she said. "You know what they say about gossip."

"I know, I know, 'He who spits in the air . . .'" I sighed and just barely suppressed an eye roll.

"'. . . gets it soonest in the face,'" she said.

"Yes, ma'am." Further protest was futile.

"And you'd better not wear those shoes to the funeral if you're try-ing to discourage Jeff Morris."

Even though I'd given in to Grandma Ruth about P. B. Harrington's funeral, I wasn't looking forward to asking for the time off from work. It was early January, and the pace at Crawford and Associates, Certi-fied Public Accountants was picking up as we headed into tax season. Mr. Crawford, however, was delighted. Well, as delighted as anyone can appropriately be about a funeral.

"P. B. Harrington was a prominent citizen of Raeburne's Ferry in his day and a long-standing client of this firm. It is such a shame how he went downhill those last few years." Mr. Crawford shook his head sadly. "I know you'll represent the firm well at the observances. Take the whole day, Miss McCready. We can hold down the fort here. Oh, and would you take care of ordering the floral tribute? Something tasteful and restrained. Just have it charged to the firm's account. Have the card say . . ." He paused, his eyebrows drawn together as if he was puzzling over a particularly tangled account. "Well, I daresay you know what to put on it. Mary Ruth has given you enough practice over the years."

"Yes, sir." I headed back to my office before he could add anything else to my Harrington funeral to-do list. So far this included attending the viewing at the funeral home, making Grandma Ruth's signature macaroni and cheese casserole, dropping it off at the Harrington homeplace before the service, attending the funeral, interment, and reception, and now ordering flowers on behalf of the firm. Oh, and I'd have to remember to sign the guest book on behalf of Crawford and Associates as well as the McCready family.

I walked across the street to the Daisy Chain during my lunch hour to get a head start on the funeral list.

"I need to order flowers for the Harrington funeral," I told Abby Claire Harper, who looked something like a flower herself. Her spiky blond hair and warm brown eyes always made me think of sunflowers. The ink was barely dry on her horticulture degree from nearby Horton-Holgate University, but Abby Claire was already making her mark. When she started at the Daisy Chain, there was talk that she was wasting her degree. There was talk about her hair, too, as nobody ever walked into the Blue Moon Beauty Emporium and asked for hair that stuck up like that. But the talk died down quickly since her arrangements were breathtaking additions to happy occasions and always struck just the right note at funerals. It was clear that Abby Claire Harper had found her calling.

Abby Claire gave me a quizzical look. "Your grandmother doesn't usually send flowers."

"Yeah, she just sends me," I said. "This order is from Crawford and

Associates. Mr. Crawford says to put it on the firm's account. He said he wants 'something tasteful and restrained.' I imagine the restrained part refers to the cost."

"That means no roses," Abby Claire said. "The service is over at St. Alban's, isn't it?"

I nodded. "It's on Thursday morning at eleven."

"I love doing flowers for that church. The rich colors in those stained-glass windows give a lot of scope for the imagination. You'll want a card to go with that," she said. "This one will go with what I have in mind." Instead of one of the umpteen variations of white lilies that characterize the cards that usually accompany funeral flowers, this one had a classy black art deco border.

"Tasteful," I said as I carefully wrote *With Deepest Sympathy, Crawford and Associates* on the card and handed it back to Abby Claire.

She clipped it to the order sheet. "He'll be missed. The boss tells me he had standing orders for Valentine's Day, his wife's birthday, and their anniversary. I was going to get to do the Valentine's one this year. They were married over sixty years, so I planned on making it really romantic. And now Mrs. Harrington won't be getting flowers from him anymore," Abby Claire said with a sigh.

I was tempted to tell Abby Claire how that "romantic" man threw plates at his wife when she burned his toast, but I resisted. Considering how many people would be ordering funeral flowers over the next few days, it would be sure to get back to Grandma Ruth. I'm never in the mood for the gossip lecture.

I worked late the night before the funeral so as not to get too far behind from taking a day off. About an hour after the office emptied, I heard the cleaning crew arrive. I worked steadily to the sound of vacuum cleaners and the emptying of wastebaskets. Along about seven, Malcolm Hartwell, owner of Hartwell Office Cleaning, stuck his head around my door. He's been in business for years and years, but he still works alongside his crew at a different office each night to make sure his people are maintaining the company's standards. He has standards for his clients, too. He's been known to threaten to drop clients who make extra work for his people. Mr. Crawford has fielded only one such complaint. It was about the men's restroom here at the firm. The male CPAs took to practicing basketball shots with wadded-up paper towels in there—and couldn't be bothered to pick up the missed shots around the base of the trash can. Apparently, there had been quite a few missed shots. Mr. Crawford tried to take a "boys will be boys" attitude, but Mr. Hartwell was not amused. Mr. Crawford had to threaten to make the guys clean their own restroom, which brought basketball practice to an abrupt end.

"Still here, Sarah?" Mr. Hartwell shook his head as he came in to empty my wastebasket. "It's late. You should be getting on home."

I shook my head back at him. "'I have promises to keep and miles to go before I sleep.' I want to finish this account, and then I have to stop by Morris's. I promised Grandma Ruth I'd go to P. B. Harrington's viewing."

"'Stopping by Woods on a Snowy Evening.' Robert Frost sure knew what my evenings are like. Minus the snow, of course," he said with a grin. "I remember Mr. Harrington in his heyday. He convinced the partners to hire me way back when I first started the company, when I cleaned all the offices myself. He was a hard worker, just like you. Plenty of times I told him to go home to that lovely wife of his, but he would still be hard at it when I was finished. Not many at that firm worked as hard as he did. Shame how he went downhill toward the end."

I was tempted to say, "You don't know the half of it," but held my tongue to keep my promise to Grandma Ruth. Instead, I lifted my feet so Mr. Hartwell could vacuum under my desk.

At seven thirty I shut down my computer and headed over to the viewing at the Morris Funeral Home. As I waited for my turn to view the deceased, I took note of the floral arrangements, especially the one from Crawford and Associates. It was, indeed, tasteful and restrained, but only in appearance. The arrangement of white gardenias and blue forget-me-nots may have looked demure, but the heady fragrance of the gardenias filled the area around the casket. My grandmother would also want to know who had sent what.

When I turned my attention to Mr. Harrington, I had to admit he looked pretty good. The face that had been furrowed with deep lines of grumpiness was smooth and peaceful. Even his sharp, straight nose seemed softened somehow. You may think it morbid that I studied a dead man's face so closely, but from long experience, I knew that my grandmother would not be satisfied with, "He looked pretty good, Grandma." She would want the color of his suit, a description of his tie, and whether or not he was being buried with his wedding ring on. (He was.)

After taking inventory of Mr. Harrington, I went in search of his widow. Instead, I found Jeff Morris hovering nearby.

"Anything I can do for you, Sarah?" he asked in a low, somber, yet eager voice. "Anything at all?"

"I'm looking for Mrs. Harrington," I told him.

"She has gone home. She is taking this very hard," he said in the tone of a professional undertaker. His puppy-brown eyes drooped sadly. All the Morris men have those droopy eyes. I wondered whether that trait had lent itself to their success as funeral directors or had developed over three generations of sympathizing with the bereaved. Either way, it was depressing.

"Thank you, Mr. Morris. I will ask a family member to convey my grandmother's condolences."

"You can call me Jeff," I heard him murmur wistfully as I headed across the room.

I went straight to Grandma Ruth's room when I got home. It's everyone's first stop when they come to the house, to say hey and tell her all the news. Before she was bedridden, we'd go to the kitchen to fill her in while she plied us with cookies. She makes sure my mother keeps her well supplied with them so she can continue to elicit that same Pavlovian response.

"So?" Grandma Ruth prompted as I settled myself into the wing chair by her bed. I reached for one of the oatmeal raisin cookies piled on a plate on the bedside table. It had been a long time since lunch.

"He looked pretty good, Grandma," I said, just to tease.

She snatched the cookie out of my hand.

"All right, all right," I said, as she held it out of my reach. "He did look good, though. He had on a navy blue suit, a pale blue shirt, and a blue-and-burgundy paisley tie. He didn't look mean or grumpy at all. He looked peaceful and . . . and, well, satisfied." The thought had not occurred to me until that moment, but it was true. Was it simply the skill of the mortician, or had that crotchety old man finished his life completely content with what he had accomplished? "And yes, he was wearing his wedding ring."

"I should say so." Grandma Ruth harrumphed as she gave me back my cookie. "There never was a man more married than P. B. Harrington. Now about Charlotte—Mrs. Harrington to you, young lady—how is she holding up?"

"I didn't see her. One of the undertakers said she's having a real hard time and went home early. I spoke to Mr. Bent instead." In Raeburne's Ferry we have our own way of telling the four generations of Preston Bentley Harringtons apart. It all started with William Bentley, Esquire, the founder of Bentley, Harrington, Harrington, and Nidden. His daughter, Cordelia, married prominent local businessman, Preston Harrington. They named their firstborn son Preston, of course, after his father. Tradition is strong in Raeburne's Ferry, so his middle name had to be his mother's maiden name. The first Preston Bentley Harrington (Preston Senior, now deceased) grew up to be a lawyer and joined the firm. His son, Preston Bentley Harrington II, has always been "P. B." Then there's the third—but Preston Bentley Harrington III is quite a mouthful, so he goes by "Bent." (Of course, that's Mr. Bent to a young person like me.) The fourth and final Preston Bentley Harrington is simply "Preston."

My grandmother nodded. "I imagine she's exhausted. He *was* a bit trying toward the end."

A bit trying? I considered reminding her of the plate-throwing incident but decided against it. As I said before, I'm not fond of the gossip lecture, especially since Grandma Ruth is so fond of it—gossip, I mean, *and* the lecture.

Mama appeared in the doorway. "Your supper's on the table, Sarah. I hope you still have an appetite after those cookies."

Back in the kitchen, I tucked into pot roast that nearly melted in my mouth.

"Plan on sleeping in tomorrow morning," my mother said. "You look worn out."

"I can't," I said around a mouthful of roasted carrot. "I still have to make the macaroni and cheese casserole."

"I thought you could use a break from putting together that everlasting casserole," she said as she opened the refrigerator. The shallow casserole dish that our family always uses for that ultimate Southern comfort food rested on the middle shelf, covered in foil. "All you have to do is bake it in the morning before you go."

"Thank you, Mama."

My mother is a genuinely kind and compassionate person. She had to be, to survive teaching eighth grade math for over twenty years. She often stayed late to tutor, since a lot of kids went into a tizzy when the x's and y's of algebra showed up right after they'd finally figured out numbers. About the time Mama couldn't stand it anymore, Grandma Ruth fell and broke her hip. I was home from college for the summer, and the two of us took care of her. By the beginning of August, it became clear that my grandmother would not be able to get around on her own anytime in the near future or maybe even anytime at all.

Mama retired from teaching, and she and Daddy moved from the bungalow where I had grown up to the McCready homeplace so they could take care of Grandma Ruth. The house was built by one of my daddy's ancestors back in the early 1800s and has been occupied by McCreadys ever since. When I came home for Christmas break, I found my room exactly as I'd left it, except it was in a different house. It wasn't that much of an adjustment when all was said and done. I'd spent a lot of my childhood at the homeplace, heading there after school while Mama talked eighth graders down from the ledge over algebra.

The thing that *did* take some getting used to was Grandma Ruth confined to bed. Before her fall, my grandmother was an elderly version of the Energizer Bunny. If she wasn't on her way to choir practice, getting her hair done, or attending a funeral, she was playing bingo, making quilts, or getting in nine holes at the country club with her friends. And the kitchen always smelled of fresh-baked cookies because she needed a steady supply to keep us all talking.

After her fateful fall, she was ensconced in a hospital bed in the front parlor with a window to look out of and a phone on the table by her bed. Before you start to feel sorry for her, though, may I remind you of the conversation in which I was railroaded into attending P. B. Harrington's funeral? Being bedridden simply meant she channeled her considerable energy into staying connected to the life of Raeburne's Ferry by any means necessary. I was so used to saying "Yes, Grandma" from the time I could talk that when I came home from college to work at Crawford and Associates, she managed to take over my life before I even realized what was happening.

I hear what you're saying to yourself. "She's a grown woman, a college graduate. Why doesn't she just say no?" Well, I dare you to come by the house when Mary Ruth McCready really wants something done and see how *you* do. Right. I'll save you a seat at the funeral she makes you attend.

CHAPTER 2

THE DAY OF PRESTON B. Harrington II's funeral dawned cold and bright. I dressed carefully in my winter funeral outfit, a charcoal-gray sweater dress with a scoop neck that shows off the pearls my daddy gave me when I graduated from high school. I went down the back stairs so as to avoid a critique of my attire. My grandmother doesn't approve of the way that sweater dress clings "in all the wrong places," as she puts it. I think it looks great on me. I don't see why I should have to look frumpy to show respect to the dead. I think it makes it all the more depressing for the bereaved to have that sea of black dowdiness stretching out behind them in the church.

I baked the macaroni and cheese, tucked it into Mama's thermal casserole keeper, and headed over to the Harringtons'. Patti Sue Seiden, another funeral aficionado, met me at the kitchen door and relieved me of my burden.

"So thoughtful," Patti Sue murmured as she patted the casserole keeper dolefully. "There's no more room in the ovens." Over her shoulder, I could see that the counters were filling up fast with food for the reception.

"How's Mrs. Harrington doing?" I asked.

Patti Sue's voice dropped to a mournful whisper. "It's pitiful, Sarah Elizabeth, just pitiful. She wouldn't eat a bite this morning, no matter how we coaxed her."

"Well, I'm sure it's a comfort to her to have you taking care of the food." The wind was whipping up as I stood at the door. I hunched my shoulders against the cold. "I'd better be going. You'd better head out soon, too, if you want a good seat."

"I'll be along directly," Patti Sue said. "The Eifflebachers are saving me a seat toward the front."

The church was filling up by the time I got there, fifteen minutes early. I never have to worry about getting a good seat. My grandmother always sat in the seventh pew from the front on the left-hand side of the church—on the aisle, of course. The Episcopalians of St. Alban's are an orderly people. They like to have a place for everything and everything in its place. This extends to people as well. Once you sit down in a service at St. Alban's, they expect you to sit in that spot every time you come to church. It didn't matter that Grandma Ruth couldn't attend church anymore. Since I was her proxy, her seat was reserved for me, defended by Mrs. Vivian Morgan's fur coat draped across the back of the pew in case some non-Episcopalian (bless his heart) took it into his head to sit there.

"Thank you," I whispered to Mrs. Morgan as I took my seat. Mrs. Morgan just nodded in that regal way of hers.

I settled back into the sun-warmed pew. My grandmother had known what she was doing when she chose her seat in church. I had a clear view of the pulpit, the altar, the casket, and the pew where the family of the deceased would sit. I breathed in the faint scent of incense that always lingered in the air of St. Alban's. When I was little, I thought it was what angels smelled like.

The church was packed by the time the family came up the center aisle to fill the front pew. Mrs. Harrington's grandson, Preston, escorted the widow to her seat. The top of her black pillbox hat barely reached his shoulder. The rest of her ensemble was equally stylish—trim black suit, gray silk blouse, pearls at her throat, and low-heeled pumps. As she passed my pew, I saw that her eyes were full and ready to spill her sadness down her face. She clutched a lace-trimmed handkerchief that was already limp with tears. I wondered how she would manage to make it through the service.

Not well, as it turned out. She sobbed and boohooed through the music, the Scripture readings, and especially the eulogy and remarks from friends and family. Every reference to what a fine, upstanding man of character and integrity P. B. Harrington had been brought fresh torrents of tears from the front pew. At long last, Father David and the deacons came around the altar rail and took their places at the casket for the Commendation.

"Into your hands," Father David intoned, "O merciful Savior, we commend your servant, Preston. Acknowledge, we humbly beseech you, a sheep of your own fold, a lamb of your own flock, a sinner of your own redeeming. Receive him into the arms of your mercy, into the blessed rest of everlasting peace, and into the glorious company of the saints in light. Amen."

P. B. Harrington would need that mercy and redemption, I reflected as Father David removed the pall and the pallbearers came forward. Surely God takes a dim view of heaving plates at wives over burnt toast. We all stood as the casket passed down the center aisle, followed by the immediate family. As Mrs. Harrington passed, almost sagging against her grandson, I heard her heave a shuddering sigh and say, "Oh, if only I knew! If only I knew!"

If only she knew what? If she'd see him again in heaven? I had no doubt Mrs. Harrington would be welcomed at the pearly gates, if for no other reason but the saintly way she made toast, but you had to wonder about the old grouch who threw it at her.

I didn't have far to go for the interment. St. Alban's has its own churchyard situated between the church and the rectory. The Harrington family plot is under a huge oak tree. We gathered, shivering, under its spreading limbs to which a few lifeless brown leaves still clung, fluttering above us in the breeze. I looked out over the churchyard. The sky had turned cloudy during the funeral service. The churchyard looked and felt dismal, with forlorn wreaths that relatives had placed at Christmas still propped against some of the weathered headstones.

"Plastic floral tributes." Mrs. Morgan sniffed her disapproval to Mrs. Fogarty, who was standing next to her. "I keep telling Father he shouldn't allow it, but he lets people bring anything they want, no matter how tacky it looks."

She said it loud enough for Father David to hear. He looked up from his prayer book at her, his gray eyes steady and unperturbed. When she looked away, he began the committal service.

"'In the midst of life, we are in death . . .'"

As the familiar words rolled past me, I took note of the mourners. Grandma Ruth would want to know who had attended the burial and who had bugged out after the service in the church. Some folks never attend the burial, even if it's in the churchyard and doesn't involve a procession to the Magnolia Cemetery on the outskirts of town. If it were up to me, I'd skip it, too. I've never liked the sound of that handful of dirt hitting the coffin lid. It is not, however, up to me. Grandma Ruth had always been fully present for every part of the funeral rite, so I had to be, too.

I spent a good portion of the graveside service sidling away from Jeff Morris, the third-generation funeral director who had the mistaken idea that I was attracted to him. (I simply had to wear those peep-toe pumps. They were too new and too cute.) Grandma Ruth often spoke to me of what a nice young man he was, with a good, steady job.

"I can find my own boyfriend should I feel the need," I would tell her through clenched teeth.

"Believe me, you need one," she'd say. "Better yet, a husband. And do you think love will walk up and tap you on the shoulder while you bury yourself in that career of yours? No, it's going to pass you by because you're not paying attention . . ." and so on and so forth.

Jeff caught up with me at the benediction.

"Remember, dear friends," Father David intoned, "how short life is and how little time we have to gladden the hearts of those who travel with us. So be quick to love and make haste to be kind and may the blessing of God the Father, Son, and Holy Spirit be upon you now and forever."

The "amen" was punctuated by a tap on my shoulder. It was Jeff. He shot his cuffs (French, with somber black onyx cuff links), cleared his throat, and offered me a ride to the reception.

"You can ride up front with me in the limousine," he said eagerly. Did he think he was gladdening my heart?

"Uh, well, I'm going to the reception, but I don't need a ride," I stammered. Good grief, if I ever did go out with him, would he pick me up in a Morris Funeral Home limousine? It'd be better to meet him at the restaurant or movies or whatever. *Wait. What?* I mentally slapped myself. *Get a grip. You are not going out with Jeff Morris, no matter what Grandma Ruth says.*

His eyes drooped a tad more as he looked down and away. "Just thought I'd ask," he mumbled, then hurried off to help the bereaved into the waiting limousine. I immediately felt guilty. "Make haste to be kind," Father David had said. But was it really kind to encourage him when I wasn't interested?

In high school, I was a sucker for boys who gave me that same pleading look, but I was never impressed with the ensuing relationships. I decided I was done going out with guys because I felt sorry for them. Then Jake Halloran—the one guy who wasn't a pity date, the one I thought was the answer to my prayers, who swept me off my feet and seemed perfect in every way—turned out to be the biggest loser of them all. Hopes and dreams and trust had died, with the dirt of Jake's betrayal heaped on top like the soil that would soon fill in P. B.'s grave. No, I wasn't in any hurry to give the time of day to any man and certainly not hangdog Jeff Morris who wanted to squire me around in the next thing to a hearse.

There was quite a spread at the Harrington homeplace. Friends, neighbors, and church ladies had gone all out. The long table in the formal dining room was spread with a white damask cloth. The family silverware, polished to perfection, was arrayed at one end in front of a stack of Haviland china luncheon plates. Everyone had brought their best funeral dishes for the occasion.

In addition to the McCready macaroni and cheese, there was a gracious plenty of chicken salad sandwiches, three plates of deviled eggs, one tomato aspic, a cheese and potato casserole that was disappearing fast, a generous platter of sliced ham, cheese straws, a basket of biscuits, and three potato salads, to name only a few of the dishes vying for space on the table.

The sideboard was laden with assorted desserts, including Patti Sue Seiden's Black Forest cake, four different kinds of pound cake, and a large bowl of banana pudding. I knew who had brought every single offering by their serving dishes. I don't know why any of us still bother to put a piece of masking tape with our names on the bottom of our platters, bowls, and casseroles.

A crowd had gathered at the far end of the dining room where a coffee urn and silver tea service were getting short shrift in favor of the wine also being served there. I filled my plate to a ladylike level and headed to the parlor to give Mrs. Harrington the condolences of the McCready family and Crawford and Associates.

She was seated on the couch, tears running down her face. Several of her friends were trying to comfort her.

"You were a good wife, Charlotte," said Mrs. Morgan. "You took good care of him right up to the end."

"Yes, dear," said Mrs. Fogarty, as tiny as Mrs. Morgan was tall. "You were patient and kind no matter what. No man could have asked for a better wife."

"I don't understand," Mrs. Harrington moaned. "I just don't understand."

"Goodness, Charlotte," Mrs. Morgan said, losing patience. "He was eighty-five years old and not in the best of health. Surely you weren't surprised."

"No." Mrs. Harrington sniffed into the tissue Mrs. Fogarty pressed into her hand. "I've known for weeks it was coming. I just wish I knew what he meant. His last words to me, his very last words, were—" Her voice caught. I saw her fight to gain enough control to get the words out. At last, she sat up straighter, took a large swallow from the glass of chardonnay she held in her other hand, and said, "His last words were 'I loved you more than Millie.'" She gripped her glass so tightly I thought it might shatter. "Who's Millie? I never knew he loved anybody named Millie. I thought I was the only one he ever loved. How could he say something like that and then just up and die without explaining?"

How indeed, I thought. Sure, he'd said he loved her *more* than Millie, but to even mention another woman in his dying breath was just plain . . . well, I told you he was mean.

CHAPTER 3

MRS. HARRINGTON TOOK ANOTHER GULP of wine and dissolved into tears again.

"Pull yourself together, Charlotte," Mrs. Morgan said. "Whatever he meant, this is not the time to talk about it. *You have guests.*"

"Yes, Charlotte, think of your guests." Mrs. Fogarty nodded. "Let me get you some of that banana pudding, dear. That'll make you feel better."

Mrs. Harrington, however, had finished off her glass of wine and thrust the empty goblet at Mrs. Fogarty. "I'd rather have more of this."

"Are you sure that's wise, dear?" Mrs. Fogarty said anxiously. "You've already had—"

Mrs. Harrington's lower lip began to tremble, and Mrs. Fogarty was undone. She hurried off to get more wine for the grieving widow. I hoped Mrs. Fogarty would "forget" to come back. I had only ever seen Mrs. Harrington sipping delicately from a teacup at funeral receptions.

I took the opportunity presented by the wine run to take Mrs. Fogarty's place on the sofa to convey our condolences. Mrs. Harrington squeezed my hand and ran on about how sweet it was for me to come in my grandmother's place.

"Mary Ruth is one of my dearesht friends," she said as she let go of my hand to accept the glass of wine from Mrs. Fogarty. Mrs. Fogarty looked relieved to see that I had taken her place and headed off to the dessert table. "An' you, Sarah 'lizabeth, so sweet to come by to visit us now and then."

"You already said she was sweet," Mrs. Morgan said irritably.

"Well, she *is*," Mrs. Harrington insisted, and spilled a little wine onto the napkin on her lap.

"Let me get you a chicken salad sandwich, ma'am," I said. Anything to start sopping up that wine in her empty stomach.

"How sweet, dear. And get me some more of this while you're at it." She waved her half-empty goblet at me.

"Just a tad," I said as I took it from her. I knew *I* could manage to misplace it on the way back from the table.

I left the goblet in the kitchen and then stood in line to fill a plate with the sandwiches for which Mrs. Bubba Morrison is famous, at least in Raeburne's Ferry. No funeral reception around here would be complete without the tiny triangles filled with her special version of chicken salad, the crusts neatly trimmed from the thin slices of white bread.

By the time I got back, however, it was too late for the sandwiches to do much good. Mrs. Harrington's grief rose to a wail as I stepped into the sitting room, plate in hand.

"I don' unnershand. I jus' don' unnershand! There was never anyone else but me! Jus' me, ever 'n always. Tell them!" She turned and peered at Mrs. Morgan. "Who are you again?" Before Mrs. Morgan could answer, Mrs. Harrington blew her ladylike nose loudly into her tissue. "If he—if he—well, if he did, I'll jus' kill him, thash all!" With this, she threw her arms around Mrs. Morgan and sobbed as if her heart would break.

Mrs. Harrington III came in and knelt in front of her mother-in-law. "It's been a trying day, Miss Charlotte. Maybe it's time you had a lie-down. I'm sure all your guests will understand."

Mrs. Harrington lifted her head from Mrs. Morgan's damp shoulder and looked at her daughter-in-law, her blue eyes bleak and bleary. "Tha's jus' it, Ly'ia. I don' unnershand. I jus' don' unnershand."

Lydia Harrington beckoned her son. "Preston, come give me a hand here." He crossed the room in two strides.

Mrs. Harrington looked up at her grandson and beamed through her tears. "Oh, Preshton, how nishe to see you. Sush a goo' boy, my grandson," she said aside to me. "Perfec' for you, I alwaysh thought."

I felt my face flame and knew I was blushing to the roots of my hair. Unlike Jeff Morris, Preston B. Harrington IV is *not* pathetic looking. For one thing, his eyes are blue, not hangdog brown. A soft shade of blue, like a pair of well-worn, comfortable jeans. They crinkle nicely at the corners when he smiles.

"I'll help you, Preston." Leslie Nidden bounced up from a chair across the room.

Preston helped his grandmother up from her chair and wrapped his arm around her tiny waist. His broad shoulders cleared a path for Mrs. Harrington through the sitting room. Leslie twittered and fussed alongside. As he guided his grandmother down the hall, Leslie shot a poisonous look at me over her shoulder. Mrs. Harrington III followed in their wake, murmuring to the guests she passed that Miss Charlotte was worn out. She urged them to stay and visit with one another.

"Don't you pay that Nidden girl no never mind," Patti Sue Seiden said at my elbow. "She thinks that just because her daddy is a partner in the firm that she's got sole rights to Preston. It's what Miss Charlotte thinks that really counts, though, so you have nothing to worry about."

It had never occurred to me to worry about Leslie Nidden—or Preston either, for that matter. Oh, I suppose every girl in my class at Raeburne's Ferry High had a crush on Preston at one time or another, myself included. He'd been so clearly out of my league, though, that the idea of dating him hadn't been worth more than sighing over a time or two. Then senior year Jake Halloran came into my life, sweeping thoughts of any other boy and a good deal of my common sense right out of my head.

"I wouldn't put too much stock in what Mrs. Harrington said just now," I said in a low voice to Patti Sue. "She's . . . um . . ." I couldn't bring myself to say out loud that Mrs. Harrington was drunk.

"*In vino veritas.*" Patti Sue gave me a knowing look and headed back to the kitchen.

"If looks could kill, they'd be carrying you out, too," Meredith Mayhew said as she slid into the space Mrs. Harrington had vacated on the couch. Meredith is a paralegal at Bentley, Harrington, Harrington, and Nidden, and has been my best friend since kindergarten. "I'd snag him right out from under Leslie Nidden's long, snooty nose if I were you."

"Is that any way to talk about your employer's daughter?" I whispered. "Mr. Nidden might hear you."

"You could do a whole lot worse than Preston. I say go for it," Meredith whispered back.

Meredith would say that. Unlike me, she is eager to get married as soon as possible, mainly to change her last name. Her mother insisted on the tradition of giving her daughter her maiden name as a middle name, even though it resulted in the unfortunate full name of Meredith Meriwether Mayhew. And yes, the nickname her family gave her—Merrie Merrie May—stuck.

She is so desperate for a different last name that she even dated my charming but no-good cousin, Reggie. I knew it would be no use to tell her that was a lost cause. Reggie inspires a *Beauty and the Beast* complex in naive young women. While they dream of being the pure flower of Southern womanhood whose influence will redeem him, Reggie just keeps on cultivating his irresistible bad-boy image. That is not to say I stood by and let him break her heart. She is my best friend, after all. I did not dash her hopes of getting him to the altar, but I did point out that as Meredith Mayhew McCready, her monogram would still be the three spiky Ms she hates so much.

"My monogram looks like 'mmm . . . yummy,'" she often complains. "Like I'm a particularly toothsome piece of peach cobbler."

It was, thankfully, enough to put her off him. Reggie had never been dumped before. She had to repeat herself three times before it started to sink in, and even then, he tried to charm her out of it. When she stood her ground, he tried to enlist me to intercede for him, crocodile tears in those chocolate-chip brown eyes that have melted so many female hearts.

"I wouldn't wish you on my worst enemy," I told him. "What makes you think I'd wish you on my best friend?"

"You're still mad about prom, aren't you?"

"That and about a million other things," I snapped. I will not go into the prom incident here. Suffice it to say that the dirty tricks my cousin Reggie has pulled on me and many other people would fill a book. "Go break some other girl's heart. Leave Meredith alone. Go on. Shoo." In the end, he'd had no choice but to shoo.

"I wonder if we could sic Reggie on Leslie," I said to distract Meredith from her plan to marry me off to Preston.

"Hmm . . ." Meredith considered this. "If anyone could distract her from Preston, it would be Reggie." There was an if-only-his-last-name-didn't-start-with-M wistfulness in her voice.

"I'll bet the banana pudding is going fast."

Meredith snapped out of her nostalgia for my ne'er-do-well cousin and joined me at the dessert table.

I stood around chatting with Meredith and ignoring Leslie's dirty looks for another hour. By then those black peep-toe high-heeled pumps were killing me. I expressed my condolences to Mrs. Harrington III, made lunch plans with Meredith, and took my leave. The macaroni and cheese casserole had been polished off long ago, but I didn't swing by the kitchen to take the dish home. Under Patti Sue's supervision, it was undoubtedly already washed, dried, and sitting on a counter, but I was under strict instructions from Grandma Ruth to retrieve the casserole dish one week after the reception, so as to visit with (read that *check on*) the bereaved.

The warmth of dinner preparations in full swing enveloped me when I stepped through the back door of the homeplace. Something wonderful was simmering in the Crock-Pot. My mother looked up from cutting biscuits.

"Your grandmother is waiting for you, none too patiently. Her phone's been ringing off the hook, but she refuses to get the news about the funeral from anyone but you."

"I *have* to get out of these shoes, Mama," I said as I limped up the back stairs to my room and a pair of comfy slippers.

"She told you not to wear those," my mother called after me.

"It's about time, young lady." Grandma Ruth greeted me when I stepped through the parlor doorway. She glanced at my feet. "I don't imagine Jeff Morris was sorry you wore those shoes, even if you are."

"My feet are cold," I said. I wasn't about to tell her anything about Jeff Morris. "It's bitter out there."

She waved her hand dismissively from the warmth of the shawl around her shoulders. "It's not as though I didn't warn you."

"Yes, Grandma," I said with an inward roll of the eyes. I settled into the easy chair that faces her bed. The lamp on the bedside table cast a rosy glow over the plate of cookies that rested there.

She passed me the cookies, and after a thoughtful bite of oatmeal raisin, I began, in the way I knew she loved best. She always wanted to start with the flowers and the names of the senders, even though we'd been over that the night before. As I did, I realized there had been no flowers from anyone named Millie, though some of the cards said only "Mr. and Mrs. So-and-So," with no first names included.

From the flowers, I went on to the music. "At the reception, I heard Mrs. Morgan say that Mr. Harrington planned his own service years ago, right down to the music. He had 'The Lord's Prayer' and 'God Moves in a Mysterious Way.'" I went on to describe Mrs. Hanson's reedy voice reaching for the high note at the end of the second line of "God Moves."

"Such a thoughtful man," Grandma Ruth said. "It's hard enough to lose someone without having to plan the funeral, too. Don't forget about my funeral book when my time comes, Sarah."

"I won't, Grandma." I averted my eyes from the bookcase where the leather-bound book that contained instructions for her final occasion rested on the third shelf from the top. It is written by hand and covers everything from the music and Scripture readings to whether we should have her casket open at the viewing. ("If I look good, casket open. If I don't look good, casket closed.") I've been to a lot of funerals, but I don't like to think about hers.

"And so thoughtful of P. B. to remind us in that last hymn that there is a plan, no matter how hard or baffling life seems to be," she said.

"Speaking of baffling," I said. "You would not believe what else I heard at the reception."

My grandmother, however, would not be lured from her accustomed funeral litany. I had to recap the rector's eulogy—complete with texts—relate the remarks of family and friends, and list everyone present at the service. Grandma Ruth nodded as I detailed the accomplishments for which Mr. Harrington was remembered. Years ago, he had spearheaded the building fund to renovate the church in which I had worshipped all my life. He'd been a Boy Scout leader and a catch-playing, fishing-trip kind of dad. He'd been a trusted lawyer and a friend you could count on.

"And someone said, kind of low, but loud enough for me to hear, 'And a da—'" I hesitated, knowing how my grandmother felt about strong language. "'—darn good businessman,'" I said.

"Who was it?" Grandma Ruth asked.

"This lady in a really sharp suit," I replied. "I didn't recognize her. She must be a relative from out of town."

When I got to the part about Mrs. Harrington's loud and tearful exit, Grandma tsked.

"He was only an old grouch for the last few years of his life, Sarah. They had a good and rich life together. I have to admit, though, I'm surprised at Charlotte. I've seen her perfectly composed in every kind of situation. When Bent had that horrible car accident, she was a rock for his wife, Lydia, and someone calm the doctors could explain things to." She smiled to herself. "I remember the time a snake got into church, and she almost knelt on it at the communion rail. She pointed it out to P. B. as cool as you please. He and the church warden removed it, and the service went on as though nothing had happened. Of course, P. B. was there, and she could face anything with him."

She nodded as I described the location of P. B.'s grave. A faithful grave visitor until she broke her hip, she recognized the exact spot where Mr. Harrington now lay.

"She'll want to plant some nice impatiens in that shade this spring. A little too close to Uncle Hubert, though," she mused. The only people not buried too close to my great-uncle Hubert were other blackhearted reprobates. Maybe she'd change her mind once I told her about Mr. Harrington's last words to his wife.

But first I listed everyone at the reception, including Father David, the church ladies, the Rotary Club, the Raeburne's Ferry Harringtons, some cousins from Chicago, and the entire staff of Bentley, Harrington, Harrington, and Nidden, Attorneys at Law.

"What about the lady in the sharp suit?" Grandma Ruth wanted to know.

I thought a moment. "She was at the graveside, but she didn't come to the house."

"Hmm," my grandmother said.

At last, it was time to drop the bombshell, to tell the juiciest morsel of all.

"I don't know, Grandma," I said. "This next part might be gossip."

"From the way my phone's been ringing, it's all over town already," she snapped. "At this rate, I'll be the last to know."

"You're not going to like it," I said.

"Let me be the judge of that."

And so I told her all about P. B. Harrington's last words to his wife, Mrs. Harrington's tears, and the chardonnay.

"She was *not* drunk, Sarah Elizabeth," Grandma Ruth told me with a look that made me quail. "Don't you go spreading that around." (As if *I* were the one we had to worry about.)

"But she was slurring her words, Grandma, and she'd had a lot of wine on a completely empty stomach," I said.

"She was worn out, as Lydia said. True ladies like Mrs. Harrington do not so forget themselves as to become intoxicated, especially in public."

Grandma could deny it all she wanted. I know tipsy when I see it.

"'I loved you more than Millie,'" Grandma Ruth mused, now that she had disposed of the inebriation question. "I don't remember any Millie from around here, at least not the right age. I had an aunt who insisted we call her Aunt Millicent. We called her Silly Milly behind her back."

"What about college?" I asked. "She could have been someone he met at college."

Grandma Ruth shook her head. "He and Charlotte were high school sweethearts. They were engaged before he left for Harvard."

"I never knew he went to Harvard." No wonder he'd looked so smug in the casket.

"Indeed," Grandma said. "He graduated in the top ten percent of his class at Harvard Law School."

"He still could have met someone at college named Millie," I said. "I'll bet Millie was some hussy who threw herself at him and he could hardly help himself."

Grandma Ruth fixed me with a stare that told me I was indulging in wild speculation that bordered on disrespect. It was just a look, but it had all those words in it.

"You'd have to have seen them together back then, Sarah." Grandma Ruth looked past my face into a time as alive to her as the present moment, a time that lives for me only in her stories. "They had this glow about them. She was only sixteen when they were engaged, but her father raised no objections. There was an undeniable rightness about them. Let me show you."

My grandmother pointed to her bookcase, where her high school yearbooks occupied the bottom shelf. She leafed through one until she found the Senior Superlatives page. Mr. Harrington had been voted "Most Intelligent" his senior year. A few pages on, there was a picture of an impossibly young Mr. and Mrs. Harrington at a school dance.

"Doesn't do them justice," Grandma Ruth murmured and reached for another yearbook. She showed me that, in the year that Mrs. Harrington graduated from Raeburne's Ferry High, she had been voted "Most Likely to Marry a Harvard Man."

"I never knew he was so smart," I said.

"It's a family trait," she said. "His father was the first Harrington of Bentley, Harrington, Harrington, and Nidden. It was always understood that P. B. would go to Harvard like his father and join the firm. He was happy enough as a lawyer, but you notice he didn't object when his son wanted to go to business school instead. At least it was still Harvard, and he was in the top ten percent at Harvard Business School."

Actually, I hadn't noticed. Mr. Bent was my dad's age.

CHAPTER 4

WHEN I ARRIVED HOME AFTER work on Monday, Mama greeted me with a plate of cookies. As it turned out, however, they were not for me.

"Take these on through to your grandmother and Mrs. Harrington," she told me. "I'm in the middle of making supper."

"There you are," Grandma Ruth said when I stepped into the parlor. Mrs. Harrington looked up from her seat by the bed, her pale blue eyes magnified by brimming tears. She blinked and sat up a little straighter.

"How nice to see you, Sarah." Her soft voice was warm and refined at the same time. "It was kind of you to attend P. B.'s funeral. I'm sorry I didn't have a chance to speak with you at the reception."

"Don't give it another thought, ma'am." I wasn't about to say anything that would imply she didn't remember because of the, *ahem*, wine—especially with Grandma Ruth's gimlet eye on me.

"Have a cookie, Sarah," Grandma Ruth said, deftly changing the subject.

"No, thank you. I should help Mama with supper." What I really wanted was to get out of my heels.

"Nonsense," my grandmother said. "Your mother can spare you. Sit down."

I sat.

"You were saying, Charlotte?" Grandma Ruth said to Mrs. Harrington.

"Yes, Mary Ruth, I was about to tell you about—" Mrs. Harrington's lower lip trembled. She pressed her lips together for a moment and then continued in a rush. "About P. B.'s last words, which I don't understand at all.

"I knew the end was near," she began. "I didn't want to miss a single moment with him. I didn't want him to die alone if I could help it, so I took to spending the night in the recliner by his bed. Preston turned it around so I could watch P. B.'s face and hold his hand while he slept." Mrs. Harrington stared off into space, as though lost in the memory. Grandma Ruth set her teacup on her saucer with a clink.

Mrs. Harrington gave herself a little shake and continued. "I dozed off, oh, around eleven or so it must have been. A while later, P. B. woke me up. He must have been trying to rouse me for a while. By the time I woke up, he was squeezing my hand hard and his voice was quite sharp. When I finally got my eyes open, his eyes were so bright you could even say they twinkled, but that could have been a trick of the light from the fireplace. He beckoned me closer. I was still waking up as I leaned toward him and looked into his eyes.

"You know what he was like those last few years." Mrs. Harrington turned to me for confirmation. "He was not himself much of the time. But in those few moments right before he passed, it was like he was all there for one last time." She paused and closed her eyes, as though steeling herself to tell the next part. "He looked me full in the face with those devastating blue eyes of his and said, 'I loved you more than Millie!' and then—and then—he *winked*, as bold as brass!"

"Do tell." I leaned forward. She had me on the edge of my seat. "Then what?"

"Then I said, 'What? What do you mean? Who's Millie? You tell me this instant, Preston Bentley Harrington!' But it was too late. He let out a long, slow sigh and was gone. The love of my life was gone, and I was so mad at him, Mary Ruth. I was so mad!" She buried her face in her handkerchief and sobbed.

"Sarah, pour Mrs. Harrington a fresh cup of tea," Grandma Ruth said.

Our guest pulled herself together enough to hold the cup and sip the tea to which I had added a restorative three lumps of sugar.

"Since then," Mrs. Harrington continued, "I've gone through his papers to try to find out who this Millie could possibly be, to no avail. He fussed with his papers a good deal about a month before he died, so maybe he was removing anything that had reference to her so as not to hurt my feelings. But then why mention her at all right at the end?" Her tears threatened to brim over again.

"As you said, Charlotte, he really wasn't himself toward the end," Grandma Ruth said.

"That's true." Mrs. Harrington dabbed at her eyes. "These last few years I had to remind myself what he was like the other sixty-odd years we were married and not take things personally."

"Maybe you shouldn't take this personally either."

Mrs. Harrington shook her head. "You should have seen his face, Mary Ruth. He was so focused for those few seconds, so intent on what he was trying to tell me. It was very important to him that I know that he loved me more than Millie. And now I don't know if I'm mourning for the man who loved me or the man who loved me *and* Millie!" Her tears spilled over again, dripping into her teacup.

At that moment, the doorbell rang. I opened the front door to find Preston on the porch and the Harringtons' forest-green vintage Rolls-Royce pulled up at the curb.

"Hey, Sarah," he said, pulling off his ball cap as he stepped into the hall. "I'm here to carry my grandmother home. Is she ready?"

Mrs. Harrington smiled through her tears when I led Preston into the parlor. "Now aren't you two a sight for sore eyes."

"Aren't they now," Grandma Ruth said.

I could feel the heat rise in my cheeks.

"Your chariot awaits, ma'am," Preston said with a low bow and a sweep of his ball cap. He helped her out of her chair and then tucked her hand into the crook of his elbow. I watched from the parlor window as he guided her down the front walk, his head bent attentively to listen to her. He settled her in the front seat, closed the door with care, and glanced up at the house. I whisked out of sight. I didn't want him to think I was watching him.

"Such a nice young man," Grandma Ruth said.

"With a good, steady job. I know, Grandma, I know." I took the chair by my grandmother's bed. "What I really want to know, though, is who this Millie person is."

"I don't know that that's any of our business," Grandma Ruth said.

"Since when is anything none of your business?" I shot back.

"Hush your mouth, young lady. You know better than to sass your elders."

"I can't bear to see Mrs. Harrington so sad, though," I said.

"And you think knowing who Millie is will cheer her up?" Grandma Ruth arched her right eyebrow. "Did knowing who Jake cheated with help you?"

"This isn't about me," I said, a little too fast. I had mixed feelings about finding out that Jake preferred Buffy Doyle, a stunning but vacuous redhead.

"Besides," my grandmother said, "there is no way on God's green earth that P. B. Harrington ever cheated on his wife."

I stared at her. "Of course, he did. He *told* her he did. That's just how men *are*."

"Not your grandpa Andy," she said, eyes blazing. "Or your father either!"

"Okay, okay! Grandpa and Daddy excepted."

"*And* P. B. Harrington," she said.

"That remains to be seen," I said.

Grandma Ruth fixed me with a stubborn stare. I met her eyes and tried to hold my ground, but I blinked first.

"Look, Grandma, I only knew the mean P. B. Harrington, so I can imagine him being unfaithful. But you knew him as a man besotted with his wife, who would never think of betraying her."

"That's right." She gave me a decisive nod.

"In addition, Mrs. Harrington has always believed," I said, "that she was his one and only love. Now her faith is shaken. The doubt is tormenting her even more than the grief over his passing. It's like she's losing him twice. I can't bear to see her like this. I have to do something. I have to find out who Millie is."

I flinched under the stare with which Grandma Ruth met this statement.

"You will not meddle in this, Sarah Elizabeth."

"But if he didn't cheat on her, like you say, what harm could it do? It would relieve her mind. She could dismiss his last words as the ramblings of a man who wasn't himself the last few years of his life," I said.

"The past is better left alone," she said.

"Tell that to Roger Burmeister," I said, referring to our local Confederate history fanatic. "It's been over a hundred and fifty years, but to hear him talk you'd think Sherman burned down St. Alban's last week."

"Exactly," Grandma Ruth said. "It's better to leave the past in the past and get on with life."

I didn't pursue the matter any further, but I had a feeling that Mrs. Harrington was going to get as stuck on her husband's last words as Roger was on Sherman's March.

CHAPTER 5

A WEEK AFTER THE FUNERAL, I stopped by the Harrington home-place to retrieve Mama's macaroni and cheese dish. Mrs. Harrington favored me with a wan attempt at a smile when she opened the door.

"Sarah, how good of you to stop by. I was about to make some tea. Will you join me?"

I followed her back to the kitchen. Mrs. Harrington insisted I sit at the table while she fussed with the tea and a plate of lemon bars. Gone were the bustling friends and church ladies of last week's funeral reception, tending to the generous offerings of food and washing up the dishes. A week later it was just me, Mrs. Harrington, the lemon bars, and . . . memories of P. B. Harrington (which was the real reason we always left the macaroni and cheese dish behind).

"These were his favorite, you know," she said as she passed me the plate. She didn't take any for herself. While I sipped and nibbled, she retrieved a recipe file from the counter by the stove. She pulled dog-eared index cards from the box as she reminisced about her husband's favorite dishes. She laid a recipe for Boston baked beans on the table between us and tapped it with her forefinger.

"Oh my, I took some teasing for this one. He came home for Christmas his freshman year of college raving about Boston baked beans. Of course, I searched out a recipe and learned how to make them. My family said there wasn't anything Boston about them. They tasted just like the beans we all have with barbecue here in Raeburne's Ferry. P. B. was so pleased when I made them for him when he came home at the end of the spring term that nothing else mattered."

"You two had it bad, didn't you?" I said and immediately regretted it as I watched her eyes fill with tears.

"We did indeed." She sighed.

I scrambled to change the subject. "I didn't know he went to Harvard until Grandma Ruth told me the other day."

"He graduated in the top ten percent of his class," she said, her eyes gleaming. "Both undergraduate and law school. Here, let me show you." She rose from the table and disappeared into the hall. Moments later she returned, her arms laden with college yearbooks.

Together we pored over the pages filled with pictures of college life up north two generations ago. I was seized with a sudden idea, an idea that my grandmother had forbidden me to pursue. Here, practically on a silver platter, was an opportunity to look for Millie. I decided that what Grandma Ruth didn't know wouldn't hurt her.

Under the guise of fascination with P. B.'s college career, I examined the yearbooks, paying special attention to the pages devoted to pictures of Mr. Harrington's senior class. There was not, however, a single Millie, Millicent, or Mildred. In fact, there was not a single woman in any of P. B. Harrington's Harvard yearbooks.

Perplexed, I asked Mrs. Harrington, "Why did they only put in the male students' pictures?"

She gave me a rueful smile. "There weren't any women to put in the yearbook back then. Harvard wasn't coeducational until the 1970s. My, but some of the alumni were upset about it, but P. B. said the only thing he regretted about it was that he didn't have a daughter to send there once they started to admit women. He was a staunch supporter of higher education for women. He was as proud of my Radcliffe degree as he was of his Harvard ones."

"You went to *Radcliffe*?"

"I had to do *something* while P. B. was in school. I was Phi Beta Kappa," she said with a modest smile.

"I would certainly hope Mr. Harrington was proud of you." I couldn't help but be impressed myself. "They only let brainiacs into Phi Beta Kappa, and you have to be really smart to get into Radcliffe to begin with."

"P. B. always said he got the whole package, brains *and* beauty," she said.

"So you were at college with him. Sort of," I said. P. B.'s college years still couldn't be completely ruled out. He could have been involved with Millie sometime during his first two years at Harvard. Mrs. Harrington had been safely tucked away in Raeburne's Ferry, finishing high school.

"Sort of is right. We studied hard during the week, but on the weekends there were dances and concerts. Sometimes we took a picnic to the park and other times we went to a museum. Those were golden years," she said with a wistful smile.

"But you had to come back home when you graduated, right?"

Mrs. Harrington shook her head. "P. B. only had one more year of law school left. We couldn't bear to be parted. We got married right after I graduated. I was able to get a job at one of the museums. P. B. and I set up housekeeping in the row house that summer."

"The row house?" I asked.

"When Harringtons started going to Harvard, the family bought a row house near campus. That way the family always has a place to stay when they visit. We call it our northern pied-à-terre."

Now she had me curious. "Do you still have it?"

"As long as there are Harringtons at Harvard, we will have the row house. Preston will be there in the fall to start his MBA," she said. "If you ever visit Boston, you're welcome to stay there, Sarah. If you go during the school year, I'm sure Preston would be happy to show you the sights."

I could see it now—the pitying glances of Preston's study group as he introduced me as his grandmother's best friend's granddaughter from Raeburne's Ferry, Georgia, wherever that was. "I wouldn't dream of taking him away from his studies," I told her and glanced at my watch. "It's been lovely visiting with you, Mrs. Harrington, but I should be getting on home to supper."

When she handed me the casserole dish I'd come to retrieve, I found that it contained a dozen lemon bars.

"Please take them, dear. I don't seem to have much of an appetite these days," she said. "I don't know why I even made them. I didn't remember that P. B. wasn't here to eat them until I was sprinkling the powdered sugar on top. If only he *was* here . . ." Her softly wrinkled face crumpled.

If he were here, you could ask him about Millie, I finished in my mind. *You could have your lemon bars and eat them, too, after you threw a few at your philandering husband.*

My father helped Mama with the supper dishes that night.

"You go on and tell your grandma all about your visit with Mrs. Harrington," he told me. I think he mainly wanted to stay in the kitchen with the lemon bars.

"Charlotte called to say how much she enjoyed your visit," Grandma Ruth said as soon as I settled into the chair by her bed. "How is she?"

"You should know," I said. "You've been calling her every day since the funeral."

"You can only find out so much over the phone. How does she look?"

"Sad. She was close to tears a few times."

"That's understandable," my grandmother said. "It's only been a week."

"She served me lemon bars but wouldn't eat any herself. She made them sort of by accident. The lemon bars were a favorite with Mr. Harrington, and she didn't remember he wasn't around anymore to eat them until she was almost done making them."

Grandma Ruth shook her head. "And now she can't bring herself to eat them."

"She said she doesn't have much of an appetite these days."

"She's so small to begin with." My grandmother tsked. "What did the two of you talk about?"

"Mr. Harrington, of course," I said.

"You have no idea what a kindness that is, Sarah." Grandma Ruth reached out and patted my hand.

"It was interesting. I never knew she went to Radcliffe. Did you know she was Phi Beta Kappa?"

Grandma Ruth nodded. "She majored in American history. She's an outstanding volunteer archivist at the county museum. Did she say anything to you about Millie?"

"No, we mostly talked about their years up North. And lemon bars and baked beans." I didn't tell her about the yearbooks. She didn't need to know that I was delving into the past when she'd told me not to.

"Maybe she's taking my advice, then, to dwell on the good memories and leave the bad ones alone," my grandmother said with a satisfied nod of her head.

Somehow, I wasn't as sure of that as Grandma Ruth.

CHAPTER 6

NOT THAT I HAD ANY idea of how to go about finding out who this troublesome Millie person was. And I had tax returns to prepare. I had taken to eating lunch at my desk and only came up for air to refill my insulated cup at the café next door. One of the perks of working at Crawford and Associates is that the firm pays our tab at the Coffee Break.

On Monday, I was taking just such a break. Mrs. Fogarty was behind me in line, so naturally we fell into conversation while we waited for the barista to fill our orders. There were the usual questions about my parents, my grandmother, and my marriage prospects.

"So sorry to hear about what happened, Sarah." She laid a consoling hand on my arm. "It just shows he wasn't good enough for you. That's what everyone is saying, dear."

A few people looked up from the café tables where they were eavesdropping and nodded encouragingly at me. *Dear Lord, take me now*, I prayed as I felt the blood rush into my cheeks. It would be two years in June, but they were still talking about my broken engagement. Raeburne's Ferry needs to get a life. Oblivious to my embarrassment, Mrs. Fogarty sailed on to a discussion of the weather and finally arrived at the most recent social occasion we had attended together.

"Poor Charlotte." Mrs. Fogarty shook her head. "She was in quite a state at the reception."

"She was," I said and filed away the phrase "in quite a state" as a useful euphemism for Mrs. Harrington's degree of inebriation.

"I was at Radcliffe with her, you know," she said.

I started—and not only because the barista had called my name. Mrs. Fogarty had been a Radcliffe girl?

"Really?" I said as I accepted my latte.

"It wasn't easy to talk my parents into it, believe me. They thought Wesleyan down in Macon was quite far enough away from home, thank you very much. And my mother had her heart set on me being an Alpha Delta Pi there, like she was and her mother before her. I didn't want to belong to some old sorority, Sarah. I wanted to see the world!"

"So you and Mrs. Harrington were in college together?" I said to get her back on track. How she got her parents to let her go to Radcliffe was a story for another day.

"Not exactly together," Mrs. Fogarty said. "I was two years ahead of her."

"You and Mr. Harrington were up there at the same time, then?" I asked. Could I play my cards right without tipping my hand?

"Oh yes." She grinned. "He cut quite a dashing figure at the dances. He took me to the first few just so I'd have a date, but it wasn't long before I had dates of my own." She preened.

"So he was popular with the ladies?"

"Oh my, yes." Mrs. Fogarty chuckled. "It was quite funny to watch. He was already engaged to Charlotte by then, so he went stag to the dances. He was every bit as handsome as Preston in those days, and how those girls vied for his attention! He would dance with one or the other to be polite. You should have seen the way they zeroed in on him for slow dances and batted their eyelashes. I told them they didn't stand a chance against Charlotte, but they kept trying. It was so much fun to watch those Yankee girls make fools of themselves." She finished with a happy sigh.

A glance at my watch told me it was time to extricate myself from Mrs. Fogarty's reminiscences and return to number crunching.

"How interesting," I murmured. "Mrs. Fogarty, I would love to hear more about your Radcliffe days sometime. Right now, however, duty calls." I waved my coffee cup toward Crawford and Associates, looking suitably regretful.

"Of course, dear. I'm sure they can't spare you for long, especially these days. They'll have to though, won't they, when you meet Mr. Right?" she said with a wink.

I really did have to get back to the office, or I would have informed Mrs. Fogarty that I had no intention of ever giving up my career. Or getting married, for that matter.

As I drove home from work that afternoon, I considered that there were plenty of women in P. B.'s college days who would have liked to be Millie, but according to Mrs. Fogarty, Mr. Harrington hadn't risen to the bait. Maybe it was because he knew it would get back to his fiancée through Mrs. Fogarty. He must have at least been tempted, though—more girls than he'd ever seen at Raeburne's Ferry High, and so many of them chasing him. Had he really been so irrevocably in love that the attention didn't go to his head? I found it hard to believe.

When I arrived home, I saw an ancient Rambler parked in front of the house. Our town is small enough that Dr. Milford (who has delivered three generations of McCreadys) makes house calls on his shut-in patients. Grandma Ruth looks forward to Doc's monthly visit. Despite all those new privacy regulations, my grandmother routinely worms information about other patients out of him. There is no vaccination against the influence of McCready baked goods.

When I went to the parlor to replenish the cookies, I found Grandma Ruth and Dr. Milford deep in consultation. Grandma was fine, apparently. It was Mrs. Harrington they were worried about.

"She's eating her heart out over this Millie thing," Dr. Milford was saying. "She's not sleeping well. She's lost weight, and she's never had that much to spare. If P. B. were here, I'd give him a piece of my mind." The doctor's handsome white mustache bristled.

"If P. B. were here, he could explain himself. Ah, there you are, Sarah," Grandma Ruth said as I stepped through the doorway.

Dr. Milford stood and shook my hand with a courtly bow. Then he held me at arm's length and looked me over.

"I don't see it, Mary Ruth," he said over his shoulder. "She looks fine to me."

I raised my eyebrows at my grandmother.

"I'm worried that you've been working too hard," she said. "You're not getting out and having fun."

"As in dating, you mean." I felt my face get hot.

"Now, Mary Ruth, you leave her be. There will be plenty of time for Sarah to go out, if she so chooses, after tax season. I, for one, want her mind on her work since I'm a Crawford's client. Wouldn't do to get audited, now, would it?" Dr. Milford said with a grin.

Thank you, I mouthed to the doctor.

"Hmph," Grandma Ruth said.

"It's time I went home to Nell," Dr. Milford said as he tucked his stethoscope into his doctor's bag. "What that woman does with pork chops is out of this world."

"Give her my love," my grandmother said. "Tell her the kettle's always on for her. I'd love a visit. And if there's anything I can do to help with Charlotte, don't hesitate to ask."

"Will do," he said.

I retrieved his hat from the hall tree and saw him to the door. "Thanks for sticking up for me, Dr. Milford."

He reached out and patted my cheek with the hand that had given me my first post-vaccination lollipop. His brown eyes were warm and kind. "Remember when you fell out of the big oak in the side yard? You were about nine, as I recall."

I nodded as the shocking *whump* of my landing reverberated through my memory.

"You had the wind knocked out of you well and good. But miraculously, when I checked you over, nothing was broken. Jake purely knocked you for a loop, dear, and it feels like your heart is broken, but everything that's best about you is still in good working order."

I wasn't too sure about that. My heart *was* broken. Nearly two years later, I was still reeling, not daring to trust any man (except Daddy and Doc Milford). For the umpteenth time, I wondered how God could have let it happen to me when I'd been such a good girl all my life.

But as I looked into those kind eyes, something stirred, as if hope had caught its breath. I took a moment to clear the lump of gratitude from my throat before I went back into the parlor.

"That does it, Grandma," I said as I settled myself in the chair by her bed and leaned forward.

"You *are* working too hard," my grandmother said. "And it's more than a year since the unpleasantness with Jake—one year and seven months to be exact. It's time you got back into circulation."

"That's not what I mean," I said, as I waved away her advice for the lovelorn (which I am *not*). "We have to get to the bottom of this 'Millie thing,' as Dr. Milford calls it. It's affecting Mrs. Harrington's health."

"We should leave well enough alone, Sarah," Grandma Ruth said. "As I told you before, it's none of our business."

"Oh, really? You were pumping Doc for information about her when I got here."

"That's different," she said. "I was asking after the well-being of a friend. That's a neighborly thing to do."

It was a nosy thing to do, but I didn't press the point. She's my grandmother, after all.

"I think you're saying we should leave well enough alone because you're afraid of what we'll find," I said.

"I am not." She bridled. "P. B. Harrington was as truehearted a man as ever lived."

"Prove it."

Grandma Ruth's eyes flashed. "It's not that easy. How do you think Charlotte would feel if it got back to her that we were trying to dig up dirt on her husband?"

"But that's not what we'd be doing," I said. "We'd be confirming his innocence. And relieving Mrs. Harrington's mind. Getting her appetite back and helping her sleep at night. You told Doc Milford you wanted to help."

My grandmother leveled a long, considering look at me. I had to look away before she finished examining my soul. When I looked back, her eyes were soft. When she spoke, her voice had a catch in it.

"All right, Sarah, we'll do it, for your sake as much as Charlotte's. We have to be discreet, though. It cannot get back to her what we're up to. I don't want to add to her pain."

"Understood."

After I helped Mama with the supper dishes, I retrieved my day planner from my briefcase and headed for the parlor. I know most people my age keep their lives on their phones, but I like paper, section tabs, and fancy writing implements. I sat by Grandma Ruth's bed, opened my planner to the blank pages in the back tabbed "Notes," and uncapped my favorite fountain pen.

"Let's start with what we already know."

"We know that P. B. Harrington was faithful to his wife," Grandma Ruth said firmly.

"We *don't* know that," I said. "That's what this investigation is all about. We're trying to prove that he was."

"That's a given."

The stubborn set of her chin told me it would be an exercise in futility to argue.

"Innocent until proven guilty, then." I capitulated, with reservations. Grandma Ruth's reasoning (if you could call her intuition and ability to judge character *reasoning*) was inductive. She had witnessed P. B. Harrington's devotion to his wife on x number of occasions, therefore he was devoted to her on all occasions. I knew from high school geometry that you couldn't put blind faith in that kind of reasoning. All it took was one counterexample, and the whole thing would fall like a house of cards. If P. B. had strayed even once . . . the riskiness of our undertaking washed over me, and I felt a sudden visceral flash of what was keeping Mrs. Harrington up at night. I wrote *Given: P. B.*

Harrington was faithful to his wife at the top of the page and hoped against hope it was true.

"We also know that he did not date anyone, much less someone named Millie, while he was at Harvard," I went on as I wrote *College Fling?* on the next line and then crossed it out. "Therefore, we can discard the hussy theory."

"I never subscribed to that theory, as you may recall," Grandma Ruth said.

I winced at the memory of her rebuke when I had first posed the possibility of a college fling. "But now I have proof."

"Do tell." She leaned forward.

I recounted my coffee break conversation with Mrs. Fogarty.

"You see." Grandma Ruth leaned back on her pillows with a satisfied gleam in her eye. "I told you so. Out of sight was not out of mind when P. B. went to college."

"So now what?" I asked. I felt I had already made a huge contribution to the investigation, and it was about time Grandma Ruth came up with something more than "P. B. Harrington couldn't possibly have cheated on his wife."

"You're sure there was no Millie among the floral tributes?" she said.

I shook my head. "There were some that only said 'Mr. and Mrs.' with no first names, though."

"I'll call over to the Daisy Chain tomorrow and check on those." My grandmother jotted herself a note on the pad she kept by her bed. She tapped the end of her pen against her chin. "I wonder . . . that lady in the sharp suit . . . you said you'd never seen her before, and she didn't attend the reception."

I shook my head again. "She didn't look old enough." Then I reconsidered. "Although, sometimes older men . . ."

"Bite your tongue, Sarah. That is *not* what happened."

"Maybe she's Millie's daughter." I didn't dare suggest that could mean she was P. B.'s daughter as well, since I like my head firmly attached to my neck, but that's what I was thinking. I didn't have to say it, however.

"You'll need to look at the mourner's book to figure out who she is," Grandma Ruth said. "I'm sure Charlotte could use another visit now that the first flurry of sympathy is dying down."

"You could call and ask her," I said.

"A little obvious, don't you think?" She raised her eyebrows.

"And it won't be obvious if *I* ask?"

"Of course, not, Sarah. I checked with Mrs. Eifflebacher, and no one has thought to take Charlotte a prayer shawl yet. Tomorrow you can stop by the church on your lunch hour to pick one up and then drop by with it on your way home from work. The conversation will flow naturally from there. You'll see."

CHAPTER 7

NEVER MIND THAT I HAD lunch plans with Meredith at the Magnolia Tea Room the next day. I sent her a text to say I'd be late and to ask her to order my usual, including dessert. If things took too long at the church, I could always take it with me in one of the Magnolia's cute little to-go boxes.

On the dot of noon, I pulled on my coat and headed to St. Alban's. A cold wind hurried me on my way and banged the door behind me when I stepped into the foyer. I nearly ran into Father David coming out of the church office. His smile illuminated his face as he swept open the door to the nave for me.

"Tough accounting problem today, Sarah?" He was used to me coming by during lunch or after work. Somehow sitting in a pew in the warm silence often helped me clear my head when the numbers weren't cooperating.

"Not today, Father," I said. "I thought I'd take Mrs. Harrington a prayer shawl after work."

"How thoughtful of you." Father David beamed at me, even though we both knew that it was Grandma Ruth's idea. "I'm sure both the shawl and your visit will be a great comfort to her."

"I hope so. It's hard to see her so upset," I said. "I wish Mr. Harrington hadn't been so mean right at the end. This Millie thing is making things so much worse for Mrs. Harrington."

Father David fixed me with a look much like my grandmother's, only softened around the edges of his kind gray eyes. "Sarah, my years as a priest have taught me that things are not always, or even often, as they seem." With that cryptic remark, he patted me on the shoulder and continued across the foyer.

There was a goodly supply of shawls in the church office. I chose one that reminded me of Mrs. Harrington. Its rose-pink lacy elegance would sit lightly on her delicate shoulders, warming her without weighing her down. I tucked it into my tote and hurried on to the Magnolia Tea Room where Meredith and my lunch awaited me.

The bell over the door jingled merrily as I stepped out of the cold into the warmth and welcome of the Magnolia Tea Room. A soft chorus of greetings went up from the round tables that filled the room since most of the women here had known me all my life. I nodded to the historical society ladies and waved at a group of St. Alban's church ladies on my way to the spot where Meredith waited. I sat down with a contented sigh at the table draped with a pastel pink cloth and leaned forward to smell the pink and white rosebuds in the crystal vase that served as a centerpiece.

"Mmm, those smell so good," I said.

"You're going to think *mmm* about something else in a minute," Meredith said. "I ordered us today's special."

"I've been looking forward to the chicken salad," I said, peeved that she'd be so high-handed when she knew exactly what I wanted—what I always wanted at the Magnolia.

"It's too cold for chicken salad," Meredith said with a dismissive wave of her hand.

I opened my mouth to tell her to let me be the judge of that. At that moment, however, a waitress bustled over to our table, tray in hand. She unloaded two bowls of soup and two salads. I felt my eyes widen as the aroma wafted up to me.

"Oh yes." I inhaled the warm, delectable steam that rose from my bowl. "I'd much rather have she-crab soup."

I dipped my spoon into the rich concoction and closed my eyes as the creamy bisque slipped down my throat and warmed me, body, soul, and spirit.

"Hits the spot, doesn't it?" Meredith said after we had savored several spoonfuls in blissful silence.

"Mmm," I said. "Better than chicken salad any day of the week."

"So, how are things going with Preston?" Meredith asked as she speared a forkful of salad. "Leslie keeps asking me about the reading of Mr. Harrington's will. I think she plans to 'just happen' to be at the office that day so she can be all sympathetic to him."

"Can't she ask her father about it?" I asked.

"Thomas Nidden, Esquire, is the soul of discretion," Meredith said. "If you don't have a legal right to know something about one of his clients, he's not about to tell you. Any and all secrets are safe with him."

"Hmm . . . I wonder . . ." What I wondered was whether P. B. Harrington had entrusted the truth about Millie to the law partner who had drawn up his will. Not that it would be all that much help if he did. I had a feeling even Grandma Ruth wouldn't be able to pry it out of him.

"I'm wondering about something, too," Meredith said. "I'm wondering when you plan to make your move with Preston. Mrs. Harrington gave you her seal of approval. You're golden."

"I'm not planning to 'make my move' with Preston, Jeff Morris, or anyone else, for that matter," I said. "You can't trust any of them."

"Who said anything about Jeff Morris?" Meredith shuddered. "I wouldn't date him even if his last name didn't start with *M*. He'd probably pick you up in the hearse."

"Exactly," I said. "But my grandmother keeps going on about his good, steady job."

"People do keep on dying on a regular basis."

"They also have to pay their taxes on a regular basis, which gives *me* a good, steady job."

"Well, I think you're crazy. If I had Mrs. Harrington's green light for Preston, I'd be taking full advantage of it. He's good-looking, smart, and comes from a good family that happens to be well off. What more could you ask for?"

"You know what more I could ask for," I told my best friend. I'd cried on her shoulder for months after the breakup with Jake.

Meredith stared. "You think he'd cheat? The Harringtons don't do that. P. B. and Charlotte were married for, what—sixty-two years? I hear he was crazy about her."

"Hmph," I said.

Meredith raised her eyebrows.

"Weren't you paying any attention at the funeral reception?" I asked. "Didn't you hear about P. B.'s last words to his 'beloved' wife?" I sketched quotation marks with my fingers.

"Oh, that." Meredith waved my words away with her soup spoon. "Mrs. Harrington was upset, worn out, not herself . . ."

"He drove her to it," I said. "She was so good to him, so patient and kind, and then she finds out he betrayed her."

"Whoa." Meredith held up her hands in mock surrender. "You don't have to get so exercised about this."

"Yes, I do." I leaned across the table and lowered my voice. "This is between you, me, and the doorpost . . ." I held out my hand, pinkie finger at the ready.

Meredith locked her pinkie with mine in the way we have sealed our promises since childhood.

"Pinkie swear," we said together. Meredith leaned forward to hear my secret.

"Mrs. Harrington was upset but completely sober when she came over to tell Grandma Ruth about her final moments with her husband. He really did say that he loved her more than Millie, and then he up and died before he could tell her exactly who this Millie person was."

"Do tell," Meredith said, wide-eyed. "I won't tell a soul. How awful for Mrs. Harrington. No wonder she cried harder every time someone said something nice about him at the funeral. You just never know about people, do you?"

"Exactly," I said as I tucked into the warm peach cobbler our waitress had brought for dessert. "Which is why y'all can hint around about Preston all you want, but I am not going to do anything about it, Mrs. Harrington notwithstanding. There's more, though."

"More dirt?" Meredith asked as she raised her eyebrows.

"I certainly hope not," I said. "Mrs. Harrington can't take much more. That's what has me and Grandma Ruth worried."

"Grandma Ruth and me," Meredith said. She's been nitpicky about everything to do with words since high school, which explains why she has taken so well to working in a law office. I'm a numbers girl and could care less. Or is it couldn't care less? Never mind—you know what I mean.

"Whatever." I slid another bite of cobbler onto my fork. "The point is, according to Dr. Milford, Mrs. Harrington is making herself sick over it. She's not sleeping or eating well. And you know Grandma Ruth. She can't sit idly by and watch her friend waste away like that."

"So—what can she do about it? She can't *make* her sleep or eat." Meredith scoffed.

"I wouldn't be too sure," I said with an inward shudder. "I've eaten more than my share of brussels sprouts under her powerful stare. Grandma is convinced that Mr. Harrington was as faithful as the day is long, so she wants to set Mrs. Harrington's mind at rest by proving it. I'm helping, as usual."

Meredith shook her head. "I wouldn't get anywhere near that if I were you. Who knows what'll crawl out once you start turning over rocks?"

"I have to try."

"Oh, *you* have to try now, do you?" Meredith gave me a considering look across the table. "It's a gamble, but if you're right, it will really pay off."

"What do you mean, if I'm right, it'll pay off? *I* can't think of any other explanation for what P. B. Harrington said on his deathbed."

"But if you find it, you'll hit the jackpot. You'll save the day for Mrs.

Harrington, and you won't have any reason not to date Preston anymore."

"Besides the fact that I don't want to date anyone ever again?"

"'The lady doth protest too much.'" Before I could protest even more, she said, "I'm in. If anything comes up at the firm about Millie, you'll be the first to know."

"You don't have to—"

"Oh yes I do, my sadly single friend. And somebody needs to put Leslie Nidden in her place. When her father's not looking, she tries to send me to the Coffee Break to get her a latte." I could almost hear Meredith's teeth grinding from across the table.

"I am not sad—and I'm definitely not sad about being single," I said.

"Hmph," she said, with one of the best imitations of Grandma Ruth that I have ever seen, right down to the piercing look in her eyes. That look separates the marrow from the bone.

Not long after five o'clock, I stepped onto the front porch of the Harrington homeplace. The pots of pansies that graced the steps looked absolutely parched. I made a mental note to offer to water them before I left and to not take no for an answer.

I laid the shawl over my arm like a waiter's napkin so Mrs. Harrington would see it as soon as she opened the door, and then pressed the doorbell. I waited. And waited. I was thinking about ringing the bell again when the door opened slowly, just enough for me to see the weary sadness in Mrs. Harrington's pale blue eyes.

"Oh, Sarah. It's you." Her hand went up to her hair, overdue for a set and style at the Blue Moon Beauty Emporium. "I must look a fright."

I held up the arm with the shawl on it. "Not at all, ma'am. You look lovely," I said with the polite denial that drives Yankees crazy and keeps Southerners sane. "I brought you something—a prayer shawl."

Her eyes filled and she opened the door wider as she beckoned me inside. "That is just so sweet," she said as she accepted the shawl and led me down the hall to the kitchen.

"Here, let me do that." I took the tea kettle from her hand and filled it at the sink. She sat at the table, her hands buried in the shawl in her lap. Once I had the kettle on the burner, I took the shawl and tucked it around her shoulders. It coaxed the barest hint of color into her pale cheeks. "It looks lovely on you, Mrs. Harrington."

She clutched it around herself with her slender, still-elegant hands. "This is so thoughtful of you, Sarah, so like your grandmother and your mother, too." I felt my heart swell. I'm not sure just how much I want to be like Grandma Ruth, but I'd love to grow up to be my mother.

"It's the least I can do, ma'am," I said, sincerely wishing I could do more, hoping against hope that Grandma and I could relieve her mind and ease her grief through our meddling—I mean, *investigation.*

I served us tea and some cookies that were on the verge of going stale in the cookie jar. It was a novel experience. Cookies are plied so liberally at the McCready homeplace that I don't think I've ever had a stale one. I obligingly ate one, however, when Mrs. Harrington pushed the plate toward me without taking any herself. I had given some thought to how I could get a look at the mourner's book without rousing Mrs. Harrington's suspicions. I didn't want to tell her the real reason I wanted to see it because I didn't want to get her hopes up. When I was honest with myself, I also didn't want her to think I was sticking my nose where it didn't belong (even though I was).

"Mrs. Harrington, the other reason I came by is that I was supposed to sign the mourner's book for both Grandma Ruth and Crawford and Associates. I usually only sign for my grandmother, so I'm worried I might have forgotten to do it for Crawford and Associates. Could I check to be sure? Mr. Crawford is a stickler for the formalities."

"He is indeed," Mrs. Harrington said. "He won't tell me a thing about the state of P. B.'s finances until the will is read, except to say he's sure I'm well provided for." She rose from her chair and returned moments later with the mourner's book. She sat down next to me, and together we leafed through its pages. Long after we ascertained that I had indeed signed for Crawford and Associates, Mrs. Harrington continued to pore over the book. Small smiles lit her face as she pointed out various names and told brief stories about their connection to her husband. For a few, she pressed her lips together and shook her head.

"I'd be breaching confidentiality if I told you about this client," she said. "Suffice it to say that he didn't see eye to eye with the terms of somebody's will. I can't say whose, you understand. P. B. was the soul of discretion."

Except at the end of his life. That thought hung between us for a moment. I looked back down at the mourner's book as the tears in her eyes threatened to spill over.

"Does that happen very often?" I asked. "People contesting wills, I mean."

"Every now and then," she said. "But no one has ever successfully contested a will drawn up by Bentley, Harrington, Harrington, and Nidden. They discuss matters thoroughly with the testator and look at things from all angles before anyone signs on the dotted line. Oh, there are the usual squabbles about who gets Great-Aunt Edna's sugar tongs, but unless those sugar tongs were specifically mentioned in the will, the firm stays out of it."

"How does it get settled, then?" I asked. "People can get pretty heated over family heirlooms."

"Pistols at dawn, perhaps?" she said.

I was grateful to see the glimmer of a twinkle in her eyes. I shared a smile with her and then looked back down at the mourner's book. That's when I saw the name M. D. Farnsworth, followed by an out-of-town address. It was a way-out-of-town address—New York City, to be exact.

"Who's this?" I asked.

Mrs. Harrington leaned over and peered at the page.

"Why, I don't know, dear. How odd. That little check mark next to the name means I've already sent an acknowledgment, but I have no idea who this person is." Mrs. Harrington fiddled with her teacup and shook her head as if to clear it. "I certainly hope the note I wrote was gracious."

"I'm sure it was, ma'am." I gave her hand a gentle pat. I also took a good look at the name and address, committing it to memory. This *must* be the lady in the sharp suit. She had come hundreds of miles to attend P. B.'s funeral. Who had Mr. Harrington been to her? Who had she been to Mr. Harrington?

A half hour later, we finished going through the mourner's book. Much to her relief, Mrs. Harrington knew all the other people who had attended the funeral. On that positive note, I excused myself to go home to supper. Mrs. Harrington saw me to the door, and as I drove away, she waved, with the shawl warming her shoulders and a smile on her face that almost crinkled the corners of her eyes.

Surprisingly, Grandma Ruth let me eat supper before she summoned me to the throne room—I mean, the *parlor*.

It took about ten minutes to get through her questions about my day at work, which prayer shawl I had picked out and why, the apparent state of Father David's health, and my lunch with Meredith.

"And how is Meredith?" my grandmother wanted to know.

"Fine," I said.

"Seeing anyone?" she asked with studied nonchalance.

"No," I said and prepared to tell her about my visit with Mrs. Harrington.

"You really should step aside and give her a chance with Jeff Morris," Grandma Ruth told me.

"I'm not in her way." I felt my jaw tighten. "And besides, she doesn't want him."

"Whyever not?" My grandmother bridled. "He's a perfectly nice young man with—"

"A good, steady income. We know, we know." I sighed. "Even if she did like him, which she *doesn't*, his last name starts with *M*."

"What does that have to do with it? She wouldn't even have to change her monogram."

"Exactly," I said. "We digress, Grandma. What did you find out when you called the flower shop?"

"Abby Claire Harper is such a sweet girl," Grandma Ruth said. "I don't know why she's not married yet either. Now that's an idea—flowers and funerals—a match made in heaven."

"Give it a rest, Grandma, please. We can find a husband for Abby Claire later. Right now, we have to find out about Millie and Mrs. Harrington's husband."

"No need to get exercised, young lady," Grandma Ruth said, giving me a quelling look. "I had a lovely chat with Abby Claire, but she was no help at all."

"She wouldn't tell you about the people who sent the flowers?"

"On the contrary—she told me about every single person who sent flowers, but not a one of them was named Millie," Grandma Ruth said. "I hope you fared better with the mourner's book."

"I did. We went through the whole book, and Mrs. Harrington recognized all the names except one, an M. D. Farnsworth from New York City. It really bothered her that she doesn't know who that is. She already sent the acknowledgment."

"Bless her heart," my grandmother said. "She doesn't know if she's coming or going these days. I assume you copied down the address?"

I shook my head. "That would have made Mrs. Harrington suspicious. I memorized it." I handed her a slip of paper with M. D. Farnsworth's address jotted on it. Then I pulled out my phone and began a Google search.

"Sarah Elizabeth!" Grandma Ruth said sharply. "This is not the kind of thing one handles over the phone. She doesn't even know us. A tasteful note is far more appropriate."

"I'm not calling, although I'm pretty sure I could find the phone number if I needed to," I said. "I'm googling her." I had to spend the next ten minutes explaining how you could find out all kinds of things about people on the internet and how I could access all that on my cell phone. By that time, I had found a Margaret D. Farnsworth on LinkedIn. Her profile picture was a dead ringer for the lady in the sharp suit.

"That's her," I said as I handed the phone to Grandma Ruth. She held it at arm's length and squinted.

"I'll take your word for it." She handed the phone back. "I don't know how you can see anything on there. What does it say about her?"

"She's a stockbroker. I've heard of the firm she's with—they're pretty successful. Oh, and here's her work email. I could shoot her an email right now."

"You will do nothing of the kind." Grandma Ruth snatched the phone out of my hand. "For goodness' sake, she doesn't even know us. And it's about a bereavement. This requires a tasteful note. Hand me my desk."

Grandma Ruth was soon settled with her lap desk, a sheet of cream-colored stationery embossed with her name and address at the top of the page, and her favorite fountain pen. She handed me the note after she signed it with a flourish. As I read it, I had to admit that she knew how to be nosy without being tacky.

Dear Ms. Farnsworth,
I am writing on behalf of my dear friend, Charlotte
Harrington, wife of the late Preston Bentley Harrington II. You
were kind enough to attend his funeral several weeks ago. While
going over the guest book, she was surprised to note a visitor
from so far away. How did you come to know Mr. Harrington?
Mrs. Harrington would treasure any reminiscences you may
have of her beloved husband.
  Sincerely, Mary Ruth McCready

I was impressed that she'd used the modern title for a woman instead of fussing over whether she was married or not. I should be so lucky.

She took the letter back and slid it into the envelope she'd addressed while I read. Then she affixed a stamp and handed the whole thing to me.

"You will see that this gets into the mailbox tomorrow morning."

"Of course," I said.

She pointed to the phone that rested in my lap. "I had no idea you could find out so much on those things. It's a shame they're so small."

"You can do the same things on a laptop or a tablet. We have Wi-Fi here at the house. And you can make the font as big as you need on those."

By the time I finished explaining laptops, tablets, Wi-Fi, and fonts, there was a gleam in Grandma Ruth's eyes that told me she was beginning to grasp the possibilities the technical world held for an inquiring mind like hers.

Upstairs in my room later that evening, I curled up on the window seat with a calming cup of hot chocolate. I was fed up with everyone and their grandmother (literally) pushing me to get back into dating. At lunch, Meredith had acted like Preston was the answer to my prayers. *Hmph.* I had not been praying for any man to ask me out, much less my way-out-of-my-league high school crush.

But truth be told, I hadn't been praying about much of anything since the breakup with Jake.

I gazed out at the night sky. Somewhere in that vast expanse of darkness was God, but it seemed like all my life, my prayers had never gone past the cool glass of the window. I'd longed and possibly prayed for a wonderful man to love me, and what had I gotten? Jake. Handsome and apparently wonderful on the outside, but rotten to the core.

What had Father David said when I'd stopped by the church for a prayer shawl? "Things are not always, or even often, as they seem." Boy howdy, wasn't *that* the truth?

CHAPTER 8

WHILE WE WAITED FOR A reply from the lady in the sharp suit, I couldn't stop thinking about that mourner's book. It represented most of the people touched by P. B. Harrington's death, but not all. We'd been assuming that Millie had attended the funeral. What if she lived too far away or didn't find out in time to go to the funeral? What if she was physically limited, like Grandma Ruth? In those cases, people usually sent flowers or cards. Grandma Ruth had already checked on those who had sent flowers, but neither of us had thought of the sympathy cards Mrs. Harrington had undoubtedly received. I decided that I had to get a look at those condolence cards.

I'd already asked so many questions about P. B. that I was worried that Mrs. Harrington's Phi Beta Kappa brain would figure out what I was up to. How could I get a look at those cards without rousing her suspicions? *Hmm* . . . I fell back on one of my grandmother's favorite ploys. With her cookies and casseroles, Grandma Ruth has taught me that food both comforts and distracts. In Mrs. Harrington's current state of distress, however, it would be a challenge to find food that would tempt her. I needed the help of an expert.

"Mama," I said as I helped my mother clean the kitchen after supper on Thursday. "I'm worried about Mrs. Harrington."

"We all are," Mama said as she handed me a glass to dry and put away.

"She's not eating well. I've been thinking that some of your special dishes might tempt her. I'll help," I quickly added. Mama's always after me to learn to cook (to make me more marriageable, I suppose), but so far, I've escaped mastering much beyond scrambled eggs and macaroni and cheese casserole.

"What did you have in mind?" she asked.

"Why, Sarah, how sweet," Mrs. Harrington exclaimed on Saturday evening as I unpacked the box of food Mama and I had prepared that afternoon. Steam rose from the shepherd's pie, crowned with real, from-scratch mashed potatoes that were browned ever so lightly and crisply on top. I turned on the oven and tucked the apple crisp inside to stay warm until we were ready to add a scoop of the vanilla ice cream I had brought to go with it. Mrs. Harrington regarded me thoughtfully as I bustled around, setting the table for two. I wondered if she was trying to figure out how she could get away with not eating.

To my relief, Mrs. Harrington plunged her fork into her mashed potatoes and took a bite. "My, my, your mama is still in fine form, isn't she?"

"I helped," I said, more defensively than I intended.

"Of course, you did, dear." Mrs. Harrington patted my hand across the table. "Now, you've come to ask for the sympathy cards, haven't you?"

I choked a little and took a sip of sweet tea. "Um, well . . . yes," I stammered.

"You're looking for Millie, aren't you?"

"Yes, ma'am," I mumbled at my plate. I couldn't look at her.

"It's all right, Sarah." I looked up to find that the kindness in her eyes matched the gentleness of her voice. "I knew you weren't really interested in P. B.'s college career when you kept leafing back and forth in the yearbooks looking for the female students."

I cringed inwardly as I realized that the Phi Beta Kappa brain under that fluffy white perm had been onto me from the beginning. "Why didn't you say anything? Aren't you mad that I'm trying to dig up dirt on your husband?"

Mrs. Harrington enjoyed a mouthful of shepherd's pie—and my

64

discomfort—before answering the question. "If I thought for a moment that's what you're doing, I would be very angry. But I know you. You're trying to help. You're not Mary Ruth McCready's granddaughter for nothing."

"So, you don't mind? Even if—?"

"Especially if," she said. "People won't tell *me* the truth if I go poking around, but I need to know if I'm grieving for the man who loved me or the man who loved me *and* Millie."

With the air cleared, I filled Mrs. Harrington in on what Grandma Ruth and I had found out so far.

"We haven't heard back from M. D. Farnsworth yet," I said, and hoped she wouldn't think of the possibility that the stockbroker could be Millie's daughter.

Mrs. Harrington tapped her lower lip with her fork. "I didn't realize Preston had a stockbroker. As proud as he was of my brains, he was a bit old-fashioned about women and money. He never went so far as to say, 'Don't worry your pretty little head about it,' but he definitely wanted me to leave it to him. I never pursued it. I knew he went to law school to please his father, but he'd much rather have gone to Harvard Business. Leaving it to him to manage our own little pile was the least I could do."

"That's kind of sad," I said. "That he didn't get to pursue the career he wanted, I mean."

"P. B. had a great deal of respect for his father," Mrs. Harrington said. "I don't think he would have gone against Preston Sr.'s wishes. And he did find estate law challenging and fulfilling. He gave people peace of mind and navigated some sticky situations with wills and estate plans. He gave his own son a choice, though, and Bent opted for business school. Preston Sr. blustered a bit, but he subsided once Bent rose to the top ten percent at Harvard Business. Preston is headed that way, too."

I did a quick mental calculation. I would have to endure seven more months of Meredith, Mrs. Harrington, and Grandma Ruth hinting around about Preston.

"I believe you've mentioned that he's going back to school," I said.

Mrs. Harrington's eyes beamed with pride. "He graduated three years ago from Harvard with an economics degree. Top ten percent, of course. He's been working in his father's company ever since. It's time for him to get his MBA. Past time, actually," she said. She sighed and the light faded from her eyes.

"Why do you say that?" I couldn't help myself. She'd piqued my curiosity.

"Preston and his father don't see eye to eye about the business . . . and that's putting it mildly. His father says Preston focuses too much on the legal aspects of the business. Preston keeps talking about business ethics. I'm beginning to wonder . . ."

"Wonder what?"

"I'm beginning to wonder if Preston ought to go to law school instead. It would be hard on Bent—he's had his heart set on passing the business down to his son."

"But he ought to be able to understand," I said. "*His* father let him do what *he* wanted to do."

Mrs. Harrington sighed and ran her fork around her plate to get up the last of her shepherd's pie. "You would think so, but I imagine it's quite different being on the other end of that decision. Since his terrible car accident, he's been even more obsessed with making sure that what he built lives on after him. I thought P. B. would have a fatherly talk with him about it, but—" Her bottom lip trembled, and then she sat up straight. "But he never did, so we'll just have to muddle on without him. My, that apple crisp smells heavenly, Sarah."

Taking my cue, I excused myself from the table to take the apple crisp out of the oven. I slid slices of one of my mother's best desserts onto our plates and added a generous scoop of vanilla ice cream to each. I closed my eyes as I took a bite. Mama had outdone herself.

"Preston would absolutely love this," Mrs. Harrington said after she savored her first bite. "You're really coming along as a cook, Sarah."

"I didn't do all that much, Mrs. Harrington. I fetched, carried, and stirred things when Mama told me to."

"Never you mind, dear," she said. "You'll be a fine cook all in good time. It's in your blood."

"That's the thing," I said. "I really don't have much time to cook, with my career and all." *And not much inclination to either*, I added mentally, *blood or not.*

Once we had practically licked our dessert plates clean, I cleared the table. Mrs. Harrington and I chatted companionably while we dealt with the dishes and leftovers.

"It's been nice to have a cheerful face across the table this evening. You're good medicine, Sarah Elizabeth."

"I enjoyed having supper with you too, Mrs. Harrington."

"'Mrs. Harrington' seems a tad formal, seeing as how you're looking into the nooks and crannies of my affairs. You may call me Miss Charlotte," she said as she handed me a shoebox full of sympathy cards.

Oh, Miss Charlotte, I thought to myself, *it's not your affairs I'm looking into. And I really hope P. B. didn't have any either.*

I finally got a lead with those condolence cards on Sunday evening. Miss Charlotte had filed them alphabetically and each one had been returned to its envelope. I not only had names but also addresses, in varying states of legibility.

I hit pay dirt in the *W*'s. In the top left-hand corner of the envelope, Mildred Wellington had written her name and address in a tidy, precise hand. She lived in Connecticut, even farther north than Ms. Farnsworth. I consulted a map of the United States and noted that Connecticut is not all that far from Massachusetts. Maybe . . . I tapped the card against my front teeth . . . maybe P. B. had managed a college fling after all.

I knew Grandma Ruth would insist on another tactful letter of inquiry. I knew a tactful letter of inquiry would get us absolutely nowhere if P. B. and Mildred had been involved. Armed with her address, I googled her home phone number. If I called out of the blue,

I reasoned, I just might surprise the truth out of her. What Grandma Ruth didn't know about my methods wouldn't hurt her.

I made the call in the privacy of my room and crossed my fingers. I was soon to discover that all the surprises would be on my end of the telephone. Mildred Wellington's approach to life was too well-ordered to allow for them on her end.

"Good evening, Wellington residence," said the voice on the other end of the line. It was a Southern voice, warm and soft around the edges. I put the college fling idea on hold.

"Ms. Wellington?" I said.

I could feel her stiffen over the phone, even before she corrected me.

"Er, yes, *Mrs.* Wellington, this is Sarah Elizabeth McCready. I'm a friend of Charlotte Harrington—"

I got no further than murmured words of agreement for a few moments.

"Yes, yes, I know," I finally said. "He *was* a fine man. Yes, it *was* sad the way he went downhill toward the end."

She finally tsked and tutted herself out and gave me a chance to get a word in edgewise.

"Mrs. Harrington has me going through the condolence cards, and when I saw the address, I wondered if you went to college with her."

"Didn't you ask her?" Her tone implied I was a highly inefficient person. I was tempted to inform her that I am the most efficient CPA at my firm but decided the investigation was more important than defending my character.

"I didn't want to bother her. She's still so upset about his passing," I said.

Mrs. Wellington clucked her tongue sympathetically. "No, I didn't go to school with Mrs. Harrington. No Radcliffe for the likes of me," she said with a chuckle. "*I* was the top graduate at secretarial school. I kept things running like a top at Bentley, Harrington, Harrington, and Nidden for forty years before I retired. I live in Connecticut now. Grandchildren, you know. Although why my son had to move all the way up here to the cold, I'll never know."

I could almost see her shiver as she said this. And I could also see her overseeing her family affairs in Connecticut with the same efficiency with which she'd run the law firm. There was that word *affair* again. I groaned inwardly. Had there been an office romance between secretary and boss? If so, how would I ferret out the sad and sordid truth?

"Um, Mrs. Wellington, did you go by Millie in those days?"

At this, the retired secretary bristled. "I have never gone by anything but Mildred. At the office I was always 'Mrs. Wellington,' the proper way to address the senior secretary." She gave a contemptuous sniff. "If you're looking for a Millie in the firm, there was that flighty Camilla Holtgrew. No *Miss Holtgrew* for her. 'Call me Millie,' she'd say. 'Everybody does.' She was dismissed—*dismissed*, I tell you, for wearing short skirts, having poor phone manners, and making goo-goo eyes at every lawyer, clerk, and male client in the firm." Mrs. Wellington's voice shook with umbrage.

"Um . . ." I hesitated. "Did she succeed with any of them?"

"Indeed not." Mrs. Wellington was adamant. "Even the greenest clerk could see she had 'gold digger' written straight across her forehead in capital letters. She even tried with young Mr. Harrington." Here she dropped her voice conspiratorially. "But ever and always, he only had eyes for the missus."

"Are you sure?" I asked.

"Absolutely," she replied in a tone that brooked no argument. "He was a faithful and careful man. He always left the door open when he had a lady employee in his office. Of course, for confidentiality, the door had to be closed when he met with a lady client, so he always had a clerk in the office for those appointments. He would tell the client it was to 'take notes,' but he had a mind like a steel trap. Never forgot a thing. And then, there was the oil painting of Mrs. Harrington in a ball gown over the credenza. Oh, there was no question of where his heart lay." Mrs. Wellington gave a slightly wistful sigh.

After a few more minutes of reminiscing about Bentley, Harrington, Harrington, and Nidden, I thanked Mrs. Wellington for sending her condolences and said goodbye with many assurances that I would convey her regards to Mrs. Harrington.

I tucked my cell phone back into my purse and reflected on what I had learned. P. B. Harrington may have held a special place in Mildred Wellington's heart, but nothing had ever come of it. Whoever Millie was, I found myself relieved to know she wasn't Mildred Wellington, former senior secretary of Bentley, Harrington, Harrington, and Nidden. But she might be Millie Holtgrew.

CHAPTER 9

LONG AFTER I FINISHED MY phone call to Mrs. Wellington, I sat on the window seat of my room, snuggled in a quilt against the January chill that seeped through the window. As I gazed out into the gathering night, the moon, round and full, rose over the tall pines at the back of the house. It was so bright I could see Mrs. Morgan's cat, Lady Jane Grey, silvered in the moonlight as she glided across the top of our fence. With that sixth sense cats have when they are being admired, she paused and looked up at my window. Her eyes, shining like tiny lamps, held mine for a moment before she continued her sinuous journey across the fence. It was a knowing look, and I wondered what she knew.

My reverie was interrupted by the strains of "Für Elise" that signaled an incoming call on my cell phone. I let it go to voicemail. It was too cozy inside the quilt to venture my hand out from under it to retrieve my phone. I closed my eyes and let myself drift, far away from tax returns, retired secretaries, and shepherd's pie.

I was on the sweet edge of sleep when my phone started playing "Für Elise" again. Once again, I let it go to voicemail. I had the vague thought that I ought to get ready for bed right before I arrived at that precipice again and slipped over into a doze.

The third time my phone rang, it startled me out of a sound sleep. I nearly fell off the window seat. What could be so all-fired important at—I checked my watch—eleven o'clock on a Sunday night? *Some* people had to go to work in the morning. I reached for the phone, which promptly stopped ringing as soon as I dug it out of my purse.

Blearily, I looked at the screen and saw that the three missed calls were all from the same all-too-familiar number. I was glad I hadn't picked up the other calls and that I had fortuitously missed this last one. Let him think I wasn't picking up because I was out on a date. Not that I planned to have any more dates ever again, thanks to him, but the man who had soured me on fully half the human race didn't need to know that. Why was Jake calling me anyway? Didn't he have a flame-haired airhead to warm his winter night?

I told myself to delete the voicemails he had left, but before I knew it I had tapped the screen to access my messages. I still could have deleted them without listening to them. Don't ask me why I didn't.

"Hey, sugar." Jake's voice, every bit as smooth and rich as molasses, came through the phone. "Pick up, darlin'. I have something special to tell you."

Again, I could have stopped right there. But Jake knew how to make the word *special* dance up and down my spine, so I hung on and listened to the second message.

"Have a heart, honey," he said, with just the right note of longing and pathos in his voice. "I really want to talk to you. I really *need* to talk to you."

I could feel my heart going out to him. Jake wanted me. He needed me. The memory of the cat's glowing eyes flashed through my mind, and I had the sudden fanciful thought that what Lady Jane Grey knew was that Jake was a low-down, rotten cheater. I snatched my heart back and put it where it belonged.

Cats and curiosity go together, however, so when the brisk female voice offered to play the next message, I let her.

"Sarah, *please* answer. I don't know what I'll do if you don't. I was crazy to let you go. *Please*, sugar, call me back."

You were crazy, all right. Crazy about Buffy Doyle, whose long, wavy auburn hair and curvaceous figure clearly made up for all the air between her ears. I shut down my phone to ward off any more calls. A girl needs her beauty sleep, after all. I lay awake, however, long into the night. Memories flooded my mind like the moonlight that spilled across the window seat.

As I've said before, my high school dating career was singularly disappointing. The only boys I seemed to be able to attract were shy, awkward types who looked at me with such pleading eyes that I didn't have the heart to say no. Pity, however, can only take a relationship so far. One after another, those relationships petered out, trailing off like the sentences my dates didn't seem to be able to finish whenever I was around. And then, during Christmas break of my senior year, Jake Halloran, home from his first semester of college, noticed me.

Meredith and I were at the Coffee Break, indulging in hot chocolate heaped with mounds of whipped cream. We'd finished the last of our Christmas shopping, our bags piled on the other two chairs at the table.

I nudged Meredith when he walked into the coffee shop. "Look who's here."

We studied him as he studied the menu board that hung over the espresso machines.

"Way out of our league." She sighed.

"Doesn't mean we can't look." I took in the back of the tall frame that stood in front of the counter, legs braced confidently. His wavy, dark hair curled over the collar of his jacket and around his ears. We watched him place his order and turn to look for a place to wait for his coffee. We quickly looked away and became deeply interested in our hot chocolate, but not before I caught a glimpse of his eyes, deep blue like the sky right before twilight gives way to night.

"Sarah McCready, is that you?"

I looked up to see Jake Halloran standing by our table, apparently—impossibly—talking to me. I nodded and hoped against hope there was no whipped cream on my upper lip. Meredith kicked me under the table and hissed, "Say something!" under her breath.

"Yes, it is," I finally said.

He shook his head in wonder. "They tell you things will be different at home the first time you come back from college, but I never expected it to be *this* different. You've really changed, Sarah."

Looking back, I realize this was a left-handed compliment. What he meant was that I hadn't been pretty enough before to merit his notice. It was all new to me back then, though. Over the past six months I had "come into my beauty," as Grandma Ruth put it. She had assured me throughout my adolescence that I just needed to grow into my "excellent bone structure." Still, I continued to agonize in front of the mirror, believing the way the popular boys treated me (or, rather, left me alone) over the vision of a relative who was clearly partial to me.

As usual, however, Grandma Ruth was right. My face cleared to a peaches and cream complexion. My smile no longer dazzled with the amount of metal it revealed, but with pearly whites in neat and tidy rows. And somehow, the proportions of my face had righted themselves—my wide mouth was now balanced by cheekbones I never knew I had. The only part of my anatomy that hadn't gotten the message was my ta-tas. Grandma Ruth dismissed my concern, assuring me that large ones were a decided liability. I disagreed with her on that point. I saw which girls were getting all the attention.

Jake, however, was not looking at my chest but straight into my eyes with that lopsided smile that made me walk into an open locker door the first time I saw it as a freshman at Raeburne's Ferry High. I flipped my hair casually (I hoped) over my shoulder the way I'd seen the cheerleaders do.

"I suppose I have," I said. I was tempted to bat my eyelashes, but from the way Jake was looking at me, I could tell it would be overkill. Meredith kicked me under the table again to remind me of my manners. "This is my friend Meredith," I added.

"Yeah, yeah, Merrie Merrie May, right?" He flicked a glance her way, then turned his attention back to me.

"Meredith," she said through tight lips. Out of the corner of my eye, I could see a flush creeping up her neck.

"Whatever," he said without taking his eyes off me. "Look, one of my frat brothers is having a party tonight. Want to go with me?"

Bells rang in my head. They should have been warning bells. He had just blown off my best friend. He had also asked me out on short notice, which was a big no-no in both Mama's and Grandma Ruth's books. My head, however, rang with *Jake Halloran asked me out! I'm going out with Jake Halloran!*

I nodded as the joyous news clamored through my head.

"I'll pick you up at eight, then."

I nodded again.

The barista called Jake's name.

"That's me," he said. "I'll see you tonight, sugar." He collected his coffee and headed out the door, throwing me one more deep-blue glance over his shoulder.

I slumped a little in my chair. "I was hoping he'd come back to the table to drink his coffee."

"Why should he?" Meredith said somewhat waspishly. "He got what he wanted. Why should he stick around?"

"What do you mean, he got what he wanted?"

"Someone to take to the party and enough adoration to keep his ego going all afternoon."

"You're just jealous he picked me and that I'm going to a college party tonight."

The flush that started up Meredith's neck again told me I had hit the mark, and I was immediately sorry I'd said it. I started to apologize, but she cut me off.

"Do you really think you're going to a college party tonight?"

I stared at her. "Of course, I am. You heard him."

"Your daddy will not let you go to a frat party, I can tell you that. And Jake won't pass inspection either."

I hadn't thought of that when I accepted Jake's invitation. All the other boys who had come to the house to pick me up over the past few years had passed my father's inquisition with flying colors, suitably cowed by his probing questions about their intentions and his precise expectations as to how they were to treat his daughter. Most of them brought me home a full half hour before my curfew, and all of them declined to kiss me good night under the porch light. When I reached sweet sixteen, I really had never been kissed.

Meredith's prediction proved to be correct. I broke the news over supper that evening. My father barely let me finish.

"Absolutely not."

"But, Daddy—"

"But Daddy nothing," my mother said. "He's too old for you and a frat party is no place for a high school girl, especially my high school girl."

"It's not a frat party," I said. "One of his frat brothers is giving the party."

"Where?" my father asked. "At his parents' house? Where I can call to find out if they will be chaperoning?"

"Daddy, they don't have chaperones at college parties," I said, ready to die at the thought of Daddy or Mama making that phone call. It was bad enough that they did it for the high school parties I rarely got to go to.

"Our point exactly," Mama said.

"But I already told him I'd go," I wailed. "He's picking me up at eight."

"That's another thing, young lady," my mother said. "It shows a distinct lack of respect—"

"To wait till the last minute and expect me to be available," I finished the familiar dictum. "I know, I know, but this is Jake Halloran, Mama. *Jake Halloran* asked me out. I might never get a chance like this again."

And wasn't there a Bible verse somewhere about God doing exceedingly more than you could ask or think? I had certainly never thought a guy as cute as Jake, a *college* guy, would give me a second glance, much less ask me out.

"As I was about to say, it also shows a lack of respect for yourself to accept such an invitation. If he really likes you, he'll ask again," she said.

I could feel tears welling up in my eyes. "I can't tell him I can't go."

"Of course, you can," Mama said. "Just phone him and say you have a family obligation."

"But I don't and I can't," I said, miserable at the thought of missing this once-in-a-lifetime opportunity.

"You have an obligation to be guided by your parents," Daddy said.

"But I can't call him," I said as a tear slipped down my cheek. "He didn't give me his number."

"Nonsense," my father said. "I'm sure his parents' phone number is in the book." He retrieved the slim volume that passes for a phone directory in Raeburne's Ferry and found the Hallorans' number in a matter of seconds. He handed me the receiver of the kitchen wall phone and dialed the number himself.

I sighed. The only thing more embarrassing than calling the Hallorans' landline would be for Daddy to turn Jake away at our front door. Maybe the number would be dead. Who had landlines anymore, anyway? Besides us.

Apparently the Hallorans did. "Can I at least have some privacy?" I said as the phone rang on the other end.

"Of course, darling," my father said as he and Mama left the room.

When Jake came on the line, I explained that I had a "family thing" this evening and would not be able to go to the party with him.

"A 'family thing'?" he asked.

"Yes," I said through gritted teeth. "You know how it is this time of year—all the get-togethers. I don't remember them telling me about it, but you know how families are . . ." Could this excuse be any more lame?

"Don't worry about it," Jake said.

I did worry about it, though. My parents had ruined my one chance to rise above the pity dates. I could have screamed, but I hung up the phone and went up to my room instead. Let Mama do the dishes all by herself tonight.

It turned out that I needn't have worried. Jake was not easily discouraged.

Don't ask me how he knew I would be at the early service at St.

Alban's that Sunday. He was there, remarkably bright-eyed and bushy-tailed for someone who'd been to a frat party the night before. I was impressed. So were my parents when he introduced himself to them during the coffee hour between services. When he showed up at church again the next Sunday, Mama invited him home for Sunday dinner.

"Let me check with my mother." Jake pulled his cell phone from the breast pocket of his blazer. "There may be family plans." Only I saw his wink. I was enthralled.

After consulting solicitously with his mama, Jake accepted my mother's invitation.

At the McCready homeplace, Jake was charming to one and all. He listened attentively to the hypochondriac aunt and answered the probing questions of the family genealogist in search of Jake's origins and connections. Grandma Ruth, however, was unimpressed.

"I don't know what you see in him," she told me as we wiped down the kitchen counters after the exodus, Tupperware containers of leftovers in hand, of the assorted aunts and cousins who had comprised the washing-up crew.

"You mean you haven't noticed how handsome he is?"

"*Hmph.*" She sniffed. "Handsome is as handsome does."

"You saw his manners!" I was indignant. "He even helped clear. He's wonderful."

"His manners are a tad too good," my grandmother said. "They're not natural. He's putting on a show. Now take Preston—his manners are as natural as breathing."

I glared at the counter. Like Preston B. Harrington IV would ever ask *me* out. Besides, who cared about him now that Jake Halloran was in the picture?

"He's too slick," Grandma Ruth said. "You be careful, Sarah Elizabeth."

Meredith told me to be careful too. She'd heard things, she said, from her brother, an upperclassman at the same university Jake was attending. I didn't want to believe any of it, though. I thought Grandma Ruth was being old-fashioned and that Meredith was jealous. Jake was going back to college in a few weeks. Why couldn't they just let me enjoy my moment in the sun?

It didn't end with Christmas break, though. After he went back to college, Jake called at least once a week, then came by the house and went to church at St. Alban's every weekend he was home. He sent me flowers on Valentine's Day, a dozen red roses. It was all calculated to sweep me off my feet and, like a fool, I fell for it hook, line, and sinker.

My eyes began to feel heavy as I lay awash in moonlight and memories. My last conscious thought was that I was glad to be falling asleep before the rest of it came flooding back.

CHAPTER 10

On Monday morning, I received a breathless call on my work phone from Meredith.

"Remember I told you I'd keep you informed? They're doing the reading of P. B. Harrington's will this afternoon. Mr. Nidden's got me polishing the silver tea service for it. Never mind I'm his administrative assistant."

"Maybe you should see if Leslie wants to polish it, since it would give her an excuse to be there and all."

"Never mind," she said. "If I'm polishing, she can't try to send me for a latte. Speak of the devil—here she comes. Gotta go!"

In my mind's eye, I could see Meredith fling her phone back into her purse to resume rubbing the life out of the firm's silver sugar bowl before Leslie Nidden could commandeer her for a coffee run.

I went back to the work that was piling up on my desk now that tax season was in full swing, and I was soon lost in capital gains and deductions. In fact, I forgot all about the reading of the Harrington will. It didn't come back to me until I stepped into the parlor after work late that afternoon to discover that Mrs. Harrington had just arrived as well.

Mama bustled in with a tray laden with tea and cookies.

"Take Mrs. Harrington's wrap, Sarah," she said as I hovered in the doorway.

When I returned from hanging Mrs. Harrington's coat and scarf on the coat tree in the front hall, Miss Charlotte was settled in the chair by Grandma Ruth's bed, thoroughly enjoying one of my mother's shortbread cookies.

"Mary Ruth . . . Sarah." She nodded at me. "I have just come from meeting with Thomas Nidden. He looks after our legal affairs, and he went over the terms of the will with the family today. P. B.'s will had a surprise. Quite a surprise, as a matter of fact."

If that buzzard left anything to Millie, I will dig him up and wipe that self-satisfied smile right off his face, no joke.

Grandma Ruth leaned forward. "Do tell."

"As expected, he left a sizable nest egg for Bent and a fund for Preston's postgraduate degree at Harvard. There are some endowments for his favorite charities, and he left the rest to me."

"I don't see what's so surprising about that, Charlotte," my grandmother said. "He was a generous man and he'd always promised to send Preston back to Harvard. And of course he'd provide for you. He loved you, and you took such good care of him."

"Of course." She nodded, then leaned forward. "It was the bequest to Preston that was the surprise. Whenever I got to fretting about the arguments between my son and grandson, P. B. would pat my hand and tell me these things had a way of working out. Little did I know—little did anyone except Thomas Nidden know—that P. B. had taken it upon himself to 'work it out' for them. According to the will, there is money for Preston to go to graduate school but only if he gets accepted to Harvard Law."

I let out a low whistle.

"Was there a scene?" I asked, thinking about what Miss Charlotte had told me about Mr. Bent's ambitions for his son.

"There was indeed," Miss Charlotte said. "Preston let out a whoop they probably heard all the way down to the feed store. Bent shot him such a look, Mary Ruth. If looks could kill, Sarah would be representing you at another Harrington funeral next week." She shuddered. "He looked at Preston and said, 'You are *not* going to law school. I don't care what your grandfather put in his will. I have enough money to send you to Harvard Business myself.'

"Then Preston jutted out his chin and said, 'And now I have enough money to go to Harvard Law.'

"'Over my dead body!' Bent yelled. His face was so red I thought he might have a stroke, then and there.

"'No,' Preston said. 'Over *Granddaddy's* dead body.' I swear, Mary Ruth, when he said that, you could have heard a pin drop in that room. Then Preston stood up, straightened his blazer, and said, 'If you all will excuse me, Mother, Grandmother, Mr. Nidden, I need to study for the LSAT,' and he left. Bent was fit to be tied, ranting on about how his father's mind went those last few years, but Thomas assured him that P. B. was of sound mind when the will was revised seven years ago. Apparently, P. B. saw which way the twig was bent before Preston even went to college."

"Do you think he'll be able to pass the test on such short notice?" I asked. I'd been counting on Preston's departure to Harvard Business in the fall as a reprieve from my grandmother's attempts at matchmaking. This was not to be, however.

"He has, unfortunately, missed the deadline for applying for this fall, so he'll have plenty of time to study. I realize now that P. B. was coaching Preston every chance he got," Miss Charlotte said. "I thought it was just something he did so he and Preston would have something to talk about during their visits, but now I know . . . he was getting Preston ready. Preston will be well-prepared for the LSAT, believe me. But I've saved the best news for last, Mary Ruth. P. B. left nothing, absolutely nothing, to Millie. There was no mention of her at all." She favored us with a triumphant smile and put three shortbread cookies on her plate.

"So how much did Mr. Harrington leave you?" I asked Mrs. Harrington.

"Sarah!" Grandma Ruth said. "You know better than to ask a tacky question like that."

"It's a professional question. Mr. Crawford is P. B.'s accountant. I hope you'll stay with the firm," I said aside to Mrs. Harrington.

"Of course, dear," Miss Charlotte said. "P. B. had nothing but good to say about Crawford's. I'll trust you all, same as he did. In fact, I have to wait to hear from Mr. Crawford as to the amount P. B. left me. According to Thomas, those two were thick as thieves over P. B.'s investments. He'll be going over P. B.'s portfolio and financial statements with me in a few days. Would you pour me some more tea, dear?" She handed me her cup.

Grandma Ruth and Miss Charlotte chatted over tea and cookies until Mrs. Harrington III came by to carry Miss Charlotte home. Preston was, of course, studying, and his father was sulking, Lydia Harrington said. She seemed unperturbed by her husband's fit of pique.

"He'll get over it. And now Preston can follow his heart," she said with a happy sigh.

"I wonder when it will dawn on Miss Charlotte," I said to Grandma Ruth when I returned from seeing the two Mrs. Harringtons to the front door.

"When what will dawn on her?"

"That the Millie question still hasn't been answered. Just because he didn't mention her in his will doesn't mean he didn't have an—"

"Don't you dare finish that sentence. She may realize or she may not. Right now, however, she's eating like a horse and she'll probably sleep better tonight than she has in weeks. I'd like to keep it that way for as long as possible."

"I have a feeling it won't be for very long," I said. "She's really sharp, Grandma."

I went on to tell her about my supper with Mrs. Harrington, how she figured out what I was looking for when she showed me her husband's Harvard yearbooks, and that she'd known ever since that I was trying to find out who Millie was.

"Well, let's let sleeping dogs lie for now, Sarah," Grandma Ruth advised. "No more sleuthing."

That was fine by me. I had tax returns to prepare. And now that Preston was holed up studying for the LSAT, Grandma Ruth would quit trying to throw me at him. He wouldn't be around for Leslie Nidden to bat her eyelashes at either.

After supper, the phone rang in the kitchen. I wiped my hands on the dish towel I was using to dry dishes and answered.

"Sarah, what's going on?" It was Meredith. "I've been calling ever since I got off work, and your cell keeps going straight to voicemail. I thought you'd want to hear what happened when my boss read the Harrington will. There were some fireworks, believe you me!"

I dug in my purse—left on the counter since I came home from work—to find my phone. *Oh, it's still off.* I was dismayed to have missed Meredith's calls, but relieved that I'd also missed any more from Jake.

"Sorry, Meredith, I turned it off Sunday night so Ja— I mean, so I could get some sleep. I forgot to turn it back on."

"Whoa, girl. Back that train up," Meredith said. "Jake called you? What did he say? What did you say?"

"Look, Meredith," I said with a sidelong glance at Mama, "I have to finish up with the dishes. I'll call you back in a little while."

"You'd better. I can't believe you didn't tell me. What are best friends for, anyway?"

"Later," I said and hung up the phone.

Mama kept me at kitchen cleanup longer than usual. I think she was hoping I'd tell her why I'd turned my phone off on Sunday night, but I kept the conversation light and hightailed it out of there before she decided it was the perfect night to rearrange the pantry.

Up in my room, I turned my phone back on. I had missed a number of calls, texts, and voicemails, but I didn't take the time to check them. Most of them were probably from Meredith, anyway.

Meredith picked up on the first ring. "*Jake* called you? What did that snake want—to twist the knife a few more times?"

I didn't even try to imagine a snake twisting a knife. Even though she's a word girl, Meredith tends to mix her metaphors when she's exercised.

"I didn't pick up," I said.

"Good for you."

"But I listened to the voicemails he left."

"*Sarah.*"

"I don't know why I did it. I couldn't help it," I said.

"Well, at least you didn't talk to him. What did he want?"

"Says he has something special to tell me, that he needs me, and that he was crazy to let me go," I said.

"Delivered with his special brand of irresistible charm, I'll bet," Meredith said.

"Yes." I sighed. "That's why I turned my phone off."

"He has a lot of nerve calling you after what he did," Meredith said. "As if all he'd have to do is sweet-talk you and you'd take him right back."

"As if." I sighed again. An all-too-familiar wistfulness crept over me.

"Don't, Sarah," said Meredith. "Not only is he not worth it, but *you're* worth far more than that. You should have blocked his number when you broke up with him."

"Why would I do that? He wasn't calling me anymore. He was calling her." I heard my voice catch and felt my eyes fill with tears.

"Don't you dare listen to any more voicemails," she said. "I'm on my way over to delete them for you—and block his number."

I heard her car door slam and the rumble of the engine starting up.

"I called to tell you about the Harrington will reading," she continued as she drove to my house. "Would you believe ol' P. B. put it in his will that he'll only pay for Preston to go to Harvard Law? I could hear his father all the way out in the reception area, ranting about how P. B. wasn't of sound mind toward the end. The kicker is that P. B. made that will before his mind started to go—before Preston even went to college. And Preston yelled right back at his father. The whole office heard every word. Then he marched right out of Mr. Nidden's office to start studying for the LSAT."

"I know," I said. "Mrs. Harrington was here to see Grandma Ruth when I got home from work. She's really happy about it. That and the fact that P. B. didn't remember Millie in his will."

"I hadn't heard that part," Meredith said. "I'll bet you didn't hear about Leslie Nidden, though. She, of course, managed to be hanging around the office at the time, supposedly doing some filing for her father. More like filing her nails, if you ask me. I have my work cut out for me every time she 'helps her daddy.' The mess she makes is unbelievable. I really don't know what she does for brains, bless her heart."

"Now, now," I said. "She's annoying, but there's no need to be catty."

"You should have seen it, though." Meredith giggled. "Preston came out of Mr. Nidden's office, letting even more of his father's tirade out into reception. Leslie popped up from her chair like a jack-in-the-box and invited Preston out for coffee to 'celebrate.' Can you believe that? His grandfather just died and she wants to celebrate. He didn't seem to hear her at first. She had to practically run after him to catch up to him at the door. He didn't even look at her until she grabbed his arm and invited him for coffee again."

"What did he say?" It's not that I cared if Preston went for coffee with Leslie, you understand. I was just caught up in the story, that's all.

"He looked real surprised and said, 'Leslie, what are you doing here?'

"Then she said, 'Isn't it wonderful, Preston? You'll go to law school, and then you'll come back and work at Daddy's firm and—and—and everything will be just perfect, that's all!' Her eyelashes were working overtime, I can tell you!"

"So what did he say to her planning his future for him?" My heart went out to him since I could imagine exactly how he felt. Grandma Ruth is intent on planning mine for me.

"He looked down at her and got those little crinkles around his eyes like he was trying not to laugh and said, 'Well, I don't know about all of that. I have to get into Harvard Law first. As you might have heard, I need to study for the LSAT.' Then he went on through the door, leaving her just standing there. Then she called after him, 'I'll bring you coffee while you study!'" Meredith snorted. "She doesn't even get her *own* coffee."

I watched out the window as she pulled up behind the house. I heard her breezy "Hey, Mrs. McCready" down in the kitchen. Moments later she burst through the door of my room and snatched the phone out of my hand. Her thumbs tapped at a furious pace to delete all my voicemails and every text message from Jake. The phone felt unaccountably light when she handed it back to me.

"Thank you," I said.

"What are friends for if they don't save you from yourself? You just put Jake right out of your head and concentrate on Preston."

Have I mentioned Meredith suffers from a one-track mind?

"He's studying for the LSAT, remember?" Besides, attracting Jake had been a stretch. What made Meredith think someone like Preston would waste any time on me?

"Minor technicality," she said with a wave of her hand. "You've got his grandmother's endorsement. You're a shoo-in."

"*After* law school, more than three years from now," I said. "By which time Grandma Ruth will have despaired of me as a confirmed spinster, if I'm lucky."

"I wish you'd get over that," Meredith said. "One bad apple doesn't spoil the whole bunch. Jake is a really rotten apple, I'll admit, but there *are* some great guys out there, and Preston Harrington is one of them."

"I'm nowhere near as sure about that as you are," I said. "They say the apple doesn't fall far from the tree. If P. B. Harrington cheated on his wife, what can anyone expect from his grandson?"

"How's that going, by the way? The investigation, I mean?"

I filled her in on Grandma Ruth's note to the stockbroker, my supper with Mrs. Harrington, and the phone conversation with Mrs. Mildred Wellington.

Meredith nodded. "She retired long before I started working for the firm, but she's legendary. She ruled the office with an iron fist, the soul of propriety and professionalism. I wouldn't be surprised if she had a crush on P. B.—have you seen his portrait in the reception area? He was extremely handsome in his prime. I'll bet Mrs. Wellington would rather die than admit it, though, much less do anything about it."

"But maybe Millie Holtgrew did something about it, something Mrs. Wellington didn't know about," I said. "Grandma Ruth wants to back off on the investigation since Mrs. Harrington is happy at the moment—she ate at least half a dozen cookies when she was here. But I'd feel better if I knew more about this flirtatious secretary, preferably before Mrs. Harrington realizes that even though P. B. didn't leave Millie any money, the question of her identity still remains."

"So you're going to keep investigating?" Meredith asked.

I nodded. "I want to find Millie Holtgrew and ask her just what she and P. B. Harrington got up to thirty-odd years ago."

CHAPTER 11

ON WEDNESDAY MORNING, MR. CRAWFORD tapped on the frame of my open office door. I glanced up to see that he was looking even more professional than usual in a charcoal-gray pin-striped three-piece suit. His pale blue dress shirt sported French cuffs adorned with his Sigma Chi cuff links. His tie was subdued and expensive. A matching silk handkerchief peeked out of his breast pocket, while a classy tie bar gleamed at his collar.

"Sarah, I know you're busy, but I need a favor today."

I suppressed a sigh and gave him my full attention. "Yes, sir?"

"I have a very important client coming this afternoon, and I was wondering if you could arrange with the Magnolia for some light refreshments. On the firm's account, of course."

"Tasteful and restrained?" I asked.

I saw the shadow of a struggle cross his face before he replied. "Tasteful, of course, but tasty, too." He chuckled at his joke. "Spare no expense, my dear. The best the Magnolia has to offer in the way of afternoon tea. The client is coming at four o'clock, so please have everything set up ahead of time. And please check that the firm's tea service is nice and shiny." He didn't need to say "and polish it if it's not." He glanced at the pile of papers on my desk and added, "Order a nice dessert for yourself, as well."

I sat at my desk and ground my teeth for a moment. I didn't mind ordering the Crème de la Crème Tea and setting it up in Mr. Crawford's office. I was getting a scone with strawberry jam and clotted cream out of it, after all. But I wasn't about to polish the tea service just because I'm the only female CPA in the firm.

I called in the order and learned that I would have to go pick it up, as the historical society ladies were arriving at 3:00 and would keep the staff hopping for a good hour and a half. Once they assured me it would be ready at 3:30, I went to the break room, climbed on a chair, and pulled the tea service, swathed in its tarnish-resistant cloth, down from a high shelf. I set it on the counter and peeked under the wrapping. Hallelujah! The treated cloth had actually worked—the insidious Georgia humidity that routinely blackens the silver we Southerners love so much had not gotten past the covering. I carried the tea service back to my office so no curious coworker would unwrap it and thoughtlessly leave it exposed to the elements. I doubted if any of the other CPAs had ever seen a polishing cloth, much less rubbed silverware with it until they could see their own reflections in the back of a spoon.

There was a bustle and buzz in the office that morning that I could hear through my open office door. I used to work with my door closed, thinking it would ensure that I'd be left alone to do my work. The accountants at Crawford and Associates are, however, a sociable bunch who worry about you when your door is closed. They feel obligated to knock or just walk in to find out if you're all right. I finally realized that the best way to discourage unwanted visitors was to leave the door open and never, ever look up when someone walked by.

To look up was to invite conversation, mostly sports related. Thank goodness, the college football season does not coincide with tax season—the SEC rankings being so much more important and all. Indeed, sports inspired those of my coworkers who had tickets to the Masters Golf Tournament in Augusta to push, pull, nag, and bully their clients into filing before that sacred first week of April.

I was pretty sure I knew what, or rather *who*, the fuss was all about, but I asked Shelby, the receptionist, on my way to the Magnolia that afternoon. She lowered her voice and flicked a glance toward Mr. Crawford's open office door.

"Mrs. Harrington has an appointment at four. Boss—I mean, Mr. Crawford says she's a VIC—a very important client."

I pondered this as I walked over to the Magnolia Tea Room. I'd thought we were going to all this trouble because Mrs. Harrington was recently widowed . . . though, come to think of it, Mr. Crawford had plenty of appointments with the surviving spouses of his clients without sending me out for the Crème de la Crème Tea. And this morning he had asked me to order tea and polish the silver for "a very important client." The firm reserved this term for those who were quite rich. Significantly so. I wondered just how rich Miss Charlotte was about to find out she was.

The order was ready as promised, and I whisked out of the tea room before any of the historical society ladies could engage me in a conversation that would take fifteen polite minutes to satisfy their concern for my grandmother's health and the sad state of my love life.

Back at the office, I set up the tea on a low table in the sitting area of Mr. Crawford's office, complete with a small lace table runner and cloth napkins. I had no sooner tucked the last cube into the sugar bowl and laid the tongs beside it than Shelby announced Mrs. Harrington's arrival.

"Thank you, Miss McCready," Mr. Crawford said. "That will be all."

I stepped out of the office to find Preston and Miss Charlotte in the reception area.

"Sarah!" Miss Charlotte beamed. "How nice to see you."

"This way, please, Mrs. Harrington," Mr. Crawford said as he ushered her into his office. Preston followed, but Mr. Crawford stopped him in the doorway. "This is a private consultation, Preston. I'm sure you understand."

Before Preston could say whether he understood or not, Mr. Crawford quietly but firmly closed the door. Preston turned around, a bewildered look on his face.

"May I bring you some coffee, Mr. Harrington?" Shelby asked. "Mr. Harrington?" she prompted when he didn't respond.

"Oh, you mean me," he said as color rose in his cheeks. "My grandfather and my father are Mr. Harrington. I'm Preston. Sure, I'll have some coffee while I wait."

He sat down in a comfortable wing chair while Shelby worked her wonders with the one-cup coffee machine tucked away in a corner of the reception area for the benefit of clients. It's just as well the CPAs get their coffee at the Coffee Break. I can't figure out how to work that coffee maker for the life of me.

I took advantage of Shelby's bustling around about the coffee to slip away to my office, get back to work, and enjoy my scone. I pulled up the tax return I was working on and opened the cute little box the Magnolia provides for take-out orders. I was about to take my first bite when I heard my name spoken by a familiar voice out in reception. I quickly closed the box and got up to close my office door.

"Do you have an appointment, sir? Ms. McCready is quite busy."

Attagirl, Shelby, I silently cheered.

"She won't be too busy to see me," Jake told her. I didn't need to see him to know he'd winked at her. Shelby's little giggle told me everything I needed to know. "Especially since I brought her favorite coffee." This last sounded like it had been thrown over his shoulder as he made for my office.

Shelby recovered enough from Jake's charm to protest. "Really, sir, you can't go back there without an appointment."

I made to close the door, but Jake was too fast and crafty for me. He slid his foot into the doorway to keep me from closing the door in his face. I was sorely tempted to go ahead and slam it, but since there was a VIC just down the hall, I refrained. It would not do to raise the kind of ruckus crushing Jake's foot would have caused.

"I'm sorry, Sarah." Shelby bobbed up from behind Jake's shoulder. "I tried to stop him."

"Thank you, Shelby, I'll take it from here," I said, not moving from the doorway.

With a worried glance, Shelby went back to her post in the reception area.

"Well?" Jake cocked an eyebrow. "Aren't you going to invite me in?"

"No," I said as I crossed my arms in front of my chest. "As Shelby told you, I'm very busy. It's tax season."

"Surely you can't say no to your favorite coffee. Caramel macchiato," he crooned as he waved the cup under my nose.

I reached for it, but he held it out of my reach. I shrugged and crossed my arms again.

"Drink it yourself," I said.

"Be that way, then," he said. "I'll just say what I have to say right here."

That's when I realized how quiet the office had become. My coworkers, with their open doors, had stopped typing on their computers, the better to hear what was going on.

"Oh, all *right*!" I grabbed Jake by the arm, hauled him into my office, and closed the door. Huge mistake.

Jake wrapped the arm that wasn't managing the coffee around my waist and kissed me before I knew what was happening. It was one of Jake's expert kisses, the kind that leaves a girl weak at the knees and hanging onto her heart with just her fingernails. I started to kiss him back before I got my wits about me. I pulled away, but he held on. I shifted the heel of one of my new black peep-toe pumps onto his instep and leaned into it (the instep, not the kiss).

Jake let go of me with a yelp and nearly dropped the coffee.

"What the— I just came to bring you some coffee and you try to impale me!"

"How dare you," I nearly shouted. "How dare you come here? How dare you try to kiss me here. This is where I work."

"Oh, I did more than try," he said. "And you kissed me back—you can't deny it. You look amazing when you're mad, do you know that, Sarah?" He reached out and tucked a stray strand of hair behind my ear. He managed to brush my cheek with his fingers too before I batted his hand away and stepped back. My heart had turned over at his words and at his touch, but he didn't need to know that.

"Leave." I reached for the door handle.

"Hear me out, honey." Jake turned the full force of his mysterious deep-blue eyes on me. "I have discovered something special that I have to tell you. It's for your ears only, but I can tell it out in the hall if that's what you really want."

He laid his hand over mine on the door handle and lightly ran his thumb across the inside of my wrist. I slid my hand out from under his before I could weaken and made for my desk chair to have the desk between us. What I would do if he came behind the desk wasn't immediately clear to me, but I did register the location of a large stapler close at hand.

"So, Mr. Halloran," I said in my CPA-to-client voice. "What is your business with Crawford and Associates today? I regret to say that I am at my full capacity for completing returns in time for Tax Day, but one of my colleagues may be able to take on the work."

"Nobody but you will do, Sarah," Jake said in a low, husky voice. "I hope you'll find it in your heart to forgive me. I was a fool to let you go."

"*I* let *you* go, as I recall. How is Buffy, by the way?" I asked.

"Out of the picture."

I raised my eyebrows, but my heart did a little dance.

"Scout's honor," Jake said. "Sarah, Buffy was just a stupid fling. She didn't mean a thing. What I feel for you, though—it's the real thing. I know that now." He leaned across the desk and reached for my hand.

Over the many months since our breakup, I had longed to hear those words. I'd played out this scene in my head a thousand times, and now I felt my heart start to melt. My hand seemed to move toward his with a will of its own—until it brushed up against the cold, hard metal of the stapler. I jerked back and clasped both my hands together in my lap, not trusting either of them.

"I am, as I said, unavailable," I said, careful to look at his forehead, not his eyes.

"Oh yes you are," Jake said. "I know for a fact you're not seeing anyone. But that could change at any moment. Just say the word, sugar. I'm lost without you."

His voice was like a siren song, just the right amount of pleading balanced by a tenderness that was like a caress. I lowered my gaze and was on the edge of falling into the deep-blue lagoon of his eyes when a knock sounded at the door. I startled, as if coming out of a trance.

Apparently, my coworkers couldn't stand not knowing what was going on inside my office.

"Sarah, are you all right?" came a voice through the door.

Not a coworker after all—it was Preston.

I hurried around my desk, giving Jake a wide berth, and flung open the door, suddenly conscious of how close to disaster I had just been.

"Preston, how sweet of you to drop by." I slipped my hand around his bicep and drew him eagerly into the room. "Mr. Halloran here was just leaving. I really don't have time to do your taxes, Mr. Halloran," I told Jake.

"That means she doesn't have time to do yours either." Jake looked Preston square in the eye.

"Unlike *you*," Preston said, returning his glare, "I wouldn't dream of asking her to. It's clear she has more than enough to do as it is." He waved his hand at the pile of tax returns in my inbox that threatened to topple across my desk.

"Thank you, Preston." I smiled up at him as I moved a tad closer. "I'm glad you understand."

Jake's eyes narrowed. "I'm beginning to understand too."

"I believe you were on your way out, Mr. Halloran." Preston gestured toward the door (rather forcefully, I thought).

"This isn't over, Harrington," Jake spat out. "You don't even have a chance." He leaned over, brushed his lips across my cheek and whispered in my ear, "See you later, sugar."

I felt my face flame.

"It's not what it looks like," I told Preston as Jake swaggered away down the hall.

Preston looked down at me with concern in his clear blue eyes, his brows drawn together ever so slightly. "Shelby asked me to see if you were okay," he said. "Are you?"

I realized that I was still holding his arm. I was, in fact, squeezing it. I eased up a bit and breathed in the clean smell of his aftershave.

"I'm fine," I replied, with more nonchalance than I felt. I could see the questions in his eyes. Why was Shelby worried about me? What was my old flame doing in my office with the door closed? I had no illusions—in a town as small as Raeburne's Ferry, everyone knew about my broken engagement. Not that everyone had all the facts straight, but they had the gist. Even Preston.

"My grandfather didn't meet with female clients alone behind closed doors," Preston said. "It's a good rule of thumb."

I felt myself bristle. As if I didn't know that. And as if his grandfather hadn't been alone behind closed doors somewhere with someone named Millie. But I wasn't about to enlighten Preston regarding Jake, open doors at Crawford and Associates, my coworkers' big ears, or my suspicions about P. B.'s behavior with Millie. I let go of his arm.

"It's complicated," I told him.

Preston searched my face. "Well, if you're all right, then, I'll let you get back to work."

At that moment, however, the door to Mr. Crawford's office opened. Mrs. Harrington stumbled into the reception area, a handkerchief clutched in her hand and tears coursing down her face. From the stricken look she cast my way, I could tell these were not the happy tears of a woman who has received good news about her financial affairs.

What could possibly have happened to the rest of P. B. Harrington's money? Lost in the stock market? Maybe M. D. Farnsworth had come all the way from New York City to attend his funeral to deliver bad news to Mr. Crawford. Or had the estate been so poorly planned that Mrs. Harrington's portion was in danger of being devoured by estate taxes? I could not believe that of P. B., who'd been an estate lawyer himself, for heaven's sake, nor of Mr. Crawford, who was adept at making sure the tax system didn't take bread out of the mouths of widows and orphans. *Something* was wrong, though. Had the Crème de la Crème Tea been meant not to pamper a rich client but to soften a heavy blow?

"It cannot possibly be true," Mrs. Harrington told Mr. Crawford, who hovered at her elbow.

"I assure you, Mrs. Harrington, it is true." He gave her a beaming, benevolent smile. "It really is."

Mrs. Harrington looked away from Mr. Crawford's smiling face. "If this is true," she said in a despairing voice, "what *else* did I not know about him?"

CHAPTER 12

I KNEW BETTER THAN TO ask Mr. Crawford what was going on when I went into his office to clear away the tea things after Mrs. Harrington's tearful departure. This was not only because it would have been un-professional, but also because it was clear that he had no idea that his VIC was upset. The way he hummed to himself at his desk while I stacked plates, cups, and saucers and boxed up the leftovers told me that he thought she had been overcome by wonderful news.

Therefore, I concluded, P. B. Harrington had left his wife a more than gracious plenty, as that was the best kind of news in my em-ployer's mind. It was this gracious plenty, however, that had sent her sobbing out of her husband's accountant's office, supported once again by the strong arm of her grandson.

There were several messages on my phone when I returned to my office. Fully four of them were probably from Jake, who had taken to using other people's phones to text me since I'd blocked his num-ber. I promptly deleted all the messages from unfamiliar numbers, I'm proud to say. The last message was from Grandma Ruth, telling me in no uncertain terms to come straight home from work. It had been only fifteen minutes, and she'd caught wind of the news already.

At five thirty I shut down my computer, tidied my desk, and headed out to my car. The wind had picked up and I was glad of my hat and gloves. My fellow CPAs and Shelby had all left on the dot of five. Only my Civic and Mr. Crawford's Mercedes were left in the lot. I stopped short when I saw a tall, dark-haired form leaning against my car in the fast-approaching darkness. I turned to go back into the office.

"Sarah, wait!" Jake called. "I just want to talk to you."

I kept walking. Gravel crunched behind me as Jake ran to catch up to me.

"Sarah, hear me out. *Please.*"

I turned with my hand on the doorknob.

"It's too cold out here to talk about anything," I said.

"Then let's go someplace warm. I'll take you to dinner, anywhere you want."

"Grandma Ruth is expecting me home directly."

Jake flinched at the mention of my grandmother, as miscreants generally do. "Then I'll take you to dinner tomorrow night. I'll pick you up after work and whisk you off to Fontanelli's."

My hand hesitated on the doorknob. Fontanelli's is the fanciest restaurant in Raeburne's Ferry. Soft music, candlelight, shrimp scampi, cannoli, and a handsome man adoring me across the table—it was tempting.

But would he be? Adoring, I mean. At that moment, it occurred to me that I had done most of the adoring in the relationship. I was so in love, so gone on him that I was practically putty in his hands. I could deny him nothing . . . except . . . well . . . except *that.*

And, when it came down to it, *that* had been the trouble. It's the twenty-first century, and nobody waits until they get married anymore. In the end, Jake made sure I felt like a colossal nobody for insisting on waiting. During our final confrontation, the one in which I threw the engagement ring at him across the room, he told me that the situation was all my fault. He would never have taken up with Buffy if I had just given in.

He said calling off the wedding was a lucky escape for him, as I was probably frigid, anyway. It was as if he never realized just how warm my heart and all the rest of me was toward him, how my blood roared in my ears when he touched me, or how many times the only thing that kept me from going over the brink was the mental image of Grandma Ruth's piercing blue eyes. Throughout my adolescence, she told me in no uncertain terms that *that* was not acceptable behavior for a person of my tender years. Right before I left for college, though, she'd sat me down for a talk over a plate of pecan sandies.

"I'll miss you," she said.

"I'm not going all that far, Grandma," I said. "I'll be home every weekend."

"Wanting your mother to do your laundry, no doubt," she said.

I started to deny it, and then realized the futility of lying to my grandmother. She sees through people as if they're plate-glass windows.

"You will have a great deal of freedom at college," she went on.

I nodded as I contemplated the glorious truth that I wouldn't have to make my bed or do dishes or be in by curfew. I'd even be able to go to frat parties if I wanted. I'd be able to go to a frat party with Jake.

"You will have much more freedom when it comes to boys," she continued, as if my thoughts had streamed across my forehead like a lighted marquee. "It seems to me that there's quite a bit of pressure at college to do what other people are doing. Don't ever forget that you are well worth waiting for, Sarah. Promise me."

I had looked into her penetrating eyes and promised. Thus it was that, no matter how tempted I was to lose myself completely in Jake's seductive gaze, another pair of blue eyes always haunted those encounters and held me to my promise.

So, according to Jake, sneering from across the room on that fateful night, it was that promise that had cost me my engagement and driven Jake, the love of my life, into another woman's arms. Frigid? I couldn't believe what I was hearing. I was as hot-blooded as the next coed, but I had promised my grandmother not to act on my desires until I was married. Didn't he want to marry someone who knew how to keep a promise? As I watched the diamond tumble and flash through the air before it hit him square on the forehead, my heart did freeze—with shock and pain. The tears that pricked my eyes felt like shards of ice.

A sudden gust of cold wind pulled me back to the present, where Jake was waiting for my answer to his dinner invitation.

"No, thank you," I said over my shoulder as I slipped through the door and leaned against it.

Mr. Crawford was in the reception area, bundled up in his hat and coat, briefcase in hand. "Sarah," he said as he peered down the hall at me. "I thought you'd left."

"I forgot something." I headed toward my office.

"I'll wait and walk you to your car," he said, like a true Southern gentleman. "It's getting dark out there."

I stepped into my office, counted to ten, and then rushed back to the reception area waving my phone in triumph.

I scanned the parking lot as Mr. Crawford tested the office door to make sure it was locked and sent up a prayer of thanks that Jake was gone. I really did not want my work life and my love life to collide.

I was soon to discover that Jake was counting on that.

When I pushed open the kitchen door, tired and windblown, I discovered why my grandmother wanted me to come straight home from work. Preston was seated at the kitchen table, where Mama was plying him with cookies and hot chocolate. He looked up as the wind from the open door ruffled the pages of the LSAT prep book on the table in front of him.

"Hey, Sarah." He greeted me with the wave of a half-eaten cookie. "Nice to see you again." I watched a cascade of crumbs and confectioner's sugar drift to the floor. "Have a cookie." He offered me the plate.

"Hey, Preston, um, nice to see you too," I answered as I felt a blush creep up my neck.

I reached for one of my mother's excellent pecan sandies. Mama put a plate of scones in my hand instead and pointed me down the hall to the parlor.

"For your grandmother and Mrs. Harrington," she told me. "Fresh from the oven."

What I really wanted was to abscond to my room with a whole plate of cookies, kick off my shoes, and lose myself in a murder mystery in which everybody got what they deserved, from the murderer to the clever and virtuous sleuth someplace far, far away from Raeburne's Ferry.

"Yes, ma'am," I replied. My feet were killing me, but I tried not to limp as I crossed the kitchen and pushed through the swinging kitchen door.

I could hear the murmur of voices and the occasional sniff as I winced down the hall.

"*There* you are," Grandma Ruth said when I entered the parlor, scones in hand. "I thought I told you not to dawdle on the way home from work."

I took one look at Mrs. Harrington's face and promptly forgot the excuses I had come up with on the way home to avoid telling Grandma Ruth about Jake. Her face was deathly pale, tears ran in a continuous stream down her cheeks, and her lips trembled.

I shoved the scones at Grandma Ruth and dropped to my knees beside the wing chair. "Miss Charlotte, what's the matter? You look like you've lost your last friend. Please don't cry. It's all right. Everything will be all right."

"No, it won't, Sarah." Miss Charlotte shook her head. "Things will never be all right again. I haven't lost my last friend." She gave my grandmother a watery smile. "But I've lost my best one." These last words were nearly swallowed up by a despairing sob.

I gave Grandma Ruth a questioning look over Miss Charlotte's bowed head.

"Mrs. Harrington has had a great shock, Sarah. Please pour her more tea." Grandma held up three fingers to indicate the number of sugar cubes to include as a restorative.

By the time Miss Charlotte drained her cup and set it on the bedside table, her hands had stopped trembling. "As you know, Sarah, I met with Mr. Crawford today regarding my husband's financial affairs, or, rather, my financial affairs now. I was in no way prepared for what he told me." She took a deep breath and then continued. "I had no doubt that P. B. would leave me comfortably provided for, but I did not have the slightest notion of being a millionaire several times over!"

I sat back on my heels, my four-inch heels that suddenly didn't hurt anymore. "How many times over?"

"Eighteen."

"Eighteen million dollars? P. B. left you eighteen million dollars? But that's wonderful, Miss Charlotte."

"No, it's not." Miss Charlotte's eyes filled with tears again.

"But whyever not?" I asked. Really, what could be so terrible about inheriting eighteen *million* dollars?

"I thought he was just dabbling in the stock market. He used to say he would leave me a million dollars when he died. I thought it was just him talking big so I wouldn't worry about the future. But he and M. D. Farnsworth were making much more than a million."

"Apparently they were quite a team," Grandma Ruth said. She handed me an envelope. I pulled out a sheet of paper and read it aloud while Miss Charlotte sobbed and sniffed.

"'Dear Ms. McCready,'" I read. "'I knew Mr. Harrington in a professional capacity, as his stockbroker for the past twelve years. I attended his funeral to pay tribute to a man of uncanny and remarkable ability. Once again, I extend my condolences. Sincerely, Margaret D. Farnsworth.'"

"Yes, just like Mr. Crawford told me today. I never knew that he was making so much money at it!" Miss Charlotte's voice rose to a wail. "This is another thing I didn't know about him. What else did he keep from me? Did I even know him at all?"

When she put it that way, I could see that she had a point. He had kept the money secret. Suddenly the idea of Millie the Mistress became even more plausible.

I felt a surge of anger. I was sick and tired of women getting blind-sided by the men they loved and trusted. If P. B. Harrington had been in Grandma Ruth's parlor at that moment, I would have shaken him until his eyes rolled around like billiard balls in his head. But no, he was tucked away in St. Alban's churchyard, untouched by the havoc he had left in the wake of his passing.

"I'm so sorry, Miss Charlotte," I finally choked out. "I wish there was something I could do."

"That's the other thing," Miss Charlotte went on. "I don't know what that man thought an old lady like me would do with eighteen million dollars. There's no mortgage to pay off, the Rolls runs like a top, I don't need or want any more jewelry, and I daresay my clothes will last me until I die. I couldn't begin to spend it all. I suppose it will go to the children when I'm gone."

"You could leave a far greater legacy than that," Grandma Ruth said.

"You mean make even more money?" Miss Charlotte said. "I don't know the first thing about investing, Mary Ruth."

"Of course not, Charlotte. Neither do I, for that matter," my grand-mother said with a sidelong glance at me. I shook my head. I only know how to keep track of money, not make it hand over fist like Mr. Harrington. "But you could do a great deal of good in this town, good that would go on long after you are gone."

"You mean give it away?" Miss Charlotte looked dubious. "I can hear Bent now, questioning whether I'm of sound mind just like he questioned his father's sanity when the will was read. No thank you." She set her mouth in a thin, firm line.

"Charlotte, I have a lot of time to think, here in this bed, day after day," my grandmother said. "It's hard to be sidelined by age, to feel like your chance to make an impact on the world is over because of your physical limitations."

I suppressed an unladylike snort. My grandmother may be bedrid-den, but her world is as big as it ever was when she was able-bodied. I'm only one of the people upon whom she continues to exert her con-siderable influence.

"And then I think about young people like Sarah here, and Preston," she said. "About how well they've turned out, in no small part due to the time they were able to spend with their grandparents as they were growing up. Do not roll your eyes at me, young lady."

The glance my grandmother speared me with stopped the eye roll immediately. I resisted the temptation to cross my eyes at her instead. It would simply have proven her point that the younger generation needs to learn manners from their elders. But honestly, it was typical of her to take all the credit, as if Mama and Daddy had simply stood by and watched.

Miss Charlotte leaned forward. Her eyes shone and not with tears. "Go on, Mary Ruth. What do you have in mind?"

"Sarah came here after school when her mother worked late, but many, many children in that situation go, not to a loving relative, but to an after-school program—or worse yet, an empty house. What if there was a place where children could go after school and be with grandparents—those older people who still have so much to give?"

"They could help with homework," said Miss Charlotte.

"And read to them," Grandma Ruth said.

"Bake cookies together," Miss Charlotte added.

"Hear about the olden days," Grandma Ruth said.

"Listen to *their* day," I put in. "The children's days, I mean."

Miss Charlotte's face lit up. "I used to love to listen to Preston run on about his day. He always came to my house when Lydia had garden club. He'd just grunt and shrug when his daddy asked him what he'd learned in school, but he'd tell me everything over cookies and milk. I like this idea, Mary Ruth."

"It would take some money, though," my grandmother said. "We'd need a building, some furniture, a kitchen or two, books . . . and cookies, for starters."

"I think I could spare a million or two," Miss Charlotte said with a smile that was like the sun coming out after a rainstorm.

I slipped away while the two friends brainstormed over their tea and scones, Millie and all of P. B.'s other secrets apparently forgotten. I hadn't forgotten, though. Then and there, I resolved to track down Millie Holtgrew and get the truth, once and for all. Miss Charlotte deserved to enjoy her windfall, not fret over it.

Out in the hall, I slipped off my pumps and padded to the kitchen for that plate of cookies I was craving. The kitchen door swung so quietly on its well-oiled hinges that no one realized I'd come in. I stood still and took in the sight of Preston bent over his book, a cookie in one hand and the mug of hot chocolate in the other. I had a sudden glimpse of him as a kid, at his grandmother's kitchen table with cookies and milk, telling her all about his day.

I felt a kinship with him. We both had grandmothers who got all up in our business and called it love. Make no mistake—Miss Charlotte might come across all fragile, fluttery, and sweet, but she usually gets her way. Just like Grandma Ruth. And in those fleeting moments, as I studied Preston's blond head bent over the LSAT prep book that represented his heart's desire, I found myself admitting that it really was love that motivated our grandmothers, not just an inveterate penchant for meddling.

"There you are, Sarah."

I blinked a few times as my mother's voice broke the spell.

Preston looked up, and I was suddenly aware of my stocking feet. I crossed the room and sat down, tucking my toes under the table.

"How is she?" Preston asked. He pushed his book aside and turned his full attention to me.

"Better, I think." I reached for a cookie. "She and Grandma Ruth are in there planning how to spend all that money."

"What have they come up with?" Preston asked. "She fretted about that money all the way over here. I really don't understand why the size of the estate upsets her so much. You'd think she'd be praising Granddaddy to the skies for leaving her so well off. Instead, she's crying. And when she's not crying, she's muttering 'Money and Millie,' and making strangling motions with her hands. What is she so mad about?"

"You know about the Millie thing, right?"

"There's nothing to that." Preston waved his hand in a gesture that reminded me of my grandmother. "Granddaddy was crazy about her. There never was anyone else."

"You can't know that for sure," I said.

"Sarah!" I instantly regretted shocking Mama.

"I'm sorry, Mama," I said to my mother.

To Preston I said, "I didn't mean to be rude. It's just that what your grandmother thinks about Millie is more important than what people like you and Grandma Ruth think they know about your grandfather."

"I don't think it," Preston said, with a handsome and stubborn set to his jaw. "I know it."

"But your grandmother doesn't," I said.

He opened his mouth to retort, but I held up my hand.

"Look at it this way. For practically her whole life, she never doubted him. And she gave him the benefit of the doubt when he got hard to live with those last few years. But now, between the Millie thing and the money thing, it seems to her like this man she loved and thought she knew kept secrets from her. She's wondering if she knew him at all, and I'll bet she's wondering what other secrets are lurking in the shadows, waiting to come out."

"Oh, I can see that," my mother said.

"But you said she seems better now that she's planning how to spend the money," Preston said. Apparently, he'd reached his limit for trying to understand things that are perfectly clear to women. "What are they cooking up in there?" He inclined his head toward the parlor.

"It's Grandma Ruth's idea," I said. "But Miss Charlotte is on board with it. It really seems to be taking her mind off her worries."

"So what is it? A new car? The Rolls is cool and all, but a red convertible might really cheer her up."

I shook my head. "The money is going to their heads in an entirely different way. They're in there plotting to take over the next generation." I outlined Grandma Ruth's idea for an after-school program manned by senior citizens.

"If it keeps my grandmother from brooding over 'the Millie thing,' as you call it, Sarah, I'm all for it," Preston said when I finished. "My father will have a fit, though. He's going to want to invest every penny, as if it were *his* money."

"I think Miss Charlotte can handle your daddy, Preston," Mama said with a smile. "She did teach him to eat with a fork, after all." She topped off his hot chocolate and swirled on some more whipped cream.

"I can see it now," I said. "After the kids finish their homework, the grandmas will teach them how to make macaroni and cheese casserole and write tasteful condolence notes. The art of the funeral will never die in Raeburne's Ferry."

"We'll teach them a lot more than that," Miss Charlotte said as she came through the kitchen door, pulling on her gloves. "This will be wonderful, for the children *and* the grandparents. I'd love to stay—Mary Ruth and I are bursting with ideas—but your mother is expecting us for supper, Preston."

Preston frowned and set his jaw. "I'll drop you by, but I'm not coming to supper."

"But, Preston, your mother's making your favorite," Miss Charlotte said.

"No, Grandmother," he said firmly. "No amount of fried catfish can make me sit through supper with my father. I'm going to law school and that's that."

"Of course you are, dear," Miss Charlotte said. "But it would mean so much to your mother if the two of you made up, came to some sort of understanding."

"I've been trying to make him understand for years, Grandmother," Preston said as he shrugged into his coat. "But the only thing he understands is money. Money talks, and the money Granddaddy left me is saying I'm going to law school. There is no more to be said."

With that, Preston grabbed up his LSAT book, thanked Mama for the hot chocolate, and offered his arm to his grandmother. I saw them to the front door and watched Preston support Miss Charlotte down the porch steps and install her in the passenger seat of the Rolls. She was talking to him the whole time, still trying to convince him to go to dinner at his parents' house, I supposed.

I sighed as they drove off. This after-school care idea and the rift between Preston and his father might distract her for a while, but eventually her mind and heart would return to the essential question: *Who is Millie?*

I devoted the remainder of the evening to trying to answer that question. Up in my room, I booted up my laptop, typed "Camilla Holtgrew" into the search engine, and came up with—nothing. I tried "Millie Holtgrew." Again, to no avail. Then I typed in simply "Holtgrew" to see what might come up. As I scrolled down the page, I saw an alternate spelling—"Holtgrewe." *Hmm.* I noodled around some more and found an entire page of Holtgrewes—names, where they lived, when they were born . . . and when they had died. There was a Minnie Holtgrewe, born in 1905, died in 1997. Mildred Holtgrewe . . . born in 1910, also deceased. My eyes lit up when I saw an actual Millie Holtgrewe but clouded over again. This Millie had been born in 1897 and lived until 1998.

It got me wondering, though, about the spelling of the name. I scrolled through my phone and found the call I'd made to Mrs. Wellington. Crossing my fingers, I called her again.

"Good evening, Wellington residence." Mrs. Wellington's well-modulated Southern voice came over the phone.

"Mrs. Wellington, this is Sarah McCready, Charlotte Harrington's friend. We spoke last week, as you may recall."

"Of course, Miss McCready. How may I help you?" Instantly, she was Mildred Wellington, senior secretary of Bentley, Harrington, Harrington, and Nidden again. I could almost see her untangling a pair of reading glasses from a chain around her neck and placing them on the end of her nose.

"Well, I know it's been a long time, but do you happen to remember the spelling of Camilla Holtgrew's last name? Was it with or without an *e* on the end?"

"Of course I remember. It was spelled H-o-l-t-g-r-e-w, no *e* on the end. I hope that helps." Bless her, she was too tactful to ask me why I wanted to know, but all she'd told me was that I'd been looking in the right place and not finding anything.

"Mrs. Wellington, do you happen to know what happened to her after she left the firm?"

"No, I certainly do not," she said. "I handed her a severance check—Mr. Harrington was generous almost to a fault—and that's the last I ever saw of her. I heard . . ." She gave a discreet cough. "That is, it may have come to my attention that she left town soon after."

Generous? I wondered . . .

"Was that Mr. Harrington's usual practice when he let an employee go?" I asked.

"Was that . . . usual practice . . ." Mrs. Wellington began to splutter. "Now, look here, young lady, if you're implying what I think you're implying, your mother ought to drag your mind out of the gutter and wash it out with lye soap. Mr. Harrington never . . . The very idea!" And with that, she slammed the phone down.

With Mrs. Wellington's rebuke ringing in my ears, I took stock of what I'd learned. Not much, really. I now knew the correct spelling of Millie Holtgrew's name and that Mrs. Wellington would *never* take a call from me again. And as far as Google was concerned, Camilla "Call-me-Millie" Holtgrew didn't exist, even in the obituaries. Which meant that she could still be out there somewhere—somehow incognito.

I didn't sleep well that night for thinking about it.

CHAPTER 13

WOULD YOU BELIEVE THAT JAKE showed up at my office again the very next day? Shelby intercepted me in the parking lot, wringing her hands. "I told him to leave it with me, that I'd make sure you got it, but he insists on giving it to you himself."

I had been nagging Hiram Fletcher to sign the electronic filing form so I could file his return, so I didn't see what Shelby was so upset about. "Well, I for one am glad that Mr. Fletcher has finally gotten around to signing that form. It's one more return off my pile." I started toward the front steps of Crawford and Associates.

Shelby barred my way and steered me toward the back entrance. "It's not Hiram Fletcher," she said. "It's Jake and he brought you a huge vase of roses. He's been here since I opened the office. You know how the boss is about personal visits at work. You go in through the back and get to work. I'll handle Mr. Halloran."

"Thanks, Shelby. I owe you." I slipped through the back entrance, tiptoed to my office, and got to work. Since I had to leave my door open to avoid interruptions, I could hear Jake in the reception area.

"She's late."

"As I said, Mr. Halloran, you can leave the flowers with me and I'll make sure she gets them," Shelby said in her most professional voice.

"She's never late," he said. "Something's wrong here."

I heard the front door open and close. I barely had time to think, *Whew! He's gone!* before it opened again.

"I knew it!" Jake cried triumphantly. "Her car's in the parking lot. She's here."

"Miss McCready is extremely busy and not to be disturbed," Shelby told him.

"I won't disturb her," he said in what I always thought of as his silky voice. I knew he was leaning over the reception desk and gazing into the receptionist's eyes. "I'll just give her the flowers and be on my way. Surely nobody can object to that."

At that moment, Mr. Crawford arrived.

"What is going on here?" he said as he eyed Jake, the flowers, and his furiously blushing receptionist. "Miss Dunaway, there is a policy in this firm about receiving personal visits during working hours. Did I not make that clear to you when you accepted this position?"

"Yes, sir, Mr. Crawford, but—"

"No excuses, now, young lady. Send your young man packing and never let it happen again."

I waited for Jake to explain, but he let Shelby hang there, taking the blame. I couldn't let her get in trouble on my account because Jake was too much of a low-down snake to set matters straight. I hurried out of my office and into the reception area.

"He's not Shelby's young man, sir," I said. "He's mine."

At this, Jake's eyes lit up.

"I mean," I backtracked, "he's not 'my young man,' but . . . he's here to see me." I gave Jake what I hoped was a piercing look that would remind him of my grandmother.

"Clients generally don't arrive for their appointments with large bouquets of roses, Miss McCready," said Mr. Crawford. "I believe I have made the office policy about personal visits during work hours clear to you as well."

"Yes, sir, perfectly clear," I said, looking at Mr. Crawford's tie bar. I was so embarrassed I couldn't look him in the eye.

"Why you didn't make this policy clear to your young man, I don't know, but I do not expect this to happen again. Now, back to work, both of you." He nodded briskly at Shelby and me. Then to Jake, he said, "This is a place of business. Since you have no business here, I must ask you to leave."

I turned and headed back to my office, muttering, "He is *not* my young man."

"But what about the flowers?" I heard Jake ask.

"Give them to her on her own time, not mine," was Mr. Crawford's clipped reply. "I cannot have my employees distracted by such extravagance when they are supposed to be preparing tax returns."

Jake, however, was not to be gotten rid of so easily. He persisted as I sat down at my desk and tried to get back to work.

"That's the thing, Mr. Crawford," he said. "I do need my taxes prepared, and I was hoping Sarah—I mean, Miss McCready could do them for me. I asked her yesterday and she said she couldn't take on any more clients. I thought the flowers might persuade her."

You had to hand it to him. Jake was slick. Too slick, just like Grandma Ruth said. But Mr. Crawford saw right through him, too.

"I can assure you, Miss McCready cannot prepare one single additional tax return, even an EZ form, which you could do quite well yourself." I heard a rustle of paper. "There you are. It's simple and self-explanatory."

"Uh, thank you, sir," Jake said, for once at a loss for words.

I wondered if he knew he'd been insulted. Mr. Crawford apparently thought very little of his earning power, large bouquets of roses notwithstanding. I heard the front door open and close and breathed a sigh of relief that he was gone at last. I gave my desk chair a little hitch and turned my attention to the task at hand—Abby Claire Harper's tax return, which happened to be an EZ form. Mr. Crawford preferred not to take on clients whose taxes were so simple they could do them themselves, but he'd said yes to Abby Claire, and what's more, we weren't charging her.

I shrugged and got down to it. Mine was not to reason why. I'm sure he had his reasons, which, as the soul of discretion, he was not about to share with me.

The rest of Raeburne's Ferry was not so discreet. It was clear that the news of Mrs. Harrington's immense inheritance was all over town by the time I met Meredith for lunch at the Magnolia Tea Room. In fact, by the time I got there, inflation had set in. Somewhere along the way, someone had misheard "eighteen million" as "eighty million."

Opinions and speculation were rife at the Magnolia. Meredith and I kept our conversation to a minimum so we could overhear. All right, we were eavesdropping, but everyone was talking loud enough that it was simply a matter of deciding which conversation to tune in to first. At a nearby table, Mrs. R. J. Hume was holding forth on the financial needs of the historical society with full assurance that Charlotte Harrington, what with her American history degree from Radcliffe and all, would jump at the chance to fully fund. Mrs. Hume thought Miss Charlotte would want to sponsor a few of the projects the United Daughters of the Confederacy had going too.

At another table, Grace Layton, president of the garden club, shot Mrs. Hume a look that said, *I hope your azaleas stop blooming* as she dreamed out loud about what they could do with the garden around the war memorial with Mrs. Harrington's help. She'd been a member of the garden club for decades, after all. Since she'd been president three times, dear Charlotte knew how much money the club needed to beautify Raeburne's Ferry and how hard that amount was to come by without begging all over town. Apparently, Grace planned on doing all her begging at Miss Charlotte's from now on.

"Did P. B. really leave Mrs. Harrington *eighty million dollars?*" Meredith whispered over her lobster bisque. The Magnolia was really spoiling us these days.

"No," I whispered back. "It's *eighteen* million."

"That's still a lot of money. What *is* she going to do with it all?" Meredith said.

"Whatever she wants," I said and turned my attention to the conversation two tables over.

"*I* think she should go to one of those fancy spa resorts and get the works," Bonnie Marsden, owner of the Blue Moon Beauty Emporium, was recommending. "It would do her a world of good to have a week or so of pampering. She looked a tad peaked last time I did her hair. I offered to do her nails for free with Heather Rose, her favorite shade, and she just sighed and said, 'Not today, dear.' I've been worried about her."

Miss Sylvia Hardcastle, one of the stylists at the Blue Moon, nodded. Not a hair of her piled-high-and-highly-sprayed platinum blond updo moved. "She sure has taken it hard. I don't know that all that money is going to cheer her up much. I bet she'd much rather have that old coot back instead."

Mrs. Hume shot Miss Sylvia a shocked glance, which Miss Sylvia caught out of the corner of her eye.

"He *was* an old coot toward the end," Miss Sylvia said, without looking at Mrs. Hume. "He got so ornery at the barbershop that Hank told him he wouldn't cut his hair anymore. P. B. wasn't about to darken the door of the Blue Moon, so the only thing to do was put him on the shut-in list. I went by every few weeks to trim him up, and I soon saw Hank's point. That old man sure was cantankerous. You'd never know it, though, from the way Miss Charlotte treated him. Sweet as pie and loving as the day is long. I know she misses him something fierce."

The talk about the money died down after that. In fact, Mrs. Hume seemed to be in a hurry to pay her bill a few minutes later. Grace Layton suddenly had a great deal to say about pruning rosebushes. Once all the old biddies were gone, I filled Meredith in on Jake's visits to Crawford and Associates.

"The roses were beautiful," I said. "There must have been two dozen."

"Down, girl," said Meredith.

"What? I was just commenting on the roses."

"Uh-huh." Meredith raised her eyebrows. "And you were pretty impressed with them too. Don't let him get to you."

"I'm not letting him get to me," I said. "But is it a crime to notice how hard he's trying?"

"No, but it would be a shame if you fell for it."

"But isn't it just possible that he's trying this hard because he really cares?" I asked.

"That's what he wants you to think," Meredith said. "I can think of several other reasons he's making such a pest of himself."

I shook my head. It boggled the mind that she thought she could see through Jake when she was completely clueless about my cousin Reggie. "Like what?"

"Like maybe Miss Buffy dumped him, so he thought he'd try his luck with you while he gets over her or finds someone else. Or maybe his oversized ego can't take the fact that *you* dumped *him*, and he wants to even the score by being the one to break up once he gets you back. Who knows what's going on in that devious, two-timing mind of his?"

By this time, I couldn't bring myself to finish my dessert. I jabbed my fork into it a few times but found no comfort in the idea of savoring any more of the warm bread pudding laced with cinnamon.

"So he couldn't possibly be in love with someone like me?" I said sadly.

"No, he couldn't." Meredith was firm. "He's incapable of appreciating what a treasure it is to be loved by someone as smart, caring, and loyal as you. And if you think that leopard has changed his spots, I've got some swampland in Florida to sell you. Now cheer up and finish your bread pudding. It's almost time to get back to work."

It was a relief to bury myself in preparing tax returns, although the pudding continued to sit heavy on my stomach and Meredith's words heavy on my heart. It wasn't long, however, before my colleagues managed to distract me. Several of them gathered in the office across the hall to discuss—what else—Miss Charlotte's inheritance, or rather, what they would do with that much money. They at least had the amount right—they're accountants, after all.

They all agreed that the stock market was too risky, however well P. B. had done. One recommended investing in gold, another in real estate. By the time they got to discussing tax shelters, I was able to tune them out and get on with work.

I was not to escape the subject for long, however. My father had been to both the feed store and the Riverside Diner that day. He told us all about it over supper that night. At the feed store, the young men in ball caps dreamed out loud about what they would do with that much money.

"Wish I was Preston," Donny Freeman had said. "I'd ask her to buy me a shiny new F150, the quad cab. I'd use it to make the flower deliveries instead of that yellow van with daisies all over it."

"If you was Preston, you'd have to go to law school," Tom Connors said, making a face.

Trevor Caldwell had laughed and said, "Donny, you'd do better to ask her for a condo or a house so you wouldn't have to live with your mama anymore."

Donny reddened to the roots of his hair. "At least *my* mama don't burn the biscuits." Then he hightailed it out of the store before Trevor could slug him.

"Boys." The high school football coach snorted. "The last thing this town needs is more rednecks ridin' around in monster trucks. What we really need is a new football stadium. Maybe even get us one of them jumbotrons."

At the diner, the old men had taken off their VFW caps and scratched their grizzled heads in wonder that ol' P. B. Harrington had that much money socked away.

"Never woulda knowed it," Hiram Fletcher said. "He always come here and set down and jawed with us, never mind his suit and tie."

"An' he wa'n't stingy, neither," Joe Simmons added. "He always bought a dozen tickets for the VFW spaghetti dinners, more'n the family needed, and give out the rest of 'em to people he knew could do with a good meal and some friendly faces."

Old Mr. Morris, founder of the funeral home and an avid fisherman, said, "And he put it all up for his missus. I used to rag him about that old fishing pole of his. I thought for sure he could afford a new one. Turns out I was right, boys—but he said his granddaddy's ol' pole suited him just fine, bein' full of memories of fishin' with his daddy and all."

"It sounds like they knew the real P. B. Harrington," I said when my father finished.

"The 'real' P. B. Harrington?" Daddy asked.

"Whenever I would go over to the Harringtons to visit for Grandma Ruth, he was such an old grouch. Sometimes I wondered how his wife could stand it. I thought that was just how he was, but Grandma and Miss Charlotte keep telling me he only got like that his last few years. I tell you, though, it's been hard to wrap my brain around. Do you think they're just remembering the good parts?"

"He really was a fine man, Sarah," my father said. "I try to be that kind of man too, so your mother will be as good to me when I'm old and cranky as Mrs. Harrington was to P. B."

He winked at my mother, who told him she would stop making him biscuits and gravy if he got cranky in his declining years.

I definitely did not want my father to be like P. B. Harrington, not if he had cheated on his wife. I pushed the thought away. Maybe P. B. really had been all Grandma Ruth and the old men at the diner thought he was. I hoped so. I hoped I could find out for sure soon so Miss Charlotte could get down to the business of enjoying that huge pile of money her husband had left her. No matter how I hoped, however, I couldn't shake the feeling that, sooner or later, the other shoe would drop.

CHAPTER 14

Days later, tongues were still wagging in Raeburne's Ferry about Miss Charlotte's amazing windfall. In fact, they were wagging all over the county, as we were soon to find out. When the news made it over to the Home Depot in Dewey Creek, the other shoe dropped. The shoe was a spike-heeled, pointy-toed pump in a garish shade of red—entirely wrong for the fifty-something-year-old woman who was wearing it, even though she did still have good legs.

On Tuesday morning, I heard my phone pinging away in my purse, announcing a text message. I started to ignore it, as Jake was still texting me from every phone he could get his hands on. I knew what Meredith would say about my weakness, but I couldn't help it. With a guilty look toward my office doorway, I fished my phone out of my purse and looked at the screen under my desk. Yes, there are also rules at Crawford and Associates about cell phone use during work hours. Business calls only. As it turned out, the text was from Meredith: *BIG NEWS!!! Meet me @ Coffee Break @ 10:30.*

Order me a caramel macchiato, I texted back.

At 10:25, I saved my work, grabbed my coat, and fielded a few coffee orders for my colleagues on my way out.

"If Jake comes by, do not tell him where I am," I told Shelby. "Tell him to go jump in the lake."

"I will escort him to the lake and throw him in," Mr. Crawford called from his office.

"Thank you, sir," I said as I dashed out the door.

The midmorning rush was in full swing at the coffee shop. Meredith waved a cup at me from a table at the back.

"I'll be right there," I called. "I have to order for some of the guys."

Three specialty coffees later, I was sitting across from Meredith.

"Make it quick," I told her. "I have to get back before these get cold." I lifted the cardboard carrier full of hot drinks.

"You will never believe who came to the law office this morning." She leaned across the table. "You'll never guess in a million years."

"Then tell me already, if you know I can't guess," I said as I took a sip of my all-time-favorite coffee.

"Brace yourself." Meredith paused for effect, cleared her throat, and then said, "Camilla Holtgrew Allen Smith Kowalski."

Luckily, I was able to grab a napkin before I sprayed coffee across the table. "Did you say 'Camilla Holtgrew'? *The* Camilla Holtgrew?"

"Allen Smith Kowalski," Meredith said with a nod. "Yep. She's been married three times, but she's not married at the moment."

Well, no wonder I couldn't find her online. I should have realized somebody would fall for those short skirts and goo-goo eyes. I had to hand it to her. She'd managed to rope three somebodies into marrying her.

"What's she doing here? What's she doing at the law office? From what Mrs. Wellington said about her, I don't think there's much chance of her getting her job back," I said.

"She doesn't want a job. Oh no—nothing so paltry as that." Meredith paused for effect again, which was starting to get on my nerves.

"Spit it out already."

"She wants part of Mrs. Harrington's inheritance."

"*What?*" I was in danger of spewing coffee again.

"Keep your voice down," Meredith whispered. "I could get in big trouble for telling tales out of the office."

I lowered my voice. "What makes her think she's entitled to any of that money?"

"The big lug she brought with her," Meredith said. "She showed up at the office this morning with her son—the one she says is Mr. Harrington's. She wants her Bentley to 'get his due,' she said."

I sat back in my chair, feeling like a wrung-out rag. I thought about myself first, I'm ashamed to say. Just when I was starting to believe that there might be something to all the great things people were saying about P. B. Harrington, here was living proof that he was a low-down cheater after all. Then I thought about Mrs. Harrington and what this devastating news would do to her. I pulled out my phone.

"Sarah, no." Meredith tried to grab the phone away from me. "You can't tell anyone else. It's confidential. I shouldn't even have told you."

I leaned back out of her reach as I pressed the call symbol next to my grandmother's name. "She'll find out soon enough anyway. They're best friends. Mrs. Harrington tells her everything."

"And we're best friends too. Don't tell her you got it from me."

"I won't tell her," I said. Never mind there was no one else from whom I could have gotten such information hot off the press. As the phone started to ring, I mouthed, *Trust me.*

"Yes, Sarah?" Grandma Ruth was delighted to have caller ID on her phone. She felt it gave her an edge.

"Grandma, please ask Mama to make her brownies today," I said. "Mrs. Harrington is going to need them." My mother's double fudge peanut butter brownies are so rich, so deeply chocolate with the perfect hint of saltiness to offset their profound sweetness, that every bite just sweeps away some of whatever is vexing you, until by the third brownie, you're feeling pretty good.

"If the news is as bad as all that, she may not want to eat," Grandma Ruth said.

"Then she might want something to drink," I said, hoping she would take the hint.

"I always offer her tea, Sarah Elizabeth. You know that," Grandma Ruth said.

"Not. Tea."

"Not tea? Oh." Grandma Ruth's voice sharpened with sudden understanding. "Then it's about—"

I cut her off before she could start to grill me. Even on the phone, out of sight of those eyes of hers, I was liable to crack. "It was told to me in confidence, though, so I can't say more than that. Just be ready. Gotta go, Grandma." I clicked off.

"See"—I gave Meredith a smug grin—"I didn't tell her, Miss Worrywart. But now she'll be prepared, and she knows it's something about P. B. and Millie."

Meredith looked confused. "And how does she know that?"

"Don't you remember Mrs. Harrington at the funeral reception? How she had to go lie down? She didn't get that way drinking tea."

"You mean she was—" The light of understanding dawned in Meredith's eyes.

"In 'quite a state,' yes," I finished for her.

"I thought she was just upset." Meredith shook her head. "Things sure aren't what they seem a lot of the time, are they?"

No, they weren't, I reflected on my way back to the office, coffee carrier in hand. And I was getting tired of it. I hated having to read between the lines, with all the suspicion and second-guessing that went with it. I hated the disappointment of finding out that my suspicions were well-founded. When I was honest with myself, I had to admit I'd suspected for a while that Jake didn't really want to marry me, even before I found out about Buffy. The missed cake-tasting appointment was easy to overlook, but the lame excuses for missing our counseling sessions with Father David should have been a whole row of red flags.

And while Jake was lying to me, I was lying to myself, trying to convince myself that what I hoped wasn't going on really wasn't going on. Miss Charlotte had the right idea, I mused. It was better to know the truth, even if it hurt, than to eat your heart out over suspicions and possibilities. I wish I'd been as brave as her when I first started having those vague, disturbing doubts about Jake.

I sighed as I pushed through the door into the reception area. It was water under the bridge now. I couldn't go back and change it, but I could take it as a painful lesson learned and never let myself get into a situation like that again. This meant not dating, as I apparently had extremely poor judgment when it came to men—Jake had fooled me for years as to his real character. That was fine by me. If this consigned me to "spinsterhood," as Grandma Ruth called it, I would be getting the better end of the deal.

I doled out the coffee and went back to my office. A stack of phone messages had accumulated in my absence. Hiram Fletcher would be by this afternoon to hand in his authorization for electronic filing (hurray—one more return in the out-box), another client couldn't find his W-2 (did we really need it? yes), and the third message was Abby Claire Harper asking me to stop by the shop after work.

The hothouse humidity of the Daisy Chain wrapped around me like a hug as I stepped into the shop that afternoon. I breathed in the fragrance of fresh flowers and admired the bouquets in the glass-doored cooler as I waited for someone to respond to the bell that jingled every time the door opened or closed.

I peered around the counter to the back, where several women were hard at work on bouquets. Abby Claire looked up from a large vase of roses and hurried out into the shop, wiping her hands on a green apron embroidered with *The Daisy Chain* encircled by a wreath of daisies.

"Thank you for stopping by, Sarah. I wanted to consult with you about an order but didn't want to do it over the phone. It seems kind of personal."

"Okay," I said. "I don't know how I can help, but consult away."

She drew me to the corner of the shop farthest from the work area and lowered her voice. "It's this order that came in for you for Valentine's Day, Sarah. It's from a Jake Halloran, and I don't know what to do about it."

It seemed pretty straightforward to me. A flower shop gets orders, makes up the arrangements, and then delivers them. I said as much to Abby Claire.

"It's that last part that's the problem," she said. "During the past week, Mr. Halloran has ordered three bouquets of roses to be delivered to your home address, and all three of them have been refused at the door. I know better than to reroute them to you at work. We all know Mr. Crawford's policy about personal celebrations in the workplace. But now I have this order for Valentine's Day, and I can't in good conscience send it to your house again, knowing it will be refused and two dozen perfectly good roses wasted. Roses are at a premium this time of year, especially red ones. When we run out, we have to substitute with white or pink and it's just not the same."

What was Jake thinking? He knew his name was mud at the McCready homeplace. And now my parents *and* Grandma Ruth knew that Jake was trying to win me back. They hadn't said word one about it, which meant they were waiting for me to 'fess up so they could pile on the advice. It was crystal clear from the way they were treating the roses what that advice would be.

"I'm sure you're right," I told Abby Claire glumly. "You can't send them to work or my house."

"So your parents don't like him, huh? So Romeo and Juliet." She gave a wistful sigh. Then her brown eyes brightened. "I know! You could pick them up here on Saturday. D-Day for Valentine's Day is the thirteenth since the big day falls on a Sunday this year."

"No," I replied. "If I brought home a huge bouquet of roses, I would have some explaining to do, and they would still end up in the trash. Tell Mr. Halloran you can't fill his order and refund his money." As it was, I would have to face the music at home about the other three bouquets. I wished they would trust me to handle this myself. I was no longer the naive teenager who had fallen hard for the devastatingly handsome Jake Halloran seven years ago. Sadder, yes, and wiser, I hoped. Even if I wasn't, I wished they'd let me come to my own conclusions instead of liberally sharing theirs.

I had a sudden inspiration. "Could you send them to someone else? This is Mrs. Harrington's first Valentine's Day without her husband. It might lift her spirits to get flowers after all."

"Funny you should mention that," Abby Claire said with a happy grin. "I won't miss out on making her arrangement from Mr. Harrington after all."

"Really? How come?" I asked.

"Mr. Harrington arranged in his will for Mrs. Harrington to receive flowers from the Daisy Chain for her birthday, their anniversary, and Valentine's Day for the rest of her life." Tears gathered in her eyes. "He even wrote out twenty years' worth of cards to include with the arrangements. The boss has kept them in a folder in her filing cabinet ever since Mr. Harrington wrote his will. That is so romantic. Mrs. Harrington is so lucky to have been married to a man like that."

Once again, I refrained from telling Abby Claire about the plate-throwing incident, and I was definitely not going to tell her the latest news about her romantic hero either.

"That *is* sweet," I said. "She'll be really surprised."

Then I had another inspiration about what to do with Jake's flowers. "I believe I will accept Mr. Halloran's roses after all, Abby Claire. Please arrange two bouquets of a dozen roses each. I'll pay for the second vase. They'll be perfect for the altar flowers at St. Alban's two Sundays from now, on Valentine's Day."

CHAPTER 15

I DROVE HOME, GRINDING MY teeth and rehearsing my confrontation with Mama, Daddy, and Grandma Ruth. Mainly Mama, since she's the one around to answer the door during the day. Besides, she's a whole lot easier to confront than my grandmother.

"Mama, I need to talk to you," I began as soon as I came through the kitchen door. She was piling brownies on a plate.

"Can it wait, dear?" she asked as she loaded the brownies and the china tea service onto a tray. "Miss Charlotte has had a great shock."

I suddenly remembered what that shock was and how I'd been the one to recommend Mama make the brownies. My own concerns immediately paled in comparison. I reached for the tray.

"I'll take it in, Mama. We can talk later."

In the parlor, Miss Charlotte sat in the armchair, pale and dazed. Without a word, I poured for them both and laced Miss Charlotte's tea liberally with sugar.

She seemed to come to a bit when I handed her the cup and saucer.

"Thank you, Sarah." She gave me a wobbly smile. The cup and saucer rattled in her trembling hand like teeth chattering on a cold day.

"Brownie?" I offered her the plate.

She teared up as she shook her head. "I couldn't." The welling tears spilled over, ran down her face, and dripped into her teacup. "Oh, Mary Ruth, what am I going to do? In my heart of hearts, I couldn't imagine that P. B. had . . . well . . . you know . . . but now I have to face it and I can't. I just can't! How could he? With *her*?" Her face crumpled. I relieved her of the untouched tea as she laid her head on the bed and sobbed.

Grandma Ruth set down her own tea and patted her friend gently on the back.

"Don't cry, Charlotte," she said, her voice soft and wise. "God is too big."

I had heard these words often from my grandmother when I was growing up. When I was little, I didn't like being told not to cry when I was sad. I really didn't like it when she said it when everything fell apart with Jake. Then, I cried and cried and felt that God *was* too big. Too big to care about me. My broken heart was a mere drop in the bucket of the vast suffering in the world.

As I stood helpless in the wake of Miss Charlotte's grief, I wondered if that bigness planned to do anything about Millie. He'd certainly never done anything about Jake. *Probably not*, I thought with an inward snort. It didn't seem like God had plans to help either of us out. She'd been such a good and devoted wife. You'd think that would count for something, but grief was piled upon grief for poor Miss Charlotte with no hope in sight. Being a good wife like Mrs. Harrington or a good girl like me didn't afford much protection at all from pain and heartbreak.

When Miss Charlotte had cried herself out and dried her tears, I handed her teacup back to her.

"Thank you, Sarah," she said after a few sugar-laden sips. "I believe I could nibble on a brownie after all." She may have started out with a nibble, but the brownie soon disappeared and she reached for another. It also vanished quickly. "I'm sure you're wondering what this is all about, Sarah." She didn't wait for my reply. "Millie Holtgrew, that flighty secretary we let go over thirty years ago, has come back to the firm, claiming that her son is . . . is . . . ." Miss Charlotte gulped and straightened her shoulders. "Is P. B.'s offspring and therefore entitled to a share of the estate."

The rich chocolate of the brownies had begun to take effect.

"I can't believe it, Mary Ruth." Miss Charlotte turned to my grandmother. "I won't believe it. He couldn't have fallen for someone like her. It was so obvious she was after a rich husband. That was one of the reasons the firm let her go."

"I know," I said and told Miss Charlotte about the results of my investigation of the condolence cards and my conversation with Mrs. Wellington. I did not tell her about my most recent conversation with Mrs. Wellington, since, unfortunately, we now knew where Millie Holtgrew was.

"There, now," Miss Charlotte said, her face brightening, "he couldn't have done it. Mrs. Wellington says so and anything Mildred Wellington didn't know about the goings-on at the firm was not worth knowing. She ran that office like clockwork and kept everyone on track."

"Maybe Millie wants revenge for getting fired," I said.

"That's a long time to hold a grudge." Grandma Ruth sounded skeptical.

"People have been known to hold grudges for decades," I said, with a sidelong glance at my grandmother. Grandma Ruth has always had it out for Great-Uncle Hubert, never mind he's been dead for twenty-odd years. The unkempt state of his grave in St. Alban's churchyard is a testament to just how angry she still is.

"But it's not P. B. who's suffering," Miss Charlotte said. "It's Bent. He won't be happy about splitting his nest egg."

"Why should he have to do that?" I asked. "Your husband left that amount to him."

"Actually, it was a part of the will that they didn't bother to revise the last time P. B. looked at it," Miss Charlotte said. "When Bent was born, P. B. revised it to include his son, and, because we planned to have more children, 'all subsequent offspring.' But Bent turned out to be our only chick and child. Even when it became clear that we were hoping in vain, P. B. couldn't bear to remove the clause in subsequent revisions over the years. But the best-laid plans of mice and men . . . and mothers . . ." She gave a heavy sigh.

"Now, now, Charlotte, that's water under the bridge." Grandma Ruth patted her hand.

"I would have liked to have had a daughter," Miss Charlotte said wistfully. "I'm grateful for Lydia. Bent chose a loving and gracious wife, but it's not like having a little girl you can dress up in smocked dresses and giant hair bows."

We were getting off track.

"So, if this Bentley is really Mr. Harrington's son, he could get half of the inheritance meant for Mr. Bent?" I asked.

"Hush your mouth, Sarah Elizabeth," my grandmother said. "He is *not* related to the Harringtons in any way, much less *that* way."

"You're probably right, Grandma," I said. "I really, really hope you are. The point I'm trying to make is that it's up to Millie and Bentley to prove it. They can't just waltz into Bentley, Harrington, Harrington, and Nidden, claim Bentley is Mr. Harrington's son, and expect the estate to simply fork over the money. Bentley will have to take a DNA test."

"Thomas might have said something about that." Miss Charlotte furrowed her brow. "I'm afraid I don't remember much of what he said after he told me someone named Millie had shown up claiming my husband had fathered her son."

"I imagine that was quite a shock," I said.

"And I must admit, I don't know how they go about it, this DNA thing." Miss Charlotte gave a helpless shrug.

I could tell that she didn't watch crime shows or Jerry Springer. This didn't surprise me. Miss Charlotte would consider such shows unsuitable for a lady. My grandmother, however, did not have such scruples. Not that she watched those shows. She was much too busy to watch television. She was, however, a voracious reader with a fondness for mysteries in nearly every form, including police procedurals.

"Scientists can compare the DNA of one person to another to see if they're related." As Miss Charlotte continued to look puzzled, Grandma Ruth went on to explain. "DNA contains the genetic code for each person. You can get samples from a person's hair, the inside of their cheek, their blood, even their saliva. Then you compare it to the DNA of the other person. They can tell the degree to which the two people are related."

Miss Charlotte's nose wrinkled at the mention of blood and saliva. "I don't know how they'll be able to find out, then. My husband is dead and buried."

"Do you still have his toothbrush?" Grandma Ruth asked. "Or some of his hair still left in a hairbrush or comb?"

Miss Charlotte's eyes filled with tears as she nodded. "I know I should clear them out. Goodness knows he doesn't need them anymore. But when I see them on the counter in the bathroom, he doesn't seem so far away."

"It's a good thing you didn't," Grandma Ruth said. "It will be easy to prove that this Bentley is an impostor. Now, don't you worry about it anymore, Charlotte."

"I'll try not to." Miss Charlotte sniffed and dabbed at her eyes with a hankie edged in tatted lace.

I poured more tea for the two friends. Miss Charlotte was halfway through her fourth brownie when the front doorbell rang.

"That will be Preston," Miss Charlotte said fondly through a mouthful of brownie. Compared to how upset she'd been at the beginning of her visit, she was now downright mellow.

I opened the front door to find Preston on the porch. Before I showed him into the parlor, I told him in a low voice that he might want to take extra care with his grandmother as he saw her down the steps since she'd had four brownies.

"Brownies?" Preston looked puzzled.

"My mother's brownies have a very . . . calming effect on people," I said.

"Oh, really?" Preston's eyes widened.

"What? No! Not that!" I said as I suddenly caught his drift. "It's chocolate, not pot. My mother would never—"

"Okay, okay." He laughed and held up his hands. "Sounds like you need one of those brownies yourself."

"The very idea that my mother would—"

"Look, I'm sorry. I should have known better than to joke about your mama's cooking."

"You two stop fussing and come on in here," my grandmother called. Was I imagining it, or did she say *you two* with relish?

"Yes, ma'am." Preston whipped off his ball cap as he stepped into the parlor.

Miss Charlotte beamed at the sight of her grandson. "Would you care for a brownie?" The plate wavered slightly as she held it out.

"No, thank you, ma'am. I need to get back to studying." Under his breath, I heard him say, "Besides, I'm driving." Then he shook his head and chuckled at his own joke as he helped his grandmother into her wraps.

I stood out on the porch as Preston and Miss Charlotte made their way down the steps to the waiting Rolls, just in case Preston needed help. None was needed, as it turned out. He patiently went at her pace and listened attentively as she explained to him that his grandfather's toothbrush was about to put that Millie what's-her-name in her place. She gave me a languid, regal wave as Preston pulled away from the curb.

Now that Miss Charlotte's problem was on its way to being solved, I decided to tackle my own problem with my mother.

"Mama." I pushed through the kitchen door. "We need to talk."

"So you said, dear." My mother took the tea tray from me and set it on the counter. "Would you mind peeling these carrots while we chat?"

I took the carrots and the peeler she held out to me and went to work, in more ways than one. "Abby Claire Harper called me today."

"How nice." Mama beamed. "How is she?"

I was not, however, in the mood for the usual dance of social chit-chat that would gracefully waltz us up to the point at some leisurely moment in the future.

"She's perplexed," I said. "It seems she has yet another order of flowers for me, this time for Valentine's Day. She wanted to know what to do about it, since the other *three* arrangements that have been delivered here have been refused."

I set down the carrot and peeler, crossed my arms, and raised my eyebrows.

"Your daddy was home for lunch when the first bouquet arrived," Mama said. "He knew he hadn't sent *me* roses, so he read the card. When he saw they were from Jake, he handed them right back to Donny Freeman. Then he told me to do the same if Jake sent any more when he wasn't here."

"And neither of you saw fit to tell me about it?" I asked. "Or ask me what *I* wanted to do about the flowers? Or even ask me what was going on?" My voice was rising to a pitch that was almost unladylike.

"Well, dear, we didn't want to pry," Mama said. "We figured if you wanted to tell us about it, you would."

"But in the meantime, you would send my flowers back and not tell me about them." I grabbed up the unsuspecting carrot and peeled with more force than necessary.

"They weren't your flowers, Sarah, they were Jake's. Your father and I don't see any point in encouraging him."

"They were too my flowers. Yes, they were from Jake, but they were mine to decide what to do with. You and Daddy just stay out of it . . . please," I added in a slightly more modulated tone, suddenly remembering to whom I was speaking.

"So do you want me to accept the Valentine ones?" my mother said. "Your daddy won't like it."

I suddenly wished that I had told Abby Claire to go ahead and deliver the flowers, just so I could show Mama and Daddy I could make my own decisions, thank you very much.

"Not to worry," I told her. "They will be gracing the altar at St. Alban's, seeing as how Valentine's Day is on a Sunday this year."

Mama's eyes widened with surprise.

"Why, Sarah, what a lovely idea." She put her arm around my shoulders and gave me an admiring squeeze. "Your daddy and I should give you more credit for being able to handle things."

"Yes, Mama, you should. I can handle Jake, believe me," I said, with more bravado than I actually felt. It was one thing to make such a confident declaration in the warmth of Mama's kitchen and another to do so in the quite different warmth of Jake Halloran at his most charming and seductive.

"I'm sure you can, dear." Mama's tone was placating, but in the very next breath she asked, "What *is* going on?"

"Mama, I said I can handle it." I gave the last carrot its last swipe with the peeler and stomped out of the kitchen.

"*Honestly!*" I muttered to myself out in the hall.

"They're just looking out for you." Grandma Ruth's voice floated out from the parlor. Had my protest been so loud she'd heard it all the way into her room? Or did she, as I have often suspected, have the kitchen bugged? I wouldn't put it past her.

I stepped into the parlor—not daring to stomp.

"I might as well have your opinion too," I said. "Seems like everybody around here has one." I looked out the window into the gathering dusk as I said this.

"You should accept his invitation to dinner," she said.

I snapped my eyes away from the window to stare at her. "How do you know about that?"

"It's a small town, Sarah Elizabeth."

I could have sworn there was no one around when Jake asked me to dinner at Fontanelli's. Had Meredith blabbed? *I need to have a talk with my bestie.* I set my jaw. Then Grandma's actual words registered.

"Wait. What? You think I *should* go out with him? Do you think he really has changed, like he says?" My heart clenched with longing.

"No, Sarah. He hasn't changed a bit, but that's why you should go to dinner with him," Grandma Ruth said.

I shook my head, trying to clear it. "If he's still the same, don't you want me to stay away from him?"

"Jake Halloran is the kind of young man who always wants what he can't have. That's what made that Buffy girl so attractive."

"She didn't exactly play hard to get," I muttered. Buffy had flirted outrageously with my fiancé, and I had foolishly trusted that his heart was mine no matter how she flipped her hair and flaunted her generous curves whenever he was around.

"But he was engaged, which made her off-limits. And if there's one thing Jake Halloran can't abide, it's limits," Grandma Ruth said.

Truer words were never spoken. He had certainly been unhappy about the limits I'd put on . . . well, would it have killed him to wait a few more months?

"If that's the case," I said, "if I married him, he'd always be hankering after someone else. I couldn't live like that."

"Who said anything about marrying him?" Grandma Ruth said. "Just go out to dinner with him and hear him out. He won't stop pestering you until you do."

"But I'll still be saying no," I said. At least I hoped I'd be able to say no. My head and my heart weren't exactly in sync on the subject of Jake Halloran. "If you're right, he'll persist until we get back together, at which time he'll lose interest and dump me. He's already broken my heart once, Grandma."

My grandmother shook her head. "Sometimes I almost despair of you, Sarah. Have you learned nothing about how a Southern lady handles the weaker sex? All that's wrong with him is a severely bruised ego. You dumped him when you caught him cheating."

"You mean he planned to dump me for her, but I beat him to it?"

"I doubt dumping you for Buffy even crossed his mind, although you can bet it crossed Buffy's," Grandma Ruth said. "Jake wanted to have his cake and eat it too."

"So how do you suggest I handle him?" I asked. "I'm not about to get back together with him just so he can have the last word."

"Of course you won't be getting back together with him," Grandma Ruth told me. "By the time you're done with him, my dear, he might *think* he had the last word, but you will have the last laugh. I promise you."

"Do tell." I settled into the chair by my grandmother's bed.

CHAPTER 16

JAKE'S EYES GLOWED WITH TRIUMPH when I accepted his next invitation to dinner. He cornered me by the coffee urn in the parish hall after church and asked me out for Valentine's Day. He had resorted to attending the late service at St. Alban's. Whatever Father David's views on Jake's pursuit of me might be, he would never give Jake the left foot of fellowship on the off chance that something in the service would hit home and bring Jake into the fold. It was an *off* off chance, but, as Father is fond of saying, "Nothing is impossible with God." It's his version of "God is too big," I suppose.

"I would be happy to," I said. "Fontanelli's, right?"

My daddy, across the room discussing putters with his golfing buddies, shot a sharp look my way. I sent a determined look back at him.

"Of course," Jake said. "Nothing but the best for you, Sarah." He started to reach for my hand, but pulled back when he caught sight of my father out of the corner of his eye.

"You might not be able to get a reservation this close to Valentine's Day," I said.

"No fear. I made it two weeks ago."

I wasn't sure how to take this. Had he made the reservation cocksure of his powers of persuasion, or did he have some other too-trusting female lined up in case I refused him again? The only thing I knew for sure was that no one in Raeburne's Ferry would ever waste a Valentine's Day reservation at Fontanelli's. Dinner reservations for that day are scarce as hen's teeth, as the candlelight, luxurious Italian food, and strolling violinist make it the prime spot in town for young men to pull a little green box from Windsor Fine Jewelers out of their pockets and ask for their ladylove's hand in marriage. Windsor's slogan was "Where Augusta gets engaged," but while the diamonds around here were usually from that special store, Raeburne's Ferry got engaged at Fontanelli's.

The restaurant even had a special dessert that looked like a miniature wedding cake for the happy couples. Was that what Jake was planning? No woman had ever said no to a proposal at Fontanelli's. I would be the first if Jake were foolish enough to pull out the ring I'd thrown at him going on two years ago.

"What time?" was all I could think of to say.

"The reservation is for eight," he said. "I'll pick you up at seven forty-five."

"No need," I said quickly. "I'll meet you there."

"I'd really like to pick you up."

I'll bet you would. There was no way I was going to be alone in a car with Jake Halloran. I remembered the parking lot overlooking the lake, where necking sessions had turned into steamy tussles over my virtue. No thank you. Not letting anything like that happen ever again.

Across the room, Daddy cleared his throat.

"On second thought, maybe that would be a good idea," Jake said with an uneasy glance at the golfers. They were all looking at Jake as though they would like to throw him into the water hazard at the fourteenth hole at the Peachtree Country Club, where a mean-spirited family of swans jealously guards all the golf balls hit into the pond.

Good news travels fast and bad news even faster. Suffice it to say that I got an earful at Sunday dinner. The uncles all agreed with Daddy. They should have horsewhipped the cur when his perfidy was discovered. Then he wouldn't have dared to come sniffing around after me again. The aunts strongly protested the canine references, at least with regard to me—and then turned on me during the washing up after dinner.

"I wouldn't touch that man with a ten-foot pole," Aunt Dahlia said.

"I wouldn't touch him with a *twelve*-foot pole even if I had on rubber gloves." Aunt Louisa was not to be outdone.

"I don't plan on touching him at all," I told them. "I'm just letting him take me out to dinner."

"Well, mind you don't let him do anything else," Aunt Marjorie said. "And make sure he pays. I've heard tell that these modern young men are so cheap that they ask a girl out and then expect her to pay her share."

"I'm sure he intends to pay for dinner, at the rate he's been sending me flowers," I said.

The aunts scanned the kitchen.

"What flowers?" Aunt Dahlia asked. "There weren't any in the hall or the dining room."

"Of course not," Aunt Louisa said. "They're in her boudoir."

"Well, I call that selfish," Aunt Marjorie said. "Hoarding them away in her room instead of letting everyone enjoy them." This was typical of Aunt Marjorie, who never let her one and only son Bruce have a private thought, much less a private life.

"They never made it through the door," I said. "Daddy sent them back to the Daisy Chain."

"I'm glad *somebody* in this house has some sense," Aunt Marjorie said. "He should put his foot down about this dinner business too."

I turned to put a platter away in a cabinet, muttering under my breath. "I am twenty-four years old, for crying out loud."

"What was that?" Aunt Marjorie said. "I swear, these young people are always mumbling these days. Bruce does it too. I'm constantly telling him to speak up."

I'll bet my cousin does mutter under his breath a lot. If he ever did speak up and say what he really thought right out loud, Aunt Marjorie would probably have a heart attack or a stroke or both. I have no fear for my aunt's health, however. Bruce is the biggest mama's boy this side of the Mississippi.

"I'm sure Sarah knows what she's doing," Mama said as she came into the kitchen with the remains of dessert. Not much remained after my uncles had been after it, believe me.

"It's just like you to defend her," said Aunt Dahlia. "You always were too soft on her, Lily. That's how she ended up engaged to him in the first place."

That was it. I might mumble under my breath on my own behalf, but when they started in on Mama, I found my voice. I drew myself up to my full height in the middle of the kitchen.

"Don't you dare blame my mother," I said. "It was my decision to say yes to Jake Halloran, mine and nobody else's. I was twenty-two— old enough to decide for myself."

The aunts were not impressed. I am, after all, only five feet tall in my stocking feet. They were also not impressed with the reference to my age at the time of my engagement.

"Twenty-two is not nearly old enough to have any sense about getting married," Aunt Louisa said, not unkindly.

I did some quick calculations in my head. The aunts were cagey about their ages, but Aunt Louisa and Uncle Beau had attended their twenty-five-year high school reunion and celebrated their silver anniversary this past summer, which meant they had been all of seventeen or eighteen when they were married.

"You were younger than that when you got married," I shot back.

There was a sharp intake of breath from the other aunts. I rarely sass them.

"My point exactly," said Aunt Louisa.

I really did not want to know why marrying Uncle Beau, who had been a wonderful source of Wrigley's spearmint gum during my childhood, had been a regrettable decision.

"Grandma Ruth married Grandpa Andy right out of high school," I said. "And look how great that turned out."

"There are exceptions to every rule." Aunt Louisa sniffed. "However, marry in haste, repent at leisure is the case more often than not."

"I dated Jake off and on for five years before we got engaged," I said. "That's hardly marrying in haste."

"That's just it, dear," Aunt Dahlia said. "Did you ever wonder what was going on in those off times? Or even during the on times when he was at UGA and you were at Horton-Holgate? You've always been such a trusting soul, believing everyone else was as honest and upright and kind as yourself."

"So now I'm gullible?" I didn't know whether to stamp my foot or burst into tears.

"That's neither here nor there right now," Aunt Dahlia replied. "The point is that Jake Halloran may be handsome and charming, but he is not worthy of a woman of your character. He might be all right for a girl like Buffy Doyle who doesn't have the sense God gave a goose. You, however, are way out of his league. We don't want to see you settle, is all."

Their meddling love washed over me all at once. I burst into tears and buried my face in Aunt Dahlia's shoulder. They closed ranks around me while I cried, even Aunt Marjorie, who pressed her hankie into my hand.

"I'm still going to Fontanelli's with him, though," I said when they let me up for air. "Grandma Ruth thinks I need to hear him out or else he'll just keep pestering the life out of me."

At this, Mama and the aunts backed off. I had said the magic words: "Grandma Ruth thinks . . ."

"Are you crazy?" Meredith said when I told her about my dinner date.

"Crazy like a fox," I said, and outlined Grandma Ruth's plan for getting rid of my (mostly) unwanted suitor.

"Are you sure you can pull it off?" Meredith sounded doubtful. "Your brain kinda turns to mush when you're around Jake. It's a good thing I'll be there. I can keep an eye on you and make sure you don't cave."

"You've got a date at Fontanelli's for Valentine's?" I asked. "Who? And why didn't you tell me before?"

"He only asked me a few days ago," she said.

"Pretty short notice." I raised my eyebrows.

"He's new in town, just got here last week," Meredith said.

"Oh, really?" I had a sneaking suspicion about this, but I didn't want to jump to any conclusions. "And he was able to get a reservation on short notice too?"

"Well, he's pretty rich." Color was creeping up Meredith's neck. "Well, not rich yet, but he will be. That might have given him some pull at the restaurant."

"Do tell."

"Oh, Sarah," Meredith gushed, her brown eyes sparkling. "It's Bentley Allen. He came back to the office on Friday especially to ask me out."

"Isn't he a little old for you?" I did not have a good feeling about this.

"There's eight years between my mama and daddy. It's a good thing. Mama's kind of flighty, but Daddy can usually talk sense into her." Her forehead furrowed ruefully. "She did still get her way about my middle name, though."

"But you're not flighty," I said.

Meredith jutted her chin, looking remarkably like her mother. I decided to appeal to the sense she'd gotten from her father.

"Are you sure you ought to get involved with someone who's got an issue with a client of the firm?"

"I wondered about that too, so I told Bentley I'd have to check my social calendar and get back to him. Besides, it doesn't do to seem too eager, especially on short notice." Meredith eyed me significantly.

"Hey, can we let that go already?" I asked. "I was only seventeen."

"Anyway," Meredith went on, after staring me down for a moment or two. "I did run it past Mr. Nidden. He said it would be fine this once and to keep my eyes and ears open, whatever that means."

I knew exactly what Thomas Nidden meant, and I was inclined to agree with him. I wasn't sure Bentley was P. B.'s real son, and I was glad that Mrs. Harrington's lawyer had his doubts as well. I had a feeling things wouldn't work out for Meredith, which was a shame, since her monogram would look nice with an *A* in the middle.

"You do that," I told Meredith. "And I will too."

"No need." Meredith tossed her head. "I can handle it. You'll have your hands full with Jake."

CHAPTER 17

I DRESSED CAREFULLY FOR MY date with Jake. When I was done, I did not head down the back stairs to avoid my grandmother's critique. I made a grand entrance down the front staircase and did a slow model's twirl in the parlor.

"Perfect," Grandma Ruth said.

Most people and things fall quite short of perfection in Grandma Ruth's opinion, so I knew I had nailed it. For my last-ever date with Jake Halloran, I wore my black velvet scoop-necked dress with three-quarter-length sleeves, a fitted waist, and a full skirt that swung grace-fully around my calves. A hint of cleavage peeked over the edge of the neckline, thanks to a push-up bra. My hair was up (with the help of enough hairspray to make Miss Sylvia Hardcastle proud), and I wore my pearls, of course. I'd borrowed some pearl earrings from Mama to match. Black pumps (not the peep-toe ones) completed my ensemble. I thought I looked a bit like Audrey Hepburn after I took a turn in front of the mirror, and Grandma Ruth was delighted.

"Now, remember what I told you. Do exactly as I said." As if I haven't been doing exactly as she said all my life.

"Yes, ma'am."

Out in the front hall, my father helped me into my coat. "I hope you know what you're doing, sugar," he said as I tucked a scarf around my neck and pulled on my gloves.

"If it doesn't work, you and the uncles can horsewhip him," I told him.

"It's a deal." Daddy laughed as he said it, but I could tell he was only half kidding.

He walked me out and swept the car door open for me with a gallant bow. He waited for me to put on my seatbelt, told me to be careful, and shut the door. I looked into the rearview mirror when I got to the stop sign at the corner. He was still standing at the curb. He looked solid and steady, as though he would stand there waiting until I got home.

As per Grandma Ruth's instructions, I arrived at Fontanelli's at ten minutes after eight, just late enough to make Jake sweat, but not so late as to lose the reservation. I saw him pacing in the foyer as one of the Fontanellis (a son, a cousin, or maybe a nephew) in a doorman's uniform held the door open for me. I also saw the relief on Jake's face when he saw me step inside. So far, so good.

"For a minute there, I thought you might be standing me up," he said with a nervous half laugh as he took my coat and handed it to the coat-check girl, another of the many Fontanellis.

I turned and gazed into his eyes. My heart pounded, but I kept my voice steady. "Now, is that the kind of thing I would do?" I kept gazing until he looked down and away.

"No," he mumbled. "That wouldn't be like you at all."

The corollary to this hung in the air, unsaid but palpable. *That's right. That would be more like you, Jake.*

He offered me his arm as we approached the hostess stand. "I have a reservation for two. The name is Halloran."

"You are late," said the maître d', Mr. Fontanelli Sr. himself. "But the lady, she is worth waiting for! You look beautiful tonight, Miss McCready."

"I was just about to say that," Jake muttered as Mr. Fontanelli led us to our table.

It was a cozy booth. I chose the side that afforded me a good view of the rest of the restaurant, since I wanted to keep tabs on Meredith. Jake's side of the table offered a view of the swinging kitchen door.

"You really do look beautiful, Sarah," Jake said, after Mr. Fontanelli handed us the wine list and tall, tasseled menus. Luciano, our host said, would be by momentarily to take our drink order. Also, he just wanted to add that the Tuscany platter was especially good tonight.

"On special tonight, you say?" I asked.

"Alas, no, signorina," Mr. Fontanelli said. "Nothing is on special tonight, but the Tuscany platter is magnificent, delectable, out of this world!" He kissed his fingers for emphasis and then bustled off to welcome another pair of diners in the foyer.

Luciano arrived shortly thereafter. Like his father, he also wore a tuxedo. His black hair was slicked back, and he carried a snowy white, perfectly pressed napkin over his arm.

"What may I bring you and the lady, sir?" he said, even though the three of us had gone to high school together.

"We'll have the Sutter Home chardonnay," Jake said.

Jake knew full well that sweet tea was my beverage of choice. But here he was trying to show off by ordering wine—never mind it was one of the cheapest wines on the list. Grandma Ruth had prepared me for this move, so I knew exactly what to do.

"I'd rather have the Veuve Clicquot," I said demurely, even though I had no intention of actually drinking it.

"Veuve Clicquot?" Jake said. I watched him scan the wine list and pale a little in the candlelight when he found the expensive champagne.

"Your lady has excellent taste, if I may say so. Quite suitable to the occasion." Apparently, Luciano thought we were here to get engaged. "Bottle or glass?" he asked.

"Glass," Jake said quickly, before I could put in my two cents again. Even by the glass, it was sure to cost him a lot more than two cents.

"Are you ready to order or do you need more time to peruse the menu?"

The way Jake closed the tasseled menu and handed it to Luciano, I could tell he thought he was on solid ground.

"Shrimp scampi and a green salad with Italian dressing on the side for the lady and chicken alfredo for me."

"I know I'm usually partial to the scampi," I told Luciano with a tiny, apologetic shrug, "but I'd really like the Tuscany platter this time. Your father said it's especially good tonight." The taste wasn't the only thing about that dish that was out of this world. It was the most expensive entrée on the menu.

"Oh, it is, signorina, it is," Luciano told me. "An excellent choice."

"Oh sure, excellent for your bottom line," I heard Jake mutter as Luciano hurried away to put in our order.

"You always get the scampi!" Jake practically hissed across the table at me.

"Mr. Fontanelli made the Tuscany platter sound so wonderful, I just couldn't resist," I said.

"But it's—"

"It's what?" I widened my eyes in innocence.

"Expensive," he said in a slightly strangled voice. "You used to be so considerate, Sarah."

"But last Sunday, you said, 'Only the best for you, Sarah.' Did I misunderstand? Here, let me call Luciano back. I can have the scampi, no problem."

"No." He looked a bit panicked. "Of course we're not changing your order. It surprised me, that's all. You were always my shrimp scampi girl, remember?" He gave me a charming, wistful smile as a lock of dark, wavy hair fell across his forehead. He reached across the table and ran his fingers lightly across the back of my hand.

As shivers pirouetted up my arm, I reminded myself that I was getting the Tuscany platter not because he wanted me to have the best, but because he didn't want to lose face in front of Luciano. Jake's pride was something Grandma Ruth and I were counting on. I wondered briefly what Buffy ordered when he took her to Fontanelli's. The manicotti filled to overflowing with ricotta, much like the low-cut dresses she wore to attract the likes of Jake Halloran? I allowed myself a moment to pity her for falling for him and then refocused on the task at hand. I had to admit, this was the most fun I'd ever had on a date with Jake.

Mr. Fontanelli glided into the dining room again, Meredith and her date following in his elegant wake. He led them to a table in the center of the restaurant. Apparently, Jake wasn't the only one who wanted to make an impression. Meredith was wearing her burgundy raw silk sheath dress with the matching stiletto pumps. Her hair swept the tops of her ears on its way to an elegant French twist on the back of her head. Garnet chandelier earrings, passed down from her great-grandmother, swung and glowed in the candlelight as Mr. Fontanelli seated her. The matching ring flashed as she shook out her napkin. Bentley stood staring at her until the maître d' swept his arm toward the chair on the other side of the table.

"Please be seated, signore."

Still dazed, Bentley sat down awkwardly and hitched his chair up to the table. From our booth, I could see them both in profile. I must say I was not impressed by my first glimpse of the new Harrington heir. The Harringtons are all remarkably handsome men, blond and blue-eyed, tall, with broad shoulders, strong jawlines, and a dimpled chin. Bentley was tall, to be sure, but his suit jacket hung loosely on his frame. I couldn't be sure of his eye color in the candlelight, but it looked dark and so was the lank hair that came halfway down his collar, sadly in need of a haircut.

He should have been over the moon to be having dinner on Valentine's Day with Meredith, but he actually looked a bit sad. He stared mournfully across the table at her and only came to when Mr. Fontanelli nudged him with the menu and wine list. Meredith had pulled out the stops for this occasion, and her date, such as he was, looked less than thrilled. For Meredith's sake, I decided to give him the benefit of the doubt. He must be overcome with awe at her beauty.

"What are you looking at?" Jake said. There was an irritable edge to his voice. I was, after all, not adoring him across the table. Following my gaze, he turned and caught sight of Meredith and Bentley. "Hey, isn't that Merrie Merrie May? Wow, she looks amazing!"

"Her name is Meredith, and you're here with me, remember?"

Jake continued to crane his neck around to look at the table in the center of the room. "Who's that with her? I've never seen him before. I heard she was dating your cousin Reggie."

I began to explain about Bentley. Then the unthinkable happened. Mr. Fontanelli appeared once again in the doorway of the dining room. Behind him was a tall man with broad shoulders and blond hair. I reached for a menu to hide behind, but of course, Luciano had taken the menus away with him after we'd ordered. I desperately did not want Preston to see me here with Jake, don't ask me why. And equally inexplicably, I didn't want to see who he was with.

I shrank back into the far corner of the booth, but not before I saw Preston carefully seat his grandmother two tables away from Meredith and Bentley. The only redeeming feature of the arrangement was that Miss Charlotte's back was to Bentley. I could only hope and pray that not only would she not turn around at any point in the evening but that Bentley would keep his voice down so Miss Charlotte wouldn't hear him. Hopefully, his present state of stupefaction would continue. That would mean Meredith would have to do all the talking, but she was good at that.

Luciano arrived with a basket of garlic knots and my salad. I contemplated the situation as I bit into the warm savory bread and poured dressing over the crisp lettuce. I blinked when Jake waved a hand in front of my face.

"Earth to Sarah," he said. "What's going on?"

"A potential disaster," I replied. "Do you see that guy with Meredith? His name is Bentley and he's claiming part of P. B. Harrington's estate."

"What!"

"Keep your voice down," I whispered. "I can't believe you haven't heard yet. It's all over town. Supposedly, he's the love child of P. B. Harrington and one Camilla Holtgrew, who was a secretary at the law firm a long time ago."

"Wow." Jake shook his head in wonder. "I didn't know the old boy had it in him."

"You knew P. B. Harrington?"

"I was a Boy Scout—briefly. He was my Scout leader. Very by-the-book, honor, integrity, loyalty, and all of that. And to think he stepped off the straight and narrow." There was a note of wondering admiration in his voice.

I laid down my fork and crossed my arms. "I fail to see what is impressive about unfaithfulness to one's wife."

"You wouldn't," Jake shot back and then chuckled when he saw the look on my face. "Aw, Sarah, you know I didn't mean that. I was just kidding."

Yeah, right.

"It's not something to kid about," I told him. "The whole thing is really upsetting Mrs. Harrington and now here they are, in the same restaurant, just feet away from each other. I really, really hope she doesn't see him. It's hard enough that it's her first Valentine's Day as a widow. It's so sweet of Preston to take her out instead of letting her eat her heart out at home."

"Never mind Preston," Jake said. "Let's talk about us."

"There is no *us*," I said. I stabbed a piece of lettuce for emphasis.

"But there could be," Jake said. He flashed his lopsided, heart-stopping smile. "There *should* be, sweetcakes. We belong together."

"There is no 'us' because it's you and Buffy now, remember?" Six months ago, my voice would have wobbled as I fought back tears. This evening, however, my voice was steady and bless-your-heart sweet. "How is she, by the way?"

"I wouldn't know," Jake said. "Don't you remember? I told you we broke up."

"Oh, that's right. I do remember you saying something to that effect. What a shame, though." I tsked. "You were crazy about each other, as I recall."

"Crazy is right." Jake leaned forward across the table and tried to take my hand. I was, however, holding a garlic knot in one hand and a salad fork in the other. With a wary look at the fork, he settled for gazing soulfully into my eyes. "I was crazy to get involved with her. I never meant it to go that far. She flirted with me and I flirted back, and before I knew it—"

"So she never meant anything to you?" I asked.

"No. Scout's honor." Jake raised his fingers in the Boy Scout pledge, and it was all I could do not to snort. Jake may have been in Mr. Harrington's troop, but he would never be a Boy Scout. "You're the one I really care about. I should never have let you go."

I was about to say, "Then, why did you?" when Luciano arrived with our entrées. The aroma that wafted up from the Tuscany platter was heavenly. I closed my eyes and inhaled.

"You'll never be able to eat all that," Jake said.

"That's what take-home boxes are for." I waved my fork blithely and then dug in.

Jake cleared his throat. "As I was saying—"

"Hm?" I said, as I savored a bite of the truly excellent ravioli.

"Sarah, I'm baring my soul here. Please try to concentrate."

I set down my fork and looked at him expectantly. "You were saying?"

"I was saying that I've been a fool. I never should have let you go."

I wanted to remind him that he had not "let me go." I had thrown the ring at him and stalked (okay, I ran—I can admit it wasn't the most dignified of exits) out of the room. But Grandma Ruth's plan didn't call for this because it was the very thing that was galling him.

"So what happened with you and Buffy?" I asked. "She must be heartbroken."

"That's not really important." Jake waved the question away. "I just came to my senses. Buffy isn't half the woman you are, Sarah."

I let his words hang in the air, an invitation to elaborate.

In this silence, Meredith's voice floated our way.

"Oh, Mr. Allen, that's not necessary. I would much rather have sweet tea and the shrimp scampi."

It was just like Meredith to remember the "first date" manners our mothers had drummed into us. One of the mandates was to choose low- or middle-priced (if we must) items from the menu, so as not to take advantage of a young man eager to make a good impression. My mother had not covered "last date" etiquette, but if Grandma Ruth's instructions were anything to go by, it included ordering the most expensive dishes the restaurant had to offer. I've never dared to order the baked Alaska before . . .

"Nonsense, Meredith, we'll have something much better than that," Bentley finally came to life and found his voice. "Waiter, what do you recommend? Money is no object," he said with a grand gesture of his hand.

Of course, Luciano was delighted to recommend an entire bottle of a good and expensive pinot noir and hurried off to get it before Bentley could come to his senses.

By this time every eye in the restaurant was on Meredith and her date. I glanced nervously over at Preston and Miss Charlotte. She leaned across the table ever so slightly and raised her eyebrows at her grandson. Preston shrugged and shook his head. I realized, with relief, that they'd had no occasion to meet Bentley yet. Neither of them knew who he was. I fervently hoped it would stay that way for the rest of the evening.

"You were saying?" I said again to Jake.

"Huh?" Jake tore his eyes away from Meredith and Bentley. It might have been my imagination, but he seemed to be focusing more on Meredith than on Bentley.

"You were about to tell me why you should never have let me go." Then I took a big bite of lasagna and settled back to listen to Jake extol my virtues. He glanced at his alfredo, which was getting cold.

"Oh. Right." Once again, he composed his face into what I knew was a mask of longing and regret. The blue eyes once again sought to capture mine, inviting me to fall in, to drown, and to do so happily.

"You are so beautiful," he began.

"So is Buffy," I said.

"But your beauty is different."

I raised my eyebrows.

"Buffy's all on the surface, but you—" He paused. I obligingly leaned forward, as though hanging on every word. "Your beauty shines from within—your kindness, your compassion, your understanding."

Ah yes, my famous *understanding*. My willingness to give him the benefit of the doubt, my trusting nature that had allowed him to get away with so much.

"Go on," I said, my voice low and breathless as I played it to the hilt. Let him think I was buying it.

"I realized what an idiot I was to let myself be led astray by someone who merely looked good, when I already had someone who *is* good. You make me want to be a better man, Sarah."

There was a true-blue sincerity in his eyes that made my breath catch in my throat. You could almost believe him. Almost. I am, however, Reggie McCready's cousin. Reggie is an expert at eliciting the savior complex in sweet young women, which is why I made sure his relationship with my best friend didn't get any further than it did.

"That is just the sweetest thing," I cooed, as if I were some naive freshman at a UGA sorority mixer.

Jake reached across the table and took my hand in both of his. He looked deep into my eyes. "And so, Sarah, I know I don't deserve it, but could you find it in your warm and generous heart to—"

"Aah!" crowed Luciano as he appeared at Jake's elbow. "You will be having dessert then! The little cake, yes?"

Jake raised his eyebrows and gave me a boyish, hopeful smile.

I beamed at Luciano. "Ooh, I would love dessert!"

"I will bring the little cake, then." Luciano beamed back. "Congratulations!"

"If you don't mind"—I smiled apologetically at Jake—"I'd really rather have the baked Alaska."

Luciano's face fell just the tiniest bit, but he recovered quickly, like a true professional.

"Of course, signorina. Baked Alaska it is. And two spoons." He hurried off to put in the order (and probably gossip about it in the kitchen).

When I looked back across the table at Jake, I saw that the mask had slipped. His handsome face was contorted with fury and his eyes flashed with ice-blue fire.

"'If you don't mind,'" he mimicked my voice, loud enough for other diners to hear. "I've been so wrong about you, Sarah. All this time I thought you were sweet and good all the way through, but you're just like a baked Alaska—sweet and warm on the outside, but coldhearted at the core. No wonder you're still single." He rose and threw his napkin on the table. "Enjoy your dessert. I'll pay for this fiasco on my way out."

CHAPTER 18

Jake Halloran left me sitting alone at a table for two at Fontanelli's on Valentine's Day, thinking he had dished out the ultimate humiliation. If he had turned around before leaving the dining room, he would have seen me grinning in triumph at his stiff, retreating back. He, of course, did not look back, so he had no idea that, far from mortifying me, he had played right into my hands. Oh, all right, I admit it, he played right into Grandma Ruth's hands. The main point was that I was free of Jake Halloran. And if he had chosen to stick me with the bill, I would have happily paid it. Jake would never bother me again. His pride would see to that.

The rest of the diners did not share my elation. The room fell silent as the other couples stared at me with looks that ranged from pity to horror. I saw Miss Charlotte lean forward and speak to Preston. He immediately got up and approached the booth where I was sitting.

"Would you care to join us, Sarah?" Preston reached for my plate, to carry it over to the table where Miss Charlotte smiled encouragement at me.

"That is very kind of you and your grandmother," I said. "I'd love to."

Preston commandeered a waiter to bring another chair and seated me himself. I was soon happily settled and suddenly ravenous. Preston and Miss Charlotte looked bemused as I tucked into the Tuscany platter with gusto.

"I'm so sorry, Sarah," Miss Charlotte murmured. "That young man is not a gentleman. You are well rid of him."

"I certainly am." I twirled some more angel hair pasta and marinara sauce onto my fork.

"I must say, you're taking it well," Preston said.

"That's because she's a lady," Miss Charlotte said. "She will save her tears for the privacy of her room tonight, won't you, dear?" She patted my hand. Her wedding rings glowed in the candlelight.

"No, ma'am." I lowered my voice. "I've cried all the tears I'll ever cry over that particular man. After tonight, I doubt I will ever hear from him again, and that's just the way I want it."

"If you say so, dear." Miss Charlotte looked somewhat doubtful.

I could tell that Miss Charlotte wanted to hear more (and so did Preston), but they had better manners than to ask me for the details. I wasn't about to recount Jake's perfidy in a public place, and especially not to Miss Charlotte, as it might remind her of the doubt and sorrow Preston was trying to help her forget, at least for a little while.

Luciano arrived shortly with my baked Alaska, three spoons, and a box for the remains of my Tuscany platter.

"The dessert," he said, with a sympathetic look in my direction, "is on the house."

"Oh no," I said. "I couldn't allow you to do that. Please charge it to Mr. Halloran's card."

"I would be happy to," Luciano replied. He bowed low, caught my eye, and winked.

Next to me, I heard a sharp intake of breath.

"That wink!" Miss Charlotte gasped. "It was exactly like that, Preston. Your grandfather winked just like that when he told me—when he told me . . ." Her face began to crumple.

"Now, Grandmother, Sarah is sharing this wonderful dessert with us. Let me cut you a slice."

With Preston to fuss over her and the baked Alaska to twitter over (she'd never had it before either), Miss Charlotte soon pulled herself together and became, if not the life of the party, a lady in command of herself, charming and charmed by her company.

Out of the corner of my eye, I saw Meredith stand and head toward the ladies' room. I also saw that Bentley didn't sit like a lump but had the good manners to stand as she left the room.

I received similar treatment from Preston when I murmured something about having to powder my nose, rose from the table, and took off after Meredith as fast as my heels would allow.

As soon as I stepped into the ladies' room, Meredith grabbed my hands and started jumping up and down. "You did it! You did it! That was amazing, Sarah. You're free! You're free!"

"Settle down," I said. "You're liable to break an ankle jumping around in those shoes."

"I can't help it," she said. "I've been so worried that he'd get around you with his charm and you'd go back to him. He'd have made you nothing but miserable if you had. And now you're sharing a dessert at Fontanelli's with Preston on Valentine's Day. It couldn't be more perfect."

"Forget Preston, already. I'm free, and I plan to stay that way. How's *your* date going?" I asked by way of changing the subject.

"He's a good listener," she said, with Southern tact that did her mama proud. "And he's generous. I won't be able to eat even half of that Tuscany platter. And I know he'll want to order dessert too."

"That's what take-home boxes are for," I reminded her. "And go ahead and order dessert. You've been playing by the rules for far too long, Meredith. Live a little."

"Well . . ." She bit her lip as she struggled with the idea of defying a lifetime of training.

"We're celebrating, remember? Jake is out of my life *and* my heart, once and for all."

Meredith's eyes cleared, and she gave me a wide grin. "Since you put it that way, I think I'll have cannoli."

"Attagirl," I said. "Now, whatever else you do, don't let Bentley anywhere near the Harringtons. I about had a cow when I saw Preston and Miss Charlotte come in. It's obvious, though, that they don't know who he is, and we need to keep it that way."

"I'll do my best," Meredith said.

Meredith went back to her table while I reapplied my lipstick. I rearranged a few of the tendrils of hair around my face for good measure.

When I was sure Meredith was seated, I made my way back to the Harringtons' table. Luciano was serving cups of coffee topped with decadent swirls of whipped cream and caramel.

"It's decaf," Miss Charlotte told me.

"Caramel macchiato," Preston said.

Two tables over, Meredith tucked into her cannoli, while Bentley looked on with satisfaction. Luciano arrived with the bill and Bentley laid a credit card on the tray. Moments later, Luciano returned with the tray and the card, leaned over, and murmured something in Bentley's ear. Bentley nodded and reached for his wallet. He exchanged the card on the tray for another one.

"This is delicious," Miss Charlotte said as she sipped her coffee. "I've never had one of these fancy coffees before. Thank you, Preston."

"It's Sarah you have to thank for it," Preston said. "It's her favorite."

"How kind of you to remember," I murmured over the rim of my coffee cup.

"Preston is a very thoughtful young man." Miss Charlotte's eyes seemed to do a happy dance as she looked from one to the other of us.

Luciano stopped by Meredith and Bentley's table again. Once again, he leaned over and spoke quietly in Bentley's ear. Once again, Bentley reached for his wallet and exchanged credit cards on the little tray. I saw Meredith raise her eyebrows at him. He shook his head and waved his hand in a gesture clearly meant to tell her not to worry. She bit her lip anyway.

My heart sank. It looked to me like the credit cards of my best friend's generous date were being declined. If push came to shove, Meredith could pay the bill and Luciano would be discreet about it, but I cringed at the thought. It was humiliating, even if no one else in the restaurant knew.

A high-pitched squeal turned every head in the restaurant in time to see a young woman throw her arms around the young man kneeling by her chair. He slipped the ring on her finger as the roomful of diners watched and applauded. She held up her left hand and waved it over her head like a trophy. Mr. Fontanelli Sr. himself served the tiny wedding cake, as it was the first proposal of the night. (Jake's possible one didn't count, as I hadn't let him finish, thus preserving the legend that no one had ever turned down a proposal at Fontanelli's on Valentine's Day. I don't think he was proposing, anyway, just trying to get me back so he could dump me.)

When I turned back to my coffee from the touching scene of the newly engaged girl texting the news to her girlfriends, Luciano was all smiles as he presented Bentley with a credit card receipt to sign. I expected to see relief in Meredith's face, but what I saw was a tightness around the corners of her mouth. I hoped Bentley wouldn't try to kiss her good night. Not only was that on our mothers' and grandmothers' list of first date no-no's, but I could tell that Meredith was mad enough to sock him if he did.

Bentley, however, was oblivious. He signed the check with a flourish.

"Shall we?" I heard him say as he gallantly gathered up her take-home box.

"Please," Meredith replied through clenched teeth.

He tried to put his hand on the small of her back as they left the dining room, but she took a delicate little skipping step that put her just out of his reach and left his hand hanging in midair. He looked momentarily confused and then hurried to catch up with her.

The movement caught Miss Charlotte's attention.

"Isn't that your friend Meredith Mayhew?" she asked. "I recognize those earrings. Her grandmother wore them to every single Social dance."

A look passed between Preston and me. We had both endured Social, where the young people of select Raeburne's Ferry families learn the social graces—etiquette, formal dress, ballroom dancing, and how to juggle a plate of hors d'oeuvres and a cup of vile-tasting punch. Miss Charlotte apparently had fond memories of it, while I could still remember the awkwardness of my dinner dance dates (arranged by Grandma Ruth, of course).

"Who's that with her?" Miss Charlotte continued as she peered at Bentley's back. "He's too tall to be your cousin Reggie."

"She broke up with him," I told her.

"Good for her," Miss Charlotte said. "Reggie's not marriage material yet. He has some growing up to do."

Personally, I doubt that Reggie will ever be marriage material, as I don't think he has plans to grow up at any time in the future.

"He reminds me of someone," Miss Charlotte mused as she stared after Meredith and Bentley. "I just can't put my finger on who."

Before she could search her memory, however, another squeal went up from across the room, where another young man knelt by another young woman's chair and Luciano hovered nearby with the "little cake." Miss Charlotte gave a sigh and I saw tears glitter in her eyes. I felt my own eyes fill as I looked at her. Was she remembering P. B.'s proposal? Was she regretting saying yes to him? She glanced at me, reached across the table, and patted my hand.

"Never you mind, Sarah. Someday it will be your turn, and it will be worth the wait."

How like Miss Charlotte to think of me when she was so sad herself, even if she was wrong about what I was feeling. As I sat with her at Fontanelli's on her first Valentine's Day as a widow, I wanted to wipe away not only her tears but all the sadness in her kind and thoughtful heart.

CHAPTER 19

THEY WERE ALL WAITING UP for me when I got home—Mama, Daddy, and Grandma Ruth.

"You can put away your horsewhip, Daddy," I said as he hugged me.

"Shoot," he said. "I was looking forward to it." But I saw the relief in his eyes.

In the cozy warmth of the parlor, I gave them a play-by-play account of the evening.

"So, you see," I said as I finished, "I can take care of myself."

"Hmph," Grandma Ruth said. "I seem to recall coming up with the plan. You're welcome, Sarah Elizabeth."

"It may have been your plan, Grandma Ruth, but I think she executed it beautifully," Mama said. "I'm so proud of you, dear. I know it wasn't easy."

"Now she can focus on finding someone worthy of her," my grandmother said to Mama and Daddy, as if I wasn't even there.

"No," I said. "Now I can focus on finding out about this Millie Holtgrew person. I'm with Miss Charlotte on this one. I can't believe Mr. Harrington would take up with someone like her when he already had someone like Miss Charlotte. And that Bentley doesn't look like any Harrington I've ever seen. Something's rotten in Denmark, and I have to find out what it is so Miss Charlotte doesn't have to be so sad anymore."

"She will be sad for quite a while yet, whatever you do," my mother said. "She lost her husband."

"But she's sadder than most widows," I said. "She's afraid she lost him long before he died. She's afraid she's lost the fairy tale she's believed in all these years that she was his one and only forever love. If I can get her love story back, she won't have as much to grieve over as she does now."

"But what if you can't?" Mama asked. "What if he really did—"

"You hush your mouth, Lily Catherine McCready," said Grandma Ruth. "He did nothing of the kind."

"Besides, it's the wondering that's getting to her," I said. "She needs to know one way or the other."

"All right." My mother heaved a sigh. Once my grandmother weighed in on an issue, resistance was useless. "I'm going to lay in a supply of brownies, though. Miss Charlotte may need them before all this is through."

Grandma Ruth was inclined to wait for the DNA results to prove conclusively that Bentley was not a Harrington.

"That could take weeks," I told her. "I might be able to find out the truth before that. Besides, we shouldn't put all our eggs in one basket."

For once, I was right. Not to say Grandma Ruth was wrong, of course. That would never do. But a glitch developed over the DNA testing. According to Meredith, my mole at Bentley, Harrington, Harrington, and Nidden, Millie was insisting that the firm pay for the test, while Mr. Nidden insisted that the burden of proof was on her end, therefore she must bear the expense of the test. Millie protested, tearfully and loud enough for Meredith to hear in reception, that she was a poor widow woman and couldn't afford one of those fancy DNA things.

"Of course, he's P. B. Harrington's son," she'd said. "Just look at him! He's the spitting image of his father!"

Meredith agreed with me. Bentley might be the spitting image of somebody, but it wasn't P. B. Harrington—not even if you turned him upside down or sideways.

Regardless, they were at an impasse. It was clear to Meredith that Thomas Nidden expected Millie to simply go away, since she had no proof. It was equally clear to Meredith that Millie had every intention of stirring up trouble until she got her way.

"So," I told Grandma Ruth after work on Wednesday, "we need to find out who Bentley's father really is."

"It all happened a long time ago, Sarah. I don't know how we'd go about it."

I stared at her in disbelief. "Grandma, I've listened to you and the aunts enough to know that there is a long memory for scandal and gossip in this town. Surely somebody remembers something about who Millie was seeing back then. We just have to track it down."

"I do not gossip, Sarah Elizabeth, nor do I pass gossip," Grandma Ruth said through tight lips.

"Of course not," I said. "You gather information."

"That's right, young lady, and don't you forget it." She pulled her shawl more closely around her shoulders. "That doesn't mean, however, that we can't make use of someone who really is a gossip. You run along and help your mama with supper, Sarah. I have a phone call to make." She reached for her phone and punched a single key. Good grief—she had gossip on speed dial.

Later that evening, I took Grandma Ruth her nightcap of chamomile tea. She looked up from the spiral notebook in her lap to give me a grimly satisfied smile.

"I should have known, Sarah," she said. "I should have known."

"You found out already?" I set the tea tray on her nightstand and sat down in the wing chair.

My grandmother gave a grim nod.

"So, who is it?"

As you may have noticed, Grandma Ruth loves a story, and for her, all stories must start at the beginning. So of course she couldn't just give me a name. I saw the story coming on and settled back in the chair.

"If anybody knew anything, I knew it would be Patti Sue Seiden," she began. So that's who Grandma Ruth had on speed dial. Patti Sue probably had my grandmother on her speed dial too. "And I was right. She did know who Millie Holtgrew was dating all those years ago. Back then, Patti Sue worked at the movie theater, selling tickets. She said Millie would arrive alone on Friday nights and buy a ticket. There was a man who also arrived alone on Friday nights and always bought a ticket for the same show."

"That doesn't mean anything," I said. "It could be a coincidence and Patti Sue just wanted to read more into it because that's the way she thinks."

"Do not interrupt, Sarah. Now, where was I?"

"Two people going to the same movie separately."

"Well, they didn't stay separate for long," Grandma Ruth snapped.

"Oh, really?" I raised my eyebrows.

"Yes, really. Patti Sue told me that the projectionist told her those two always met up in the back row and necked from the time the lights went down until they came up again. He said people always think no one sees them in the back row in the dark, but they never think about the projectionist. He said the only time they ever think about the projectionist is when something goes wrong with the movie—which is really hardly ever. According to Patti Sue, he was quite bitter about that at the time."

"So this man spent the whole movie kissing Millie Holtgrew," I said. "That doesn't necessarily mean he's Bentley's father."

"It does, however, mean he might be. Kissing sometimes leads to—"

"To what, Grandma?" I asked with feigned innocence.

"Never you mind. There's no need to spell it out. Suffice it to say that considering who it was, I wouldn't be at all surprised."

"So who was it, already?"

Grandma Ruth sucked in a disapproving breath. "I should have known."

"But *I* don't know," I said. "I have no way of knowing, seeing as I wasn't even born yet when all this was happening. Who was it?"

"Your great-uncle Hubert, that's who!" She spat out the words and then pressed her lips together.

"G-Uncle?" I said, using his family nickname. "You mean Bentley might be my cousin?"

"Second cousin," she replied. "My nephew. To think one of my own in-laws is mixed up in tormenting my dearest friend. More of an out-law, if you ask me. It's just like Hubert, just like him, to only think of himself and not how his actions would affect others. And him married and all!"

"I thought G-Uncle and Aunt Helen were divorced." As long as I had known her, my great-aunt Helen had lived in the apartment over Haviland's Dress Shop, not in the big house on the hill my great-uncle had built when his ship came in.

"That's a story for another time," said Grandma Ruth. "They may have been separated at the time (and mind you, I don't blame Helen one bit), but Helen and Hubert were married when he was carrying on with Millie. I wouldn't put it past him to father a child and then refuse to accept responsibility for it. He certainly refused to accept responsibility for—" She stopped herself and pressed her lips together again.

"For what, Grandma? You never have told me what he did that's kept you mad at him all these years."

"And I won't," she said. "We never speak of it in this house, do you hear? It was bad enough the way people all over town talked about it when it happened. I expect they've forgotten by now, and I want to keep it that way."

"Yes, ma'am," I said. I doubted whatever it was really had been forgotten, but I could pursue that after all this was over. But I don't hold a lifelong grudge against Great-Uncle Hubert, so I wasn't as willing to jump to conclusions as my grandmother was. "If G-Uncle was Bentley's father, and I think it's a big if, how can we prove it? He's been dead for over twenty years."

"There are no ifs about it, Sarah. Of course, he's the father," Grandma Ruth said firmly. "It's as plain as the pert little nose on your face, which you get from my side of the family, by the way. We'll tell Thomas. He'll confront Millie, who will confess all."

"You think she'd admit it, just like that? I don't think I'd want to admit to sneaking around with Hubert McCready, if he was as bad as you say he was."

"You let me worry about that." She patted my hand. "I can take it from here."

CHAPTER 20

I WAS HARD AT WORK on tax returns on the Thursday after Valentine's Day when someone tapped on the doorframe of my office.

"I have absolutely no opinion about the results of the Super Bowl," I said, without looking up. Professional football was the main topic of office conversation at the moment—never mind the season was finally over.

"I don't either, so may I come in?"

I looked up to see Preston in the doorway. "Oh. Sorry. I thought you were—" I could feel myself blushing.

"I know," he said. "There's a huddle going on in an office up the hall. So may I come in? It'll just take a minute. I know you're busy."

"I'm not supposed to have visitors at work," I told him. "Office policy. Mr. Crawford's a stickler about it."

"Really?" Preston's eyebrows drew together. "Because he's the one who said it would be fine. I came by to drop off some papers for Grandmother Harrington and mentioned that she wanted me to give you a message."

"Oh, that explains it," I said. "She's a client, so it's work-related. No rules at all against that around here. What's the message?"

"She hopes you can have lunch with her at the Magnolia tomorrow. She apologizes for the short notice, but she really wants to see you."

"Of course," I said. "I can meet her there at noon. Did she tell you what's so urgent?"

"I'm just the grandson," he said with a laugh that crinkled the corners of his eyes. "I simply do her bidding."

"I can relate," I said. "My grandmother does a whole mess of bidding. I come to work to get a rest."

He laughed again. "I'll let you rest, then. Have a great morning, Sarah." And with that he was gone.

I turned back to my computer, and the sunniness of his laughing eyes stayed with me all morning.

Mama texted me in the late afternoon to ask me to pick up a few things at the store. Thus it was that I found myself standing in line at the Bi-Lo with Camilla "Call-me-Millie" Holtgrew (Allen Smith Kowalski). In true Southern style, she was chatting away with the person behind her in line. In true Sarah style, I was all ears, four people back. I didn't miss a word, as she had a very carrying voice.

"I never would have known he'd died if I hadn't needed a toilet flapper a few weeks ago."

I looked up from the magazine headlines to see an overprocessed blonde wearing a ton of makeup that only accentuated her age, which must have been around fifty or so.

"I'm a poor widow, so I have to do my own plumbing," she went on. "My son Bentley, bless his heart, isn't very handy."

I couldn't catch what the woman behind her in line said, but she sounded sympathetic and slightly embarrassed, the topic being toilet flappers and all.

"So there I was," Camilla Holtgrew continued, "standing in line at the Home Depot with a toilet flapper in my hand, chatting with the handsome man behind me. He was handsome in that rugged I-can-fix-anything kind of way, you know what I mean?" Camilla didn't wait to find out if the woman knew what she meant or not. She just sailed on with her story. "He said he lives in Dewey Creek, but he was born and raised in Raeburne's Ferry. I said I used to live in Raeburne's Ferry, a long time ago. I mentioned I'd worked at Bentley, Harrington, Harrington, and Nidden when I lived there.

He said, now wasn't that funny. He'd just been to a funeral over in Raeburne's Ferry and it was for P. B. Harrington, one of the lawyers at the firm. And I said I was sorry to hear he had died and that I hoped the funeral was nice. He said yes, it was, but the widow was really upset. I said, of course she was. I'm a widow myself. I know how hard it is." Camilla paused a moment to flutter her eyelashes at the men in line. "Then he said it was more than that. At the reception, she'd been crying her eyes out over her husband's dying words."

Camilla Holtgrew paused for effect. When she got no response from her captive audience (by now everyone in line was listening, especially the men), she continued.

"The last thing P. B. Harrington said to his wife was 'I loved you more than Millie.' Well, you could have knocked me over with a feather, right there in the checkout line at Home Depot. Because, you see, *I'm* Millie!"

Complete silence descended on the grocery checkout line. We weren't sure where to look, but we sure didn't want to look at Millie. I'm all for the friendly exchange of chitchat in the checkout line, but there are some things you just don't say in the midst of complete strangers, even if they're Southern and probably related to you somehow, however distantly.

"I was overcome." She dug in her Kate Spade bag for a tissue. "To think that he remembered me on his deathbed." She sniffed and dabbed the tissue at the corners of her eyes. "So then, of course, I had to come back to Raeburne's Ferry to find out if he had left Bentley anything in his will, because, well, I'm sure it's obvious to anyone who looks at him, Bentley is P. B. Harrington's son. That's why I not only left the firm but left town altogether. The scandal would have ruined his career and then there wouldn't have been any money to leave to Bentley, now would there? But now that he's passed, it can all come out and Bentley will get what's coming to him."

I certainly did hope Bentley would get what was coming to him, which in my opinion was exactly nothing.

Miss Charlotte was seated and eagerly awaiting me when I arrived at the Magnolia for lunch the next day. Preston stood and held my chair for me.

"I didn't know you'd be here too," I said to him.

"Of course, he's here," Miss Charlotte said. "He's my designated driver."

The sip of water I had just taken caught in my throat when she said this. *Designated driver* reminded me of the state Miss Charlotte had been in at the funeral reception. I managed to keep from coughing, but I could feel my eyes water with the effort.

"And I'm happy to drive you wherever you want to go," Preston said.

"He planned to just drop me off and come back for me after lunch. Can you imagine? I insisted he stay. After all, he has to eat lunch anyway, and the Magnolia is so much nicer than the diner."

I was sure Preston would have preferred the hearty food at the diner to the tiny sandwiches, soups, and salads served at the tea room, but he ordered she-crab soup and chicken salad sandwiches for us with good grace.

"We so enjoyed having dessert with you at the restaurant, didn't we, Preston?" Miss Charlotte said in her most gracious Southern manner.

"Yes, ma'am, we did." Preston smiled across the table at me.

"It was kind of you to invite me to join you," I said. The words came out automatically, the proper response Grandma Ruth had trained me to give. Otherwise, I would have been left dazed and tongue-tied by the light and warmth in his eyes.

"And now that that young man is no longer distracting you, you can focus on finding the truth about Millie." Miss Charlotte leaned toward me, eyes bright.

"Grandmother!" Preston looked shocked. "You need to let Mr. Nidden handle it. You have enough to deal with right now."

"Pooh," Miss Charlotte said. "All he plans to do is stonewall her until she gives up and goes away. I want there to be no doubt, one way or the other."

It was that "other" that worried me. What if Bentley really was P. B. Harrington's son?

At this moment, the little brass bell over the door of the Magnolia jangled, and a fiftyish woman in red stiletto heels pushed her way into the tea room.

"Come *along*, Bentley," she called over her shoulder.

I sucked in my breath and braced myself. A waitress hurried forward and seated the new arrivals as far away from our table as possible. Given the size of the tea room, this was not nearly far enough.

"Maybe we should ask for the check and leave," I said to Preston out of the corner of my mouth. I could feel my face redden as Camilla passed our table, pocketbook on her arm, nose in the air, and Bentley lumbering along in her wake. Why were the menus always gone when I needed one to hide behind?

"Nonsense," Miss Charlotte said. "I've been looking forward to dessert."

"But that's—"

"I know who they are, dear," Miss Charlotte said. "And they are certainly no reason to forgo a piece of peanut butter pie. Besides, I want to get a good look at them."

I widened my eyes at Preston, trying to telegraph, *Let's get her out of here before something happens.*

With an understanding wink, he said, "Grandmother, why don't we get the peanut butter pie to go. I really think it would be better . . ."

Miss Charlotte paid her grandson no mind, proceeding to polish her soup spoon with her napkin and angle it so as to capture a reflection of Camilla Holtgrew and her son, Bentley. She turned the back of the spoon this way and that, her eyebrows drawn together in a puzzled frown.

"Why, that's the young man Meredith was with at Fontanelli's. *That's* Bentley? He puts me in mind of somebody," she said. "But not P. B."

Out of the corner of my eye, I saw Camilla look up sharply from her menu.

I lowered my voice and leaned across the table. "Grandma Ruth thinks Great-Uncle Hubert could be Bentley's father. Patti Sue Seiden told her that G-Uncle and Camilla Holtgrew used to have clandestine meetings at the movies. The projectionist told her."

Preston called our server over and ordered three slices of peanut butter pie. "To go, Grandmother," he said.

Miss Charlotte shrugged a shoulder at him and continued to peer at the back of the soup spoon.

"That young man does not run to flab the way Hubert did," she said. "And the eyes are all wrong. Your uncle had shifty eyes. No, somebody else is that boy's daddy, Sarah, and I need you to find out who it is, once and for all."

"Oh, you needn't bother *her* about it. Bentley's ready to take the test any time," Camilla called from across the room.

The air was thick with anticipation. Every eye in the place was fixed on the two women, every ear stretched to hear the argument that was brewing.

At that moment, however, our slices of pie arrived at the table, tucked into the cute Magnolia to-go boxes and tied with the tea room's signature sage-green satin ribbon.

"Preston, the peace of the Magnolia must be preserved. Shall we?"

Preston left more than enough bills on the table and helped us into our coats.

I couldn't be sure, but I thought I heard a collective sigh of disappointment as Preston ushered us through the door. The gossips of Raeburne's Ferry do love a good catfight.

CHAPTER 21

I GOT A BREAK IN the case on Saturday afternoon at the Blue Moon Beauty Emporium. Warm air from the hair dryers fogged up the windows and wrapped around me like a blanket when I stepped out of the cold into the shop. Every chair was filled with ladies in various stages of beautification, from heads full of tinfoil for highlights to final comb-outs. Miss Bonnie smiled at me in the mirror of her station as she whisked a midnight-blue cape from around Mrs. Eifflebacher's shoulders.

"I'll be with you in a minute, Sarah," she called.

Mrs. Eifflebacher took one last look at the back of her hair in the hand mirror, nodded at Miss Bonnie, and trundled off to the reception desk to pay and make her next appointment. At the Blue Moon, you always make your next appointment before you leave. "That way, Blue Moon ladies always look their best," Miss Bonnie often reminded us. It would have embarrassed her to death if a Blue Moon lady was ever seen with her roots showing.

"Well, now, Sarah, I heard that you sent Jake Halloran packing," Miss Bonnie said as she worked the shampoo into my hair.

"Shh," I said. "Don't let him hear you say that. He thinks he dumped me, and that's the way I want it."

Miss Bonnie chuckled. "We *heard* that he dumped you, but I figured you were too smart to get dumped except on purpose."

"Smart enough *now*," I said. "I sure was a dumb bunny back when we were dating. I never suspected he was seeing other girls."

"Don't feel bad, Sarah," Miss Sylvia Hardcastle called over from her beauty station. "We all kiss our share of frogs before we wise up. And to think I almost married Virgil Thompson." She shuddered.

"I'm sorry you got cheated on, Miss Sylvia," I said.

The big-haired blonde laughed. "He didn't cheat on me, honey. He just wanted me to cheat myself. He was all for getting married until I got accepted to cosmetology school. He'd just gotten his plumbing license and was unclogging drains left and right, but he wanted me to deny my calling, stay home, and wash his socks."

Miss Sylvia's client shuddered, as if imagining her hair without Miss Sylvia's gifted ministrations.

"Good riddance to both of them," said Miss Bonnie. "Some men are just not worth breaking your heart over."

There was general assent among the comb-outs and tinfoil.

As Miss Bonnie rinsed out the shampoo and applied conditioner, I thought about everything she must have heard in the more than thirty years that the Blue Moon had been beautifying the women of Raeburne's Ferry. What had she heard about P. B. Harrington and Camilla Holtgrew?

"Miss Charlotte thinks P. B. is worth breaking her heart over," I said. "I don't want to believe he did it either, but after Jake—"

"That Camilla Holtgrew is full of it." Miss Bonnie snorted as she wrapped my hair in a midnight-blue towel. "Go on over to the chair, honey."

I settled into the chair while she snapped open a blue cape spangled with gold stars and draped it around my shoulders with a flourish.

"I remember when she was in Raeburne's Ferry the first time. Do you want the same cut, darlin'? So becoming, I think."

I nodded, willing her to go on.

"P. B. Harrington wasn't the only man Millie Holtgrew batted her Maybelline Great Lash at, believe you me."

"I heard she went out with my great-uncle Hubert," I said, and couldn't help making a face.

Miss Bonnie laughed. "You're right. He wasn't much to look at, what with that paunch and that cigar he was always chewing on, but he was well-off and nearly divorced. She wanted a man with money so she wouldn't have to work as a secretary. Probably a good idea, since she wasn't much of one. Mrs. Wellington used to give me an earful every time she came to have her hair done. There were other men, though, besides your uncle."

"Who? I really don't want Bentley for a cousin," I added to cover up my nosiness. I needn't have worried. Miss Bonnie was off and running.

"I heard that she and Jimmy Boudreaux had something going on. He was a handsome devil back then and quite the bad boy, drinking and smoking and flashing around wads of cash he said he won at poker."

"Did he? Win at poker, I mean."

Miss Bonnie shrugged. "I don't know, but Camilla obviously thought he did. She went after him like a barracuda. I wouldn't be surprised if she took a bite or two out of him. That must be where Camilla's boy got that dark hair. The Harringtons are all blond."

"He *never!*" a voice cried from the shampoo station. Pearl Sanford Boudreaux stormed across the shop, hair dripping and suds flying. "He might have flirted with her, but it never went any further than that."

"Now, Pearl, we know you caught that man hook, line, and sinker, but you have to admit there were other girls before you. A man can't be that handsome and women not take notice."

"Just leave the past in the past, then." Pearl flounced back to the shampoo sink, red in the face, her chest heaving in outrage.

That's the problem, I thought, as Miss Bonnie snipped away. *Camilla Holtgrew is not willing to leave the past there—not by a long shot.*

"Your hair looks very nice," Mama said when I stepped through the back door into the kitchen. The room smelled heavenly.

"Peach cobbler? But it's not Sunday," I said.

"Grandma Ruth's visitor needs some sweetening up." Mama gave me her disapproving teacher look. "It seems you stirred up some trouble at the Blue Moon today."

"Mrs. Boudreaux is in there?"

Mama nodded.

"I'll have you know, Mama, it was Miss Bonnie who brought it up, not me." I headed for the back stairs.

"Not so fast, young lady."

I turned to see my mother holding two plates of steaming cobbler, a scoop of vanilla ice cream melting cozily against each serving.

"Can't you take it in?" I pleaded.

"It's about time you learned that meddling upsets the innocent as well as the guilty, Sarah. If you can't be discreet about it, you have no business prying the way you and your grandmother have been doing. Remember, 'If your lips you would keep from slips, five things regard with care—'"

"I know, I know. 'Of whom you speak, to whom you speak, and how and when and where.'" With a sigh, I turned back and took the plates.

Mama gave me a reassuring smile as she held open the swinging kitchen door for me. "Your hair really does look nice, dear," were her parting words.

Mrs. Boudreaux's hair was the only thing about her that looked nice. Her mascara ran in rivulets down her face, and there were two angry red blotches on her cheeks where no one would ever apply blusher.

She glared as she accepted her dessert plate and pointed her fork at me. "Sarah Elizabeth McCready, you should be ashamed of yourself."

I took a step back and handed Grandma Ruth her cobbler without taking my eyes off that fork.

"How dare you dredge all that up," Mrs. Boudreaux went on, jabbing the fork in my direction for emphasis. "It's bad enough that woman is back in town and doesn't look half bad for her age, but to bring it up at the Blue Moon! I thought we'd never live it down. We finally did, but now—now! It'll start up all over again. I just can't go through it all again."

"Now, Pearl, why don't you take a bite of Lily's cobbler while it's still warm," Grandma Ruth said.

I waited until Mrs. Boudreaux's fork was buried in peaches and pastry before I turned pleading eyes on my grandmother.

What did I do? I mouthed at her.

"I'm sorry, Sarah," Grandma Ruth apologized sotto voce. "There's no way you could have known because"—and here she raised her voice—"not only did it happen before you were even born, the whole thing was forgotten long ago."

"Not anymore, it isn't," Mrs. Boudreaux snapped as she swallowed her first bite of cobbler. "People put one and one together back then and came up with three. You don't think they'll do it again now that Sarah has reminded them about Jimmy and that hussy? I can hear them now, pointing out that Camilla's son has dark hair just like Jimmy and wondering what he would look like with a mustache." She turned tear-filled eyes at me. "How *could* you?"

"I—I—" At that moment, the doorbell rang. "Excuse me." I fled across the front hall and opened the front door.

The man standing there under the porch light tipped his hat to me. "I understand my wife is here. May I come in?"

Even in his fifties, Jimmy Boudreaux had a dashing look about him. His hair was still black, except for some gray at his temples, combed back from his face in thick waves. He'd never run to fat the way my uncles had. His figure was as trim as his Rhett Butler mustache. Rumor had it that he still had a penchant for high-stakes poker games.

My grandmother's voice floated out into the hall. "Of course, people were going to talk back then, Pearl. Jimmy was a handsome devil—"

"Still am a handsome devil," Jimmy Boudreaux said as he stepped into the parlor. "If you're going to talk about me, Mary Ruth, let's not have any of this 'used to be' malarkey."

He handed me his fedora, topcoat, and scarf. I hung them on the hall tree and hurried back to the parlor. I didn't want to miss a word of what promised to be a very interesting confrontation—I mean, *conversation.*

"Vain as ever, I see, Jimmy," Grandma Ruth said.

He threw back his head and laughed. "Guilty as charged."

Meanwhile, Mrs. Boudreaux had set her cobbler down and was scrubbing at her face with a tissue.

At the sight of his wife, Mr. Boudreaux's breezy confidence disappeared. In one swift motion, he was on his knees beside her chair. "What's all this, darlin'?"

"Oh, Jimmy." Mrs. Boudreaux's eyes filled with fresh tears. "I know you didn't, but they'll say you did, I just know it. You didn't, did you?" Her eyes pleaded with his.

"Didn't what, Pearl? And who's saying I did?"

"Everybody!" Mrs. Boudreaux wailed. "And it's all *her* fault." She waved her tissue in my direction.

Mr. Boudreaux gave me such a sharp look that I found myself preferring to face the fork of a few minutes ago.

Grandma Ruth fixed Jimmy Boudreaux with her own penetrating stare. "Hear Sarah out, Jimmy. And wipe that look off your face before it freezes that way." She turned encouraging eyes on me. "Tell them what happened."

"We were all just talking," I said, "the way you do at the Blue Moon, and we got on the subject of Mr. Harrington and Camilla Holtgrew, and I said that I'd heard that she went out with my great-uncle Hubert, in which case Bentley might be my cousin. Then Miss Bonnie said that Camilla went after other men too, and you were one of them. That's all, really."

"Bonnie should have known better than to bring it up, with Pearl right there," Mr. Boudreaux said with a grim set to his jaw. "But you're still not off the hook, young lady. I've heard you've been poking around, asking questions."

"Well, Grandma Ruth and I are looking into the situation," I said.

"By situation, you mean Millie Holtgrew's claim that P. B. Harrington is her son's daddy?"

"Er, yes. We can't quite picture Mr. Harrington fooling around with anybody, much less Camilla Holtgrew. If it wasn't Mr. Harrington, then who was it? That's what Grandma Ruth and I are trying to find out."

176

"And upsetting my wife in the process." Mr. Boudreaux grunted. "All right, I'll tell you the real story, as long as you make sure it gets around. I want this laid to rest, once and for all."

"Have a seat," Grandma Ruth said, indicating the other armchair in the room. "Sarah, bring Mr. Boudreaux a piece of cobbler."

Mama must have been listening at the kitchen door because she had the cobbler for Mr. Boudreaux and a folding chair for me ready to hand.

Back in the parlor, Mr. Boudreaux savored a bite of cobbler before he began. "Every bit as good as yours, Pearl."

"The real story, Jimmy," my grandmother said.

"Ah yes. What I'm about to tell you is the truth, the whole truth, and nothing but the truth, so help me God." He raised his right hand as if he were swearing on a Bible.

Grandma Ruth looked at him over the top of her reading glasses. "It had better be."

"Yes, well, of course." Mr. Boudreaux shifted uncomfortably in his chair under her gaze. "That Millie Holtgrew, she sure had a nose for money and men. She wasn't above having a drink or two at the Chanticleer, and that's where she saw me flashing my cash before the poker game they used to have every Saturday night in the back room. She wiggled and wangled her way back there to watch the game. Pretty soon she was a regular, trying to hang all over me while I played."

"That's what everybody said back then," Mrs. Boudreaux said miserably.

"She tried, but she didn't succeed," Mr. Boudreaux said. "I don't let nobody hang on me when I'm playing. I need to concentrate, and I don't want nobody to see my cards, even if she couldn't tell a full house from a royal flush if her life savings depended on it. Sure, I took her out some and we had a good time, but it didn't mean anything. I had a lot of pretty girls on a string in those days, before I fell hard for Pearl."

"What do you mean by 'a good time'?" Grandma Ruth asked, her voice sharp.

"Not that," Jimmy told her, and gave his wife's hand a squeeze. "I may have been young and foolish enough to brag and flash my money around, but I never took a gamble with women. The stakes were too high, especially with scheming connivers like Millie. I'll admit she tried, and tried hard, but I never let it get far enough for Bentley, or any other baby for that matter, to be mine. I promise, Pearl."

"But when she left town so suddenly, some people said . . . and now she's back and she really was in a family way when she left . . . and her son is tall and thin like you." Mrs. Boudreaux's lower lip trembled.

"Somebody speculates at the Blue Moon, and before you know it, it's the gospel truth at the Lutheran Lenten supper," Mr. Boudreaux said. "I expect you and your cronies to set the record straight, Miss Mary Ruth, and I expect you"—he turned to his wife—"to hold your head high and ignore all those people who have nothing better to do than bring up old dirt. How anyone could think that sorry-looking Bentley looks anything like me—" He caught a glimpse of himself in the mirror across the room and smoothed his mustache.

"Do you believe him?" I asked Grandma Ruth after Mr. and Mrs. Boudreaux left, hand in hand. "All that 'so help me, God' was a little over the top, I thought."

"That's pure Jimmy," Grandma Ruth said. "He never can pass up a chance to showboat."

"But he's a poker player," I said. "That means he knows how to bluff."

"Sarah, this is much more about Pearl than it is about Jimmy. She's never been able to quite believe that Jimmy would choose her over all the girls who threw themselves at him." Grandma Ruth shook her head. "I wish she could see how much he loves her. He's as besotted as P. B. was with Charlotte."

"Not a good comparison, Grandma," I said. "Mr. Harrington's be-sottedness is still up for debate, which is how I got into today's mess in the first place."

"P. B.'s faithfulness is not up for debate as far as I'm concerned, young lady," my grandmother snapped. "I think, however, that we can cross Jimmy Boudreaux off the list. My money's still on Hubert."

"You sure have it out for G-Uncle," I said. "Whatever did he do to you?"

"Never you mind, Sarah Elizabeth. We do not speak of it." She shuddered and clamped her mouth shut.

CHAPTER 22

"So, how are things going with Preston?" Meredith asked. We had managed to coordinate a midweek coffee run and were snatching a few minutes to catch up with each other while we waited for our orders to be filled. Well, maybe we'd stay at the Coffee Break a bit longer than that, but with tax season in full swing, I really needed to come up for air now and then. Mr. Crawford didn't need to know how crowded the shop was or wasn't, just as long as the coffee was still hot when I brought it back.

"You first," I said. "How are things going with Bentley?"

Meredith wrinkled her elegant nose. "I'd like *him* to be going, but he asks me out every time he comes into the office with his mother. I keep saying no, but he just won't take the hint. He's a lot like his mother that way."

"She's still trying to get the law firm to pay for the DNA test?"

Meredith nodded. "And it'll be a cold day in you-know-where when Mr. Nidden does that. It would have to come out of the estate, and he's not about to let a penny of Mrs. Harrington's money go without a really good reason. Besides the fact he's made it clear that the burden of proof lies with Camilla and Bentley, not Mr. Harrington's estate. She doesn't even try to make an appointment anymore, just barges in and expects him to see her."

"And you're on the front lines, insisting she can't see your boss without an appointment."

"And fending off Bentley." Meredith rolled her eyes. "All he can see is that he's going to be rich, ergo, I should be panting to go out with him."

"So he thinks you're shallow."

"Don't get me wrong, Sarah, money matters in a relationship. And it's money that turned me off to him."

"The thing with the credit cards?" I asked. We had already discussed it ad nauseam in the week since Valentine's Day, but Meredith was still pretty exercised about it.

"It's like he had no idea of how it looked when the waiter kept bringing back his cards," she said. "It was bad enough that his credit cards were maxed out and it looked like I'd have to pick up the check. But he also didn't know which of his cards he'd maxed out. That says he doesn't pay attention to his money and probably lives beyond his means. So, it doesn't matter if he comes into an inheritance or not. It'll be gone in no time, and he'll have no idea where it went."

"Probably to his mother," I said.

"And that's another thing." Meredith was off and running. "It's all I can do to behave like the professional I am around her. Mr. Nidden told me not to schedule any more appointments with her, but she swans in every single day and demands, in the sweetest and most pathetic way—for the benefit of the real clients in the reception area—to see Mr. Nidden. Then she accuses me of making a mistake when I say he's busy with a client and cannot be seen without an appointment. She complains to other clients in the waiting room that she is sure she *did* have an appointment and makes me look like I'm incompetent.

"The day she leaned across my desk and tried to look at Mr. Nidden's appointment calendar, I almost snatched her bald-headed. If I ever did that, I'd lose my job for sure. Mr. Nidden is an understanding boss, but he insists on the highest standards of professionalism, no matter how provoking a client may be. And to top it all off, he wants me to go out with Bentley again to keep tabs on Millie Holtgrew. Does the man even understand the term 'professional boundaries'?"

I rolled my eyes. "This is the same man who thinks polishing the tea service is part of your job description. Didn't you tell him about the credit card fiasco?"

Meredith nodded. "But Mr. Nidden said that's the kind of thing he needs to know."

"Tell him he ought to reimburse you if you have to pick up the check, then. If he's anything like Mr. Crawford, that'll put a stop to it right there."

"Hmm . . . good idea." Meredith nodded, as though filing this idea away for future reference. Then she leaned forward. "Now what about Preston? I heard you had lunch with him at the Magnolia the other day. You have to admire a guy that's man enough to hang out at a tea room."

"I had lunch with *Mrs. Harrington*," I clarified, marveling again at the speed at which the Raeburne's Ferry rumor mill spun. "Preston just came along because he was driving the Rolls for her."

"That's not how the ladies at the tea room saw it," she whispered under her breath.

"I'm sorry, what?" I was amazed that anyone at the Magnolia had paid attention to Preston and me in light of the close call between Camilla and Miss Charlotte.

"Nothing," Meredith said. "So, ah, she brought him along," she said archly. "She's trying to set you up with him. I told you, you're golden."

"I am *not* going there, *ever* again, and especially not with a Harrington. Grandma Ruth can try to pin this on my uncle Hubert as much as she wants. Miss Charlotte can deny Bentley looks like P. B. until the cows come home. But I can't get away from those last words, 'I loved you more than Millie.' P. B. said it, practically confessed to having an affair with Millie Holtgrew. As my grandmother is fond of saying from time to time, the apple doesn't fall far from the tree."

"Well, I think you're crazy, Sarah Elizabeth McCready," Meredith said. "If Mrs. Harrington was waving Preston under my nose, I'd be cozying up to him fast. It's about time you got over Jake."

"I *am* over Jake," I said. "You saw me get rid of him."

"Then it's time you got over getting cheated on. Not all men are like that."

"Sarah!" At the sound of my name, I saw that my order was ready. I retrieved the cardboard carrier and went back to the table to say goodbye to Meredith.

"You'll have to take the risk sometime, Sarah," she said. "I hate to see you miss out on love because of that rat."

"For pity's sake, P. B. is giving Mrs. Harrington grief even from his grave. I don't think I'm missing anything, thank you very much. And the only thing I *have* to do is take this coffee back to work."

"Oh, Sarah, don't be like that," I heard behind me as I headed out the door.

As is my wont during tax season, I worked late that night. The office cleared out by five o'clock, and I was able to work in peace for several hours. At about seven fifteen I heard the cheerful voices of the cleaning crew. A few moments later, I also heard a knock on the doorframe of my office. I looked up to see Malcolm Hartwell in the doorway with a brown paper sack in his hand.

"Your mama was bringing this by on her way to her quilt guild meeting, and she asked me to bring it on in to you. Up to old tricks, I see. Working harder than anybody else in this place."

I peered into the sack and found a pulled pork sandwich—still warm—a container of coleslaw, and a couple of brownies, also still warm. "Thank you, Mr. Hartwell, but I think I must just be slower than everyone else in the office."

"Or more careful," Mr. Hartwell said.

"Maybe."

Malcolm Hartwell took off his ball cap, creased the bill a few times, and then put the cap back on his head, tilted back far enough that I could see his eyes as he spoke to me.

"I hear you're doing double duty," he finally said, once he got the cap settled to his liking.

"Hmm?" The aroma wafting up from the paper sack was distracting me.

"Helping Mrs. Harrington. She's had more than her share of troubles lately. It's kind of you and Miss Mary Ruth to try to help her."

"I don't know how much we've been able to help her yet. My grandmother is convinced Mr. Harrington is innocent of fathering Bentley, no matter what he said when he was dying. That leaves us with trying to find out who else could have been the father," I said.

"How's that going?" Mr. Hartwell asked, a little too casually.

"We've been able to rule out Jimmy Boudreaux, but the less said about that the better. Mrs. Boudreaux was really upset when someone dredged up old gossip about it at the Blue Moon."

"I could have told you that," Mr. Hartwell said. "There was nothing going on between those two, hard as Camilla tried." He looked a little sad as he said this.

"Grandma Ruth really wants to blame my great-uncle Hubert," I said, "because he used to meet Camilla at the movie theater every Saturday night."

"She'd blame global warming on your uncle if she could," Mr. Hartwell said with a chuckle.

"That's why I'm not convinced it's him. Just because, according to her, it's something he'd do, isn't proof. By the way, do you happen to know what my uncle did to make her so mad?"

"Shh," Mr. Hartwell said gravely. "We don't speak of it. And you especially do not want to bring it up at the Blue Moon."

"Don't worry," I said as I raised my hands in mock surrender. "I've learned my lesson about that. I just wish I knew where to go from here. I really don't want Bentley for a cousin. There just has to be somebody else."

Mr. Hartwell's face took on a look of sadness again. "Camilla did play the field far and wide," he said.

"Wait a minute." I leaned across the desk. "You know something, don't you?"

He looked away, over my shoulder, and sighed.

"I do. But I promised myself I'd never speak of it, for her sake."

"You promised yourself, not her?" I asked.

"She never knew that I knew."

"Please, Mr. Hartwell, if you know something that would set Mrs. Harrington's mind at ease—"

Malcolm Hartwell adjusted his ball cap again so that his eyes were in the shadow of the bill when he looked at me. "You just tell Mrs. Harrington and your grandmother that you have it from an anonymous source that Bentley is not P. B.'s son. He's not Hubert's either, if that makes you feel any better." He turned to go.

"Wait." A thought struck me like a sweet left hook. "Is Bentley yours?"

Mr. Hartwell stopped in the doorway with a sharp intake of breath. His back stiffened. When he turned around, I thought I glimpsed a flash of watery brightness in his eyes before the ball cap once again cast its shadow.

"If only," he said. His shoulders slumped as he turned away.

"Malcolm Hartwell knows something," I told Grandma Ruth over a cup of chamomile tea that evening. I filled her in on my conversation with the owner of Hartwell Office Cleaning.

"Sounds like he's carrying a torch for her," my grandmother said. "Might explain why he never married. I always assumed it was because he was so devoted to his business—he built it up from nothing to the thriving concern it is today. But this puts it in a different light."

"I can't imagine a kind, sensible person like Mr. Hartwell falling for someone like Camilla Holtgrew," I said.

"He was much younger then," Grandma Ruth reminded me. "And she was very attractive. Sometimes people are blinded by a person's outward appearance." She raised an eyebrow.

I felt myself redden. "I know, I know. It took me a long time to see past Jake's good looks, so I can't judge Mr. Hartwell for doing the same thing when he was my age. But if you ask me, he hasn't learned his lesson. I think he still sees her like he did back then. That's why he wouldn't tell me what he knows."

"He'd have known it was hopeless, poor man," Grandma Ruth said. "He was just starting out then, cleaning every office himself in the evenings and keeping up with all the billing and paperwork during the day. As hardworking as he was, it was clear that it would pay off someday, but of course Camilla would only have seen that there were no dollar signs right then. From what I've been able to gather, she wanted money and she wanted it now. She would never have given him the time of day, much less gone on a date with him."

"Probably a blessing in disguise," I said. "Well, at least we can put Miss Charlotte's mind to rest about P. B. Mission accomplished."

"I hardly think Charlotte will be satisfied with the word of an anonymous source." Grandma Ruth sighed. "Even if the rumor mill gets hold of the idea that someone else is Bentley's father, there will always be a lingering doubt if we can't find out who that someone else is. Look at how easy it was to revive the whole Jimmy Boudreaux story. And I can't see Camilla letting go of an opportunity to be rich unless we can prove she's not entitled to a piece of P. B.'s inheritance."

"Miss Charlotte should just pay for the DNA test and be done with it," I said.

"She's adamant she won't. And it's not about the money, or even Bent having to split his share. I think she's afraid. Afraid of the what-if. I've tried to reassure her, but I can tell it's always at the back of her mind."

"So we're back where we started," I said, feeling defeated.

"I wouldn't say that," my grandmother said. "We've been able to eliminate four suspects—P. B., Jimmy Boudreaux, Hubert, and Malcolm Hartwell. And with P. B. out of the picture, you should have no problem dating Preston."

"Besides the fact that (a) he's busy studying for the LSAT, and (b) he hasn't asked me? Not to mention, I wouldn't say yes even if he did."

"He will," Grandma Ruth replied with a blithe wave of her hand. "And you will," she added for good measure.

CHAPTER 23

Saturday was one of those February days in Georgia that carried a hint of spring. The sky was full of sunshine and puffy clouds. A soft breeze played with my hair as I walked from the parking lot of Crawford and Associates to put in a half day at the office. Mama had tried to get me to stay home, "to enjoy the beautiful weather and besides, you work too hard, Sarah." I resisted. I get a lot done on Saturdays because I'm almost always the only one there, even during tax season. I can even close my office door on Saturdays if I want to. Mama finally contented herself with giving me a list of things she needed from Bi-Lo before two that afternoon so she could get dinner on the table on time that night, to ensure that I really only worked a half day.

I made a good deal of progress over the course of the morning and dutifully pulled into the crowded Bi-Lo parking lot at half past twelve. On my way into the store, I noted the Harrington's Rolls parked in a far corner of the lot to protect its shiny forest-green paint from door dings and the assault of runaway shopping buggies.

I wrenched a buggy free from its closest neighbor in the return and hurried into the store. I pulled out Mama's list and made my way up and down the aisles, aisles that were strangely empty, given the number of cars in the parking lot. I arrived at the produce department, always last in my shopping itinerary, in record time. Over by the tomatoes, I saw why the rest of the store was deserted.

Miss Charlotte and Camilla Holtgrew were faced off next to a bin of beefsteak tomatoes. The way they gripped the handles of their buggies made it look like they were going to ram each other any minute. A crowd had gathered in an avid semicircle around them.

I almost expected to hear the schoolyard chant of "Fight! Fight! Fight!"

I parked my buggy over by the bananas and worked my way to the front of the crowd over on Miss Charlotte's side of the conflict. She was standing as tall as her tiny stature and sensible pumps would allow (and maybe just a tad more), eyes blazing.

"I don't know what my husband meant when he said 'I loved you more than Millie,' but I am quite sure he didn't mean you."

"Now, Grandmother." Preston hovered anxiously behind her. By contrast, I caught a glimpse of Bentley disappearing down the bread aisle.

Camilla also drew herself up, teetering on her four-inch red stiletto heels. "And just what is that supposed to mean?"

"It means that if my P. B. stepped out on me, *which* he would never do, it wouldn't be with a—"

"Grandmother!" Preston's voice was both shocked and authoritative.

"You're right, Preston. I must not forget that I, at least, am a lady." She looked levelly at Camilla, but I saw her hand move along the handle of her buggy, toward the tomato display. I couldn't be sure, but I thought I heard my cousin Reggie quietly taking bets at the back of the crowd.

"Are you saying I'm not a lady?" Camilla's voice rose to a shriek.

"If the shoe fits," Miss Charlotte replied with a delicate shrug. Her glance swept up from Camilla's low-cut blouse to her scarlet lipstick and caked-on makeup, all the way to her eyes, framed by generous false lashes.

Camilla's face reddened under Miss Charlotte's gaze. "For your information, Mrs. High-and-Mighty Harrington, P. B. *didn't* say 'I loved you more than Millie.'"

"How would you know? *You* weren't there when he was dying." Her voice caught, as though she were fighting tears, but I saw her hand creep a little closer to the beefsteaks. "I ought to know what my own husband said. I was there. And *you* weren't."

A gasp of sympathy rose up from the crowd.

"I didn't need to be there to know what he really said." Camilla tossed her head. "I know what kind of a man he was. He was the kind of man who would do right by me and our son. What he said was 'I *left* you more than Millie.'"

"Left me more what?" Miss Charlotte asked.

"Why, money, of course," Camilla said.

Miss Charlotte's hand closed around a tomato, gave it an experimental squeeze. "And just how do you figure that?" Her voice was much too quiet.

"Well, of course," Camilla replied, cocking a hip and gesturing with her hands, "he couldn't very well leave me more than you, no matter how he felt about me. You're his wife, after all. But he knew it would all come out after he died, so he wanted to reassure you that you were getting more than me."

"How dare you!" Miss Charlotte cried. "As if love can be measured with dollars and cents."

She raised the hand holding the tomato amid groans and cheers from the crowd. (I wondered what odds Reggie had given on whether or not Miss Charlotte would so forget herself as to throw a tomato at Camilla Holtgrew.) Preston, however, reached over his grandmother's head and plucked the tomato from her hand right before she let it fly.

Cries rose up from the crowd.

"Hey, no fair!"

"Pay up, Reggie. She woulda done it if Preston hadn't stopped her."

"Nothin' doin'," I heard Reggie say. "You bet she'd throw it, and she didn't."

I could have told them not to bet with Reggie. By hook or by crook, he always comes out on top. Some people never learn. The folks who bet on Miss Charlotte not throwing the tomato were moderately happy, as I watched Reggie pay out. The odds must have been short, which says a lot about Miss Charlotte.

"He didn't leave you anything," Miss Charlotte said as I turned my attention back to Miss Charlotte and Camilla Holtgrew. "Why would he? He was *not* Bentley's father."

"That's not what your son thinks." Camilla smirked.

"And just what do you mean by that?"

I saw a panicked look cross Preston's face as he edged between his grandmother and the tomato bin.

"Well, you know, I have to practically haunt P. B.'s lawyer's office to try to get any justice whatsoever." She fanned herself with her grocery list. "So I just happened to be there when your precious Bent was consulting on the matter with Mr. Nidden. Mr. Nidden's office door was not completely shut, so I couldn't help but hear Mr. Harrington suggest—well, actually he *strongly urged*—that the estate pay me a certain sum to settle things. I would never accept it, of course. The amount mentioned was not nearly enough."

"Oh, really?" Miss Charlotte said, her voice still way too quiet.

"Yes, really." Camilla nodded.

Miss Charlotte removed her pocketbook from the seat of her buggy and hooked the handle over her arm. She turned to her grandson. "We are leaving, Preston."

"But, Grandmother, what about your groceries?" Preston said.

"Leave them," Miss Charlotte said through clenched teeth. "I have lost my appetite."

The crowd parted as she swept out of the produce department, past the piles of grapefruit and onions and potatoes, without a backward glance at her would-be nemesis, Camilla Holtgrew. Preston's gaze met mine for a split second, his blue eyes clouded with concern. My heart went out to him as he turned to follow her.

At that moment, I would not have been his father, Preston B. Harrington III, for anything, not even an exemption from attending funerals until it was time for my own. From the look on Miss Charlotte's face, Mr. Bent might be occupying the family plot a lot sooner than his retirement plan allowed for.

Daddy was waiting for me in the driveway when I returned home from the store. "For goodness' sake, Sarah, get on in there. The phone is ringing off the hook, and your grandmother's about to have sixty fits. Go on and tell her what really happened at the Bi-Lo. I'll put up the groceries."

I left him to it and hurried into the parlor.

"What took you so long?" Grandma Ruth said. "This is no time for your lollygagging."

"The checkout lines were long," I said. "I couldn't very well push my way to the front, telling everyone I had to get home to tell Mary Ruth McCready all about what happened in the produce department this afternoon."

Grandma bridled at this defense. "I don't see why not."

"Well, I'm here now."

"Yes, you are indeed." Grandma Ruth smiled as she reached for the plate by her bed. "Here, have a cookie. And start from the very beginning."

When I finished recounting every word and nuance of the scene at the grocery store, my grandmother frowned and shook her head.

"I should have seen this coming. That is Bent Harrington all over. He thinks money can cover a multitude of sins, like paint over dirty walls."

"No wonder he and Preston are arguing over ethics," I said.

"Preston has a sterling character," Grandma Ruth said. "You two should work together on getting to the bottom of this."

"Preston does not have time to dig around in gossip, old or new," I replied. "He has to prepare for the LSAT."

"So supportive of his goals and dreams." My grandmother favored me with an approving smile. "Such a wonderful quality in a wife."

"It's also something friends do for each other," I said with exasperation.

Grandma Ruth's eyes lit up like a blue sky on a summer morning. "So, you and Preston are friends now. That's just the right way to start, Sarah, with friendship that grows into love."

"I am not marrying Preston—or anybody else for that matter," I replied through gritted teeth. "Can we *please* just get back to the subject at hand?"

"Mind how you speak to your elders, young lady," she snapped. "You won't catch Preston sassing his grandmother. Now, where were we?"

And this was supposed to endear Preston to me? To be forever compared to this paragon of virtue every time I dared to speak my mind? *No, thank you . . . ma'am.*

"We were discussing how Mr. Bent thinks it's all right to buy Camilla off to make her go away," I said. Enough about Preston already.

"Granted, money can solve any number of problems," Grandma Ruth said. "But this is not that kind of problem. The true identity of Bentley's father needs to be cleared up once and for all, not swept under the rug with a pile of money on top of it. Otherwise, the doubt will linger, people will talk, and Charlotte will be left wondering for the rest of her life."

"I agree," I said. "We have to find out what Mr. Hartwell knows. But how?"

"How indeed," my grandmother replied. "I have no doubt that misguided man will take Camilla's secret to his grave."

"Think, Grandma," I said. "Who else would Camilla have been interested in back then? Who else had money? And don't discount the married ones. She's already shown she has absolutely no scruples in that regard. What about Dr. Milford?"

Grandma Ruth shook her head. "He was in debt up to his eyeballs back then. It takes more than a few boxes of tongue depressors to open a medical practice. He's well off thirty-odd years later, but she wouldn't have been willing to wait."

"So it would have to be someone who was already established back then," I said.

"Someone with a good, steady job," Grandma Ruth added. "Perhaps your Mr. Crawford. Didn't he inherit the firm from his father?"

I was speechless for a moment. The thought of Mr. Crawford . . . No, it was unimaginable. For one thing, he would not have considered Camilla tasteful or restrained in any sense of either word, but especially in the financial sense. A man as careful about money as

Mr. Crawford would have a moat around his heart to keep out gold diggers—probably one stocked with alligators.

"I can think of someone else with a good steady job," I replied testily. "And they've been around for three generations."

"You don't mean Gaylord Morris, do you?" Grandma Ruth said with surprise. "Granted, the Morris Funeral Home was doing well by then, but he's a straight arrow, Sarah."

"So is Mr. Crawford," I shot back. "What about old Mr. Morris's son, Fred? He'd have been in his twenties then, learning the business, sure to step into it in due time. I'll bet Camilla wouldn't let a corpse or two or the smell of embalming fluid put her off a cushy life."

"He'd only been married a few years when Camilla left town. I went to the wedding," Grandma Ruth said. "Surely he wouldn't—"

"But Camilla would," I said. "She wouldn't let a little thing like a wife get in her way."

"Wife and child," my grandmother amended. "It was a rather . . . sudden wedding. Lurleen Sinclair had to wear an off-the-rack wedding dress instead of a custom one from Haviland's. It had an empire waist too, if memory serves me right."

I had no doubt that her memory, sharp as her tongue, served her with complete accuracy. "So, Fred Morris had to get married?"

"It's the only logical explanation for that dress," Grandma Ruth said. "And Jeff's older brother Greg *was* born a bit shy of nine months."

"Didn't people talk?" I asked.

"If she hadn't gotten married, then people would have talked," my grandmother said. "Back then what really mattered was that Fred Morris did the right thing and married her before the baby was born. That's what a gentleman did if he got a lady in a family way."

"But if they'd behaved like ladies and gentlemen in the first place . . ."

"Exactly," my grandmother replied. "See that you remember that, young lady."

"No fears here, Grandma," I said. "I'm not dating anymore, ever."

"Preston would never—"

"La la la la la!" I stuck my fingers in my ears. I didn't want to hear her even come close to finishing that sentence.

"Oh, for goodness' sake, Sarah Elizabeth, stop being childish."

I took my finger out of my left ear. "Are you done talking about Preston?"

"For the moment." She passed me another cookie. "We need to find out more about Fred Morris."

"I'll leave you to it, then. Patti Sue is probably just dying to talk about the showdown between Camilla and Miss Charlotte." I stood to go.

Grandma Ruth reached for her phone, then stopped. "I may need you to see what you can find out at Morris's too. You're there so often for viewings, Fred won't think anything of you dropping by to chat."

"I have never 'stopped by' Morris's 'to chat,'" I said. "What in the world would I chat about to Fred Morris? I only go there when someone dies."

My grandmother considered a moment. "Hand me my funeral book, Sarah."

I crossed the room and retrieved the leather-bound book from the shelf. She flipped back and forth among its pages and then finally looked up.

"I might want a mahogany casket."

"Mahogany?" I said, surprised. "That's really expensive, isn't it? Whatever happened to 'just a pine box next to dear Andrew'?"

"I still want a pine box next to your grandfather, but Fred Morris doesn't need to know that. If he thinks I want a big upgrade, he'll be so excited you'll be able to get all kinds of information out of him."

"Just how am I supposed to steer the conversation from mahogany caskets to Camilla Holtgrew?" I asked. It was bad enough having to go to Morris's for viewings. I sure didn't want to go there when nobody had died.

"I'm sure you'll think of something." She gave an airy wave of her hand. "Now shoo. I have phone calls to make."

CHAPTER 24

NEXT THING I KNEW, PATTI Sue Seiden was ringing our doorbell and peering through the narrow windows that flank the front door. I took her coat and ushered her into the parlor.

"Tea, Sarah," Grandma Ruth said to me. "And more cookies, please."

"Lots of cookies," Patti Sue said as she settled her ample bottom in the wing chair by the bed. "We have so much to talk about, Mary Ruth."

Mama had the tray almost ready when I pushed through the kitchen door, cookie plate in hand. She raised her eyebrows at me.

"Patti Sue Seiden," I said.

"Gossip gives that woman a powerful appetite." Mama added a dozen more gingersnaps to the plate.

"So, you see, Mary Ruth, it's entirely possible—" Patti Sue broke off when I stepped into the doorway with the tray. "Little pitchers," she whispered to Grandma Ruth and pressed her lips together primly.

"I haven't been a little pitcher for quite a while, Mrs. Seiden," I said as I set the tray down on the nightstand.

"I would not want to be responsible for sullying a young mind with what Fred Morris got up to back then," she said.

"Too late, ma'am," I said. "What Jake Halloran got up to with Buffy Doyle sullied my mind well and good. You may speak freely with no fear of corrupting me."

Patti Sue cut her eyes over at Grandma Ruth.

"Sarah is assisting me in my investigation of this matter," Grandma Ruth said. "She needs to know what I know."

With that, Patti Sue Seiden, whose knowledge of the scandals of

Raeburne's Ferry is both broad and deep, was off like a racehorse. "You may not know this, Mary Ruth, but Lurleen Sinclair *had* to get married."

"I always thought so. That off-the-rack dress—"

"With the empire waist," Patti Sue added archly. "But I had it straight from her maid of honor, who was exercised about her bridesmaid's dress. She told me that if Lurleen got to wear a white dress in her condition, the least she could do was let her best friend wear a dress that didn't make her look like a zucchini."

"Brides never want their attendants to outshine them," Grandma Ruth said.

"I would never make Meredith wear an ugly dress at my wedding just so I could look better," I said.

My grandmother forbore to comment, but I caught the glint in her eye. I mentally kicked myself. The comment was about my friendship with Meredith, not a sign that I was getting married someday.

"And she wouldn't do that to me either," I added.

"*Anyway*," Patti Sue continued after giving me a quelling look. "Lurleen wasn't too upset about the hurry-up wedding, even if it did mean she didn't get a dress designed just for her from Haviland's. But the groom—whoo-ee!"

I leaned forward. "Do tell."

"Fred Morris was playing the field back then. He was tall, dark, and moderately handsome. He was also the strong, silent type, which lent him an air of mystery. Some girls find that combination irresistible."

"Lurleen, for one," I said.

"Ahem." Grandma Ruth cleared her throat.

"Right," Patti Sue said. "Fred was still enjoying his popularity when Lurleen turned up pregnant. He tried to get out of his obligation, hinting that he wasn't the only one who had ever enjoyed Lurleen's favors. That nearly sent Lurleen's mother into hysterics. Lurleen's father excused himself and returned with an honest-to-goodness shotgun. We didn't have those DNA test thingies like they do nowadays, so it was Fred's word against Lurleen's (and the shotgun). But once that baby was born—nearly two months early, I might add—there was no doubt. He was the spitting image of his father and every other Morris man, especially around the eyes. Gaylord was thrilled, since those deep brown sympathetic eyes are such an asset in the funeral business."

"But what if Greg didn't want to be a mortician?" I asked.

Patti Sue looked aghast. "Why wouldn't he? It's the family business and a good steady job."

"Which is why Camilla Holtgrew was interested in Fred," Grandma Ruth said.

"Ah yes." Patti Sue gave a sage nod. "Now is when it gets interesting." She paused for effect.

"Go on," Grandma Ruth prodded.

"Camilla Holtgrew was born and raised on the wrong side of the tracks, but she had no intention of staying there," Patti Sue said. "She wanted more, and she worked hard to get it. She always had nice clothes in high school because she worked evenings and weekends at the Dairy Queen. But I think we all thought she'd never rise above waitressing, if we thought about her at all."

"So you weren't friends with her?" I asked.

Patti Sue looked down for a moment, as if she was remembering something that she was ashamed of. "She tried to sit with us at lunch a few times, but we ignored her. We were all in after-school clubs and student government and Social. She couldn't do those things because she was working after school."

"She did that so she could buy clothes so she could fit in with you and your friends," I said.

"She didn't understand that it was about so much more than clothes," Patti Sue said defensively.

"I don't suppose the boys ignored her, though, did they?" Grandma Ruth asked.

"No." Patti Sue's face reddened. "They buzzed around her like flies, always hanging around the Dairy Queen, arguing about who would get to drive her home from work."

"Ah," Grandma Ruth said.

The doorbell rang again. This time I admitted Miss Charlotte and Preston. Preston held up his LSAT study book and made a beeline for the kitchen (and Mama's hot chocolate). After showing Miss Charlotte into the parlor, I followed Preston to the kitchen for another teacup and an extra chair. Preston gallantly carried the folding chair and set it up for me next to his grandmother.

"There you are, Sarah." He leaned down and I felt his warm breath on my neck. "Thank you," he said into my ear before heading back to his studies.

Thank you? Thank you for what? My mind buzzed, even as my neck tingled.

"Such a gentleman." Patti Sue sighed. "A credit to you, Miss Charlotte."

"He is indeed." Miss Charlotte gave me a meaningful glance.

"How many lumps?" I raised the sugar tongs to change the subject and ward off the blush that was creeping up my neck from where Preston had breathed on it.

"As I was saying," Patti Sue said after accepting three lumps of sugar and polishing off another gingersnap. "Millie Holtgrew certainly was popular with the boys in high school, but she never really had time to go on dates, what with working all the time and all."

"What about after high school?" I asked.

"She got hired on at the diner," Patti Sue said, "on the strength of her experience at the Dairy Queen. Next thing we knew, though, she was dating Luigi Fontanelli. *I* think it was because she wanted a hostess job at the restaurant."

"Bentley's father could be Luigi Fontanelli?" I asked hopefully.

"No, dear, that was several years before she worked at the law firm," Miss Charlotte told me.

"And things with Luigi didn't last long once she found out that Fontanelli's only hires family—girlfriends don't count," Patti Sue said. "After that, she went to secretarial school."

"It sounds like she was trying to better herself," I said.

"Or find a better way to snag a rich husband," Patti Sue said.

"P. B. was inclined to believe the former, at least at first," Miss Charlotte put in. "He admired ambition, and he was willing to give her a chance. Unfortunately, he came to regret it. She was not suitable at all." She pressed her lips together.

I nodded. "Mrs. Wellington told me."

Patti Sue's head whipped around, her face alight with interest. "What did she tell you, Sarah Elizabeth?"

I glanced at Grandma Ruth, who gave me an almost imperceptible nod. "She said that Camilla had poor phone manners—"

"And her a receptionist." Patti Sue sniffed.

"Wore her skirts too short—"

"Just like in high school." Patti Sue nodded.

"And made goo-goo eyes at every lawyer, clerk, and male client in the firm," I finished.

"I told you she was after a husband, by hook or by crook," Patti Sue said.

"Mrs. Wellington tried to work with her, to no avail," Miss Charlotte said. "The firm finally had to let her go."

"And not long after that, she left town, never to be heard from again," Patti Sue said.

"Until now," Miss Charlotte said. Her eyes flashed with anger or tears, I couldn't tell which. Maybe both.

"Which brings us to why you are here, Patti Sue," Grandma Ruth said. "What do you know about Camilla Holtgrew and Fred Morris?"

Patti Sue washed down her latest cookie with a sip of tea and dabbed at her lips with a napkin.

"Well," she said. "Fred Morris was not about to let a little thing like a wife and family get in the way of sowing the wild oats he wasn't done sowing yet. He still spent his Friday nights in the back room of the Chanticleer losing money at poker to Jimmy Boudreaux."

"Camilla went to those poker games too," I said. "She was trying to snag Jimmy."

"Got it in one." Patti Sue nodded. "She caught Fred Morris's eye instead."

"And you know this how?" I asked.

Patti Sue laid her forefinger on the side of her nose. "I have my sources."

"We need more than 'somebody said' to lay this thing to rest," I said.

"Oh, all right." Patti Sue heaved a huge sigh. "But it goes no further, understood?"

We nodded. I wondered if Grandma Ruth was crossing her fingers under the covers.

"My brother also spent his Friday nights in the back room of the Chanticleer, but he didn't have Jimmy Boudreaux's luck. Daddy had to pay off his debts and then sent him to work at our uncle's sawmill, which was the saving of him. Uncle worked the gambling fever right out of Otis Lee."

"So, Otis Lee told you that Camilla was trying to cozy up to Jimmy Boudreaux, I take it," Grandma Ruth said.

"Right." Patti Sue nodded. "But she got Fred Morris instead, never mind he was married."

"Maybe he said he'd leave his wife," I said.

"More like she thought he'd leave his wife," Patti Sue said.

"Poor girl." Miss Charlotte clucked her tongue.

"Charlotte!" Grandma Ruth was shocked.

"I know, Mary Ruth. She's caused me a lot of pain and trouble, but—"

"But nothing!" Grandma Ruth said. "A few hours ago, Preston had to keep you from throwing a tomato at her!"

"I heard about that," Patti Sue said.

"Think about her upbringing, Mary Ruth," Miss Charlotte said. "She didn't have what we did, and I don't mean the money. I mean all those people who pushed and prodded and nagged us to 'be a lady' and act right, like we do with the young people in our families. It looks like she's mainly after money, but maybe what she really wants is to belong."

Grandma Ruth shook her head. "She still shouldn't be going around spreading lies about a man who can't say any different, whether it's for money or some other reason."

It fell to me to keep things on track. "What you're saying, Mrs. Seiden, is that Fred and Camilla were an item. You know this for sure?"

"It was about that time that Jimmy fell so hard for Pearl Sanford, as you may recall." Here she nodded at Miss Charlotte and Grandma Ruth. "Fred Morris was right there to pick up the pieces. He didn't mind Camilla hanging all over him on poker night, no sirree. Fred Morris is Bentley's father, you mark my words."

"And he wouldn't leave his wife when Camilla got pregnant," said Grandma Ruth. "Camilla left town instead."

"It's still all speculation and hearsay," I said. "We have to find out for sure."

Patti Sue's eyes were focused on the cookie plate as she dithered over which of the two gingersnaps left to devour next, but Grandma Ruth and Miss Charlotte fixed their gaze on me. Between my grandmother's blue laser beams and Miss Charlotte's limpid blue pools, I didn't stand a chance.

"Oh, all right, I'll go to Morris's." I capitulated with a shudder.

"I'll go with you, Sarah."

I jerked around to see Preston standing in the parlor doorway, holding a plate of gingersnaps. Mama's cookie-timing was impeccable. She knew just how long it would take for Patti Sue to deplete the first plateful.

"But you have to study," I said.

"I could use a break. But only if you want me to." His eyes crinkled at the corners as I basked in his smile.

I sat there sunning myself in his gaze until Patti Sue poked a pudgy elbow in my ribs. "Do you want him to go with you or not?"

I drew on my training at Social to reply. "I would be delighted for you to accompany me to the funeral home, Preston. Thank you so much for asking."

Once the plate of gingersnaps was empty and Bentley's parentage apparently settled, Patti Sue took her leave. I saw her to the door, and while I helped her into her coat, I decided to take advantage of the freely flowing gossip.

"Mrs. Seiden, I'm glad G-Uncle has been cleared in this matter. Grandma Ruth is mad enough at him as it is."

Patti Sue gave a little snigger. "Yes, indeedy. That she is."

"Um, you wouldn't know why, would you?"

"Of course I know why." Patti Sue laid her finger alongside her nose.

I raised my eyebrows, trying to look skeptical.

She put a finger to her lips and glanced around. Grandma Ruth and Miss Charlotte were chatting and even laughing some, paying no attention to what was going on out in the hall.

"All right, Sarah, but this goes no farther, do you understand? It would just kill Mary Ruth if it got dredged up again."

"I promise," I whispered.

She gave me a hard look.

"Cross my heart," I said, and did so.

"All right. I swear, Sarah, I don't know why people kept buying used cars from McCready Motors. Your great-uncle cheated people left and right. But somehow he charmed people out of their money—and then wouldn't give it back when they complained about the rotten deal they'd gotten. He'd just point to the sign in his office, where customers had signed the papers for their vehicles."

"The one that says All Sales Final?"

"That's the one." Patti Sue said. "And family was no exception."

"Did he cheat Grandpa Andy?" I asked. "His own brother?"

"Keep your voice down," Patti Sue whispered. "And yes, he did."

I shook my head. "Grandma Ruth has been mad about a car for over forty years? There must be more to it than that."

"There is," Patti Sue said with a furtive look toward the parlor. "But

I've said too much already. Not a word to your grandmother, you hear? And you did not hear any of this from me."

"Yes, ma'am. No, ma'am." I watched thoughtfully as she made her way down the front walk to her car. Patti Sue Seiden loved to gossip, but she'd shown incredible restraint about G-Uncle, which showed just how powerful my grandmother was in this town.

CHAPTER 25

I HAD NO IDEA HOW I was going to work a conversation with Fred Morris about switching up my grandmother's casket around to his affair with Camilla Holtgrew, but it turned out that I couldn't get anywhere near Mr. Morris when Preston and I stopped by.

When we walked into the subdued light of the foyer at the Morris Funeral Home on Monday afternoon, Jeff materialized from the direction of the offices and glided over the thick carpet, right hand outstretched and eyes cast down in sympathy.

"Welcome to Morris's," he murmured as he grasped my hand and laid his other hand consolingly over mine. "How may we be of service?"

Only then did he raise those hangdog eyes and look into my face. His eyes lit up for the briefest moment, like a match flaring in darkness. Just as quickly, the flame went out when his eyes flicked over to Preston.

"It's not your grandmother, is it?" he asked anxiously as he turned his attention back to me.

I was grateful for the dimness of the foyer as I felt a flush rise from my neck to suffuse my face with embarrassment. It was *my* grandmother, only not the way he meant it.

"She's as feisty as ever," I told him. "She wants to—" I felt my throat constrict and I was grateful to have Preston standing just behind my right shoulder.

"Yes?" Jeff prompted.

"She wants a different casket," I blurted.

"A mahogany one," Preston added. His rich baritone made it sound like this was no more than my grandmother's due.

Jeff perked up considerably at this news. He didn't seem to notice how hard it was for me to discuss Grandma Ruth and the word *casket* in the same sentence.

"Mahogany? Well, well, well." He rubbed his hands together. "Please step into the showroom, Miss McCready and, er, Mr. Harrington."

"Actually, Grandma Ruth wants me to work with your father."

Jeff's face fell and the eager light faded from his eyes.

"No offense," I hastened to add. "You know how old-school she is."

Jeff drew himself up, looking for all the world like an English butler. "I am quite capable of rendering the same fine service as my father, in the same style and manner. And he is occupied at the moment. In the embalming room."

"Oh." I've been to countless viewings over the years, but the thought of what the dearly departed went through to prepare for the occasion rattled me. "Well . . . then . . ." There was no graceful way out. "Then in that case I will talk with you about this matter. My grandmother will just have to understand."

Jeff brightened considerably. "Really? Great! I mean, please step this way." He swept his hand toward the showroom.

"Don't you have, well, a catalog or something that I can take back to my grandmother so she can choose it herself?"

"I suppose," Jeff said. "But you'll get a much better sense of the quality and suitability of the piece if you see it for yourself. There are some things a photograph simply cannot capture—the softness of the lining, for example."

A mental picture of a real casket awaiting Grandma Ruth's demise was not something I wanted to carry around in my head during the many (I hoped) years before my grandmother would need it. I felt the comforting warmth of Preston's shoulder against mine. It was as if he'd read my mind.

"I would rather look at a catalog," I said again.

"If that's what you really want," Jeff said, with a slight shrug. "Please have a seat in my office while I retrieve one."

Jeff steered me across the carpet with a solicitous hand at my elbow. He fussed over seating me and bringing us cups of chamomile tea, no doubt a staple at Morris's for soothing the bereaved. Moments later he returned with a glossy catalog, open to a full-page spread of mahogany caskets. I stifled a gasp as I glanced at the prices. Grandma Ruth has made sure that I've seen the paperwork for her prepaid plan, tucked into a pocket on the inside cover of her funeral book. The cheapest of the mahogany caskets was easily twice the cost of her pine one.

"May I borrow this to show my grandmother?" I asked. "I'm sure she'll want to pick it out herself."

"Of course," Jeff said. "I'm sure she'll find something to her liking. Tell her we can"—he cleared his throat and lowered his voice discreetly—"work out a payment plan for the difference in price."

"I will." I stood to leave, as it was clear we wouldn't get a chance to interrogate Fred Morris. I began to think that Grandma Ruth had sent me on a wild-goose chase. In light of Lurleen Morris's daddy's shotgun, would Fred have told us anything about his relationship with Camilla anyway? I wondered if this was all just in aid of throwing Preston and me together. I wouldn't put it past our grandmothers.

Jeff, however, was not about to let me go so easily.

"While you're here, why don't you arrange a plan for yourself?" he urged. "It's never too early, you know. Abby Claire Harper was in just last week to plan hers, and she's even younger than you. It gives you and your loved ones such peace of mind to not have to trouble about the arrangements. I can work with you personally to arrange a tasteful and meaningful occasion. We could go over things here in my office, or perhaps you'd be more comfortable discussing it over dinner at Fontanelli's." A hopeful look peered around the edges of his professional manner.

Next to me, I heard a sharp intake of breath. Out of the corner of my eye, I saw Preston push back his shirt cuff to consult his Rolex.

"Sarah, we really should be going if we're going to make our dinner reservation." He held out his hand for my coat.

"Our . . . what?" Then it dawned on me that the only place in

Raeburne's Ferry that requires reservations is the aforementioned Fontanelli's. "Oh yes, of course. Thank you so much for your time, Mr. Morris. I'll make sure my grandmother gets this." I transferred the catalog to my other hand as Preston helped me into my coat.

Shoulders slumped in defeat, Jeff walked us out. At the door he took one more opportunity to press my hand between his damp ones. He looked mournfully into my eyes. "You really should give some thought to your final occasion. I am at your service." Then he bowed so low over my hand I thought he was going to kiss it.

"Er, I'll keep that in mind, Mr. Morris," I said as I extricated my hand.

As the door shut behind us, I heard him say, "You can call me Jeff."

"That sure was quick thinking. Thank you," I told Preston, digging around in my purse for my hand sanitizer. "I really don't want to plan my funeral yet."

"And I get the impression you don't want to have dinner with Jeff Morris either." He grinned down at me as he opened the passenger door of the Rolls.

"No," I said, unable to suppress a shudder.

"Do you want to have dinner with me instead? I might could get a reservation for this evening. I really enjoyed the last time we were at Fontanelli's. You can have baked Alaska again if you want."

"Oh no, I couldn't." I shook my head. "Have baked Alaska, I mean."

"Why not?" He tilted his head closer to mine.

"Mama's rules. I think it's rule number three. 'On a first date, order from the lower-to-middle-priced items on the menu so as not to take advantage of a young man eager to impress.'" I felt heat rising in my cheeks at the word *date*. Preston Harrington IV had, indeed, just asked me for a date.

"Far be it from me to tempt you to break rule number three," he said, a smile tugging at the corners of his mouth. "You can have the cannoli, if it makes you feel better."

I was sorely tempted. He looked so handsome in his black dress coat, those eyes of his smiling down at me like a summer sky. "Oh, Preston, I can't. Rule number one."

"Which is?"

"A lady does not accept last-minute invitations."

He nodded. "We certainly can't break rule number one. Another time, perhaps? Say Friday?"

My heart leaped, and before I knew what I was doing, I nodded back, never mind his grandfather's dying words, never mind the pain of my breakup with Jake, never mind it was still just a tad last-minute.

What was I thinking? Maybe I could back out . . . But no, there was rule number four: A lady does not break a date unless it is for family obligations. And somehow, I didn't think Mama would let me use that excuse this time.

"You owe me," I told Grandma Ruth when I got home that evening.

"Jeff Morris is a very nice young man," she reminded me yet again. "I don't know what you have against him."

"I think I'll let Abby Claire have a shot at him," I said. "Jeff said she came by to look at plans last week. Did you by any chance have anything to do with that?"

"Why, no, Sarah." Grandma Ruth was the picture of innocence. "But I wish I'd thought of it. Flowers and funerals, you know . . . they'd be wonderful together."

"I don't know," I said. "You haven't seen Abby Claire's hair lately. It's . . . well . . . exuberant. The exact opposite of the vibe at Morris's."

"I have heard about Abby Claire Harper's hair," my grandmother said. "I wouldn't want to see it on you, but Miss Sylvia assures me it's charming on her. Jeff could use a bit of vim and vigor, dealing with bereavement all the time as he does."

"Be that as it may," I said. "I've got nothing except a catalog for a casket you don't want and an invitation to plan my funeral. I never got anywhere near Fred Morris." I wasn't about to tell her about Preston's invitation to dinner.

"I wouldn't say you have nothing," Grandma Ruth said. "You have an excuse to go back to Morris's. You'll need to let Jeff know that I've changed my mind about upgrading my casket, not to mention finalizing your very own funeral plan. You could take Preston with you again."

My skin was still crawling from Jeff Morris's clammy attentions, and for once, I rose up in rebellion. "You can call Morris's on the phone and tell them yourself that you've changed your mind. And I absolutely do not want to plan my funeral yet. My life is just getting started. You're on your own when it comes to Morris's, Grandma."

I held my ground with a look as determined and steely as any she had ever sent my way. Nobody, not even Grandma Ruth, was making me plan my six-feet-under at the tender age of twenty-four.

Grandma Ruth is not nearly as helpless as she makes out to be when she's trying to get other people to do things for her. This truth was borne out by the sight of one of the Morris Funeral Home limousines parked at the curb when I arrived home, chilled to the bone, from work on Tuesday.

"Brr! The temperature must have dropped thirty degrees since lunch," I said to my mother as I came through the kitchen door.

"There's a storm coming." Mama stirred a large Crock-Pot of chili. "Snow and maybe even ice," she said with a shudder.

"Do you need me to go to the store?" I asked. Now that I thought about it, the parking lot at Bi-Lo had seemed pretty crowded when I passed it on the way home.

"Oh no. You're home safe, and you're not going anywhere else," Mama said. "I stocked up as soon as I heard it on the news, while there was still bread and milk and tomato soup left on the shelves. We'll be fine."

"We sure will," my father said cheerfully as he came through the door with an armload of firewood. "If the power goes out, we'll camp out in the parlor in front of the fireplace. Did you remember the marshmallows, Lily?"

"Of course," she said. "And the chocolate and graham crackers too."

Honestly, it was a wonder we weren't all tipping the scales. We'd be in trouble without the McCready metabolism.

I glanced out the window over the sink, hoping for snow, a rare event in Raeburne's Ferry. I found myself even hoping for a power outage, so we could have s'mores. Instead of fluffy white flakes, however, a steady rain had begun to fall. The thermometer outside the window registered thirty-six degrees.

"Shouldn't we be sending Mr. Morris on his way?" I asked. "I wouldn't want him to get caught in this."

"I've been in twice to warm up his coffee and give him the weather report, but he won't budge. He seems to be trying to get your grandmother to upgrade her casket. I've never known him to pressure people to upgrade after they've paid for their plan."

"Blame Grandma Ruth," I said, and told her about my mission to Morris's the day before. "She has no intention of changing to a mahogany casket. That's just to lure him here to interrogate him about Camilla Holtgrew."

"I hope she gets her information soon," Daddy said. "It's dropped another two degrees since I came inside."

"I'll see what I can do," I said as I picked up the coffee carafe. "You wouldn't have any brownies, would you? The chocolate might mellow him out enough to leave making a sale for another day."

Mama shook her head. "Not in this weather, Sarah. Mr. Morris will need all his wits about him to get home in that mess out there. And when it comes to my brownies, nobody can eat just one."

"A warm-up for your coffee before you go, Mr. Morris?" I asked when I stepped into the parlor. "It's raining."

"A little rain never hurt anyone, Sarah," Grandma Ruth said. "Mr. Morris and I have not yet concluded our business."

"Perhaps your business can wait," I said. "Not only is it raining, but the temperature has almost dropped to freezing."

"I'm sure I can handle driving home in a bit of freezing rain, Miss Mary Ruth," Mr. Morris told my grandmother. "Now, back to the business at hand—" He broke off to give me a pointed look.

"It's quite all right, Fred," she said. "Sarah is my representative when it comes to my funeral arrangements. When the time comes, you'll be working directly with her to make sure everything is done the way I want it."

This was news to me. It made me blink and swallow hard.

Mr. Morris shrugged and plunged ahead. "Here is what you've got on your plan now." He laid a piece of polished pine and a swatch of rose-colored satin across her lap. "But this is what you would get with the upgrade." With a flourish, he produced a piece of polished mahogany and a swatch of pale blue silk. "You will look lovely on this fabric. It even matches your eyes."

"My eyes will be closed for the occasion, I most certainly hope," Grandma Ruth snapped.

"Of course, of course," the funeral director said. "But it does complement your coloring. I wish you could see the casket itself, Miss Mary Ruth. It is magnificent, befitting a citizen of your stature in the community."

At this point, my father came in with the news that the roads had already begun to ice over. Mr. Morris had best be going if he planned on getting home safely. Grandma Ruth gave Daddy *the look*, but he ignored her.

"I'm sure your business with Mr. Morris will keep, Mama," he told her.

Reluctantly, Fred Morris rose from his chair, stowed his samples in his briefcase, and stepped into the front hall. I handed him his hat, overcoat, and umbrella. A blast of frigid wind assaulted us when I opened the front door.

"Be careful on the steps," I said. I watched anxiously as he grasped the railing and gingerly made his way to the sidewalk. He slid more than stepped to the limousine, much like the car that came fishtailing down the street. We both gasped as the blue sedan narrowly missed the limousine's back fender on its way past. The woman behind the wheel looked absolutely terrified.

"On second thought," Mr. Morris called to me, his face pale in the fading light, "perhaps I can't handle a bit of freezing rain."

My father joined me in the doorway and beckoned to Mr. Morris. "That's a good idea, Fred. No sense risking your safety and that fine vehicle in this mess. Come on back in."

Safe inside the parlor again, Mr. Morris called his wife.

"Yes, Lurleen, I'm at the McCreadys'."

I faintly heard a shrill female voice as he held the phone away from his ear.

"Yes, I know the storm is bad. That's why I'm calling." Mr. Morris let out a sigh and gazed out the window as he continued to listen.

"No, I am not planning to try to drive home in it," he replied to the voice that had now taken on a hysterical note. "Yes, I'll stay right here until it's safe to be out again. Don't you worry none. Are you all right?" Mr. Morris's tone had turned soothing. He nodded as he listened. "It sounds like Jeff has everything under control. I'll see you later, sugar." He gave the barest of smiles as he ended the call.

"She worries," he said sheepishly as he stowed his phone away.

"With good reason," Grandma Ruth said archly. In response to the startled look on Mr. Morris's face, she added, "The weather being so bad and all."

Over our supper of chili and corn bread, Mr. Morris tried to chat me up about my funeral plan, but Mama intervened.

"How are those grandbabies of yours, Fred?"

Mr. Morris was soon regaling us with the antics and accomplishments of his three granddaughters. His only regret, apparently, was that there wasn't a boy among them.

"To pass the business on to, you know," he said.

"You don't think any of them will want to join the business?" I asked.

"They're girls," Mr. Morris said, as if their unfitness for the family business were obvious.

"But it's the 'Morris Funeral Home,' not 'Morris and Sons,'" I said.

"Hopefully Jeff will have a boy someday," Mr. Morris said and turned away from me to compliment my mother on her cooking.

Reason number 672 for not dating Jeff Morris.

While Mama and I washed and put up the dishes, Daddy and Mr. Morris started a fire in the parlor fireplace, tested lanterns and flashlights, and gathered supplies for s'mores. Knowing Daddy, we'd be having them whether the power went out or not. I helped my mother carry down extra quilts and pillows from the linen closet. Soon we were snug in the parlor, prepared for anything. Well, almost anything, as it turned out.

CHAPTER 26

WE (MAMA, DADDY, MR. MORRIS, and I) were deep in a cutthroat game of Scrabble when the lights flickered the first time. Daddy reached for the lantern, but then the lights steadied. In the distance, a siren's wail waxed and waned on the way to some emergency. The phone on Grandma Ruth's bedside table rang, sounding shrill against the heavy rain.

"No, Patti Sue, we still have power here. The lights tried to go out but came back on right away." Grandma Ruth said it as if the lights wouldn't dare go out on her watch. "My goodness! You called the power company, didn't you? Don't go outside until they take care of it, you hear?"

All eyes turned to Grandma Ruth as she hung up the phone.

"There's a power line down right in front of Patti Sue Seiden's house," she told us. "The ice brought it down. She said the line is sparking all over the place."

Daddy moved to the front window and pulled back the curtain. Mr. Morris and I peered over his shoulder at the power lines in front of our house. They sagged under the weight of the ice that had formed on them.

"Only a matter of time." My father reached for a lantern.

"What a mess," Mr. Morris said.

Meanwhile, my grandmother was dialing the phone. "Charlotte? The power's out at Patti Sue's. Are you all right?" She listened and then sighed with relief. "Preston will take good care of you. He's such a thoughtful boy. Wait a minute," she said as my father signaled frantically at her. She listened as my father talked and gestured toward the window. "Charlotte? Dean says there's ice on the power lines. Do you have plenty of flashlights and batteries? Has Preston gotten a fire going in the fireplace yet? Oh, good. It sounds like he has everything under control. And you tell him Sarah's just fine. She's looking particularly lovely today in a powder-blue sweater dress that brings out the blue in her eyes."

"Do you mind, Grandma?" I said when she got off the phone with Miss Charlotte.

"Not at all, dear. I love telling my friends about my beautiful grand-daughter." She turned back to the phone.

The call to Miss Charlotte was the first of many as Grandma Ruth checked on all her friends who were either shut-in or lived alone, although what she would do if some of them didn't have what they needed to weather the storm, I had no idea. I, for one, had no intention of stepping foot out of the house until this was all over. As she neared the end of her list, I saw the power line in front of our house fall away from its pole in a shower and sizzle of sparks. The streetlights went out like snuffed candles.

"Well, well," Daddy said as he turned on the lantern by my grand-mother's bed. "Who's up for s'mores?"

We were toasting our second round of marshmallows when we heard a crash, followed by a sickening crunch. Mr. Morris rushed to the window and peered into the darkness.

"Oh no," he groaned. "My beautiful limousine!"

I joined him at the window to see a dark sedan cozied up to the crumpled rear end of the Morris Funeral Home limousine. Through the lashing rain, we watched two people struggle out of the wreckage, perilously close to the downed wire that waved and writhed in the wind. I ran out of the parlor and flung open the front door.

"Be careful!" I shouted to the pair who inched along the side of the limousine on the ice that now coated the road. "Come around this way, away from the power line!"

Their heads jerked up at the sound of my voice and the two of them nearly went down when they caught sight of how close they were to something even more dangerous than the ice. They edged their way back around the end of the sedan. Daddy came out with a flashlight and guided them as they slipped and slid across the sidewalk and up onto the porch. Mama was ready in the front hall with towels to dry them off and quilts to wrap around them, while Mr. Morris came out of the parlor lamenting over his limousine.

"I'm so sorry about your car!" said the taller of our new guests through his towel. "I swear I didn't see it until it was too late. You can't see anything out there, what with the rain and no streetlights."

"He tried to stop, but the car just slid," came a familiar feminine voice from the depths of my mother's Jacob's Ladder quilt. A glance down at the sodden red stiletto heels dampening the front hall carpet assured me that we were in the process of rescuing Public Enemy #1 and her son, Bentley. Another glance, this one from my mother, made me clamp my mouth shut. Everything in me wanted to escort them back out into the storm. My mother's commitment to hospitality would not, however, allow this. If General Sherman himself had come to our door in such weather, I believe she would have given him shelter (at least until the storm let up and as long as he stayed away from her grandmother's silver tea service).

"Come in and warm yourselves by the fire," Mama said. "We're having s'mores. Would you care to join us?"

Mr. Morris was, however, not inclined to be gracious to our new guests. "What kind of idiot are you!" he shouted at Bentley. "Anyone with any sense has been out of this mess for hours!"

Camilla gasped and stepped in front of her son. "How dare you speak to my son like that! He certainly didn't mean to run into your old car!"

"Old car! *Old* car!" Mr. Morris said. "That is a vintage limousine! It was the first one my father bought when he founded the family business. Your insurance better be good because it will cost plenty to repair it."

Bentley slunk off and sidled up to the toasting forks by the fireplace. I absently handed him the bag of marshmallows, intent on the confrontation between Camilla Holtgrew and Fred Morris, who didn't seem to have recognized each other yet.

"What were *you* doing bringing an antique car out in this mess?" Camilla shot back.

Fred Morris drew himself up and said, "I was conducting business. And it wasn't raining *or* freezing when I arrived. I, at least, had the sense to stay put when the weather got bad, unlike some people." He glared at her.

Grandma Ruth's eyes glittered in the firelight. She loves a good fight—I mean, *discussion*. My mother, however, does not. Mama put her arm around Camilla.

"Really, Fred, there will be time enough later to exchange insurance information. This poor lady has had quite a fright, not to mention the fact that she is soaking wet and chilled to the bone. Come over and sit by the fire, dear. I'll go upstairs and find you and your son some dry clothes."

Under Mama's gentle but firm gaze, Mr. Morris subsided into a seat at the card table, looking none too happy to be minding his manners. Camilla's eyes widened. It looked to me like she was really seeing Mr. Morris for the first time since we'd rescued her from the storm. I watched her lips form the word *Fred*. Then she quickly turned away.

"Here, Bentley, let me do that." Camilla took charge of her son's place in front of the fire as well as the toasting fork, edging him into the shadows. "He always burns the marshmallows," she said to the room at large.

Good grief, I thought as Camilla elbowed her son away from the fire. *She could give Aunt Marjorie a run for her money. Come to think of it, my cousin Bruce probably doesn't get to toast his own marshmallows either.*

"I like them burned," Bentley muttered.

"So do I," Mr. Morris chimed in.

Camilla turned her back and focused on browning the two marshmallows on the toasting fork to golden brown perfection.

"Where are my manners?" Mama exclaimed as she appeared in the parlor doorway with her arms full of clothing. "I haven't made introductions. I'm Lily McCready. Over there is my husband, Dean." My father waved his toasting fork. "This is my daughter, Sarah." My grandmother cleared her throat. "And my mother-in-law, Mary Ruth McCready. And this is Fred Morris, our local funeral director." Mama raised her eyebrows encouragingly at our new guests.

"Mrs. Kowalski," Camilla said tersely. "And my son, Bentley."

"Kowalski?" my father said. "I thought—"

Mama, however, bustled into the room before he could finish his question. She distributed dry clothes and flashlights to our sodden and shivering guests, with directions to the bedrooms upstairs where they could change.

"I thought her name was Holtgrew," Daddy said, when our guests were out of earshot. "Isn't she that woman who's trying to get part of the Harringtons' estate?"

There was a sudden clatter as Fred Morris's hand jerked and over-turned his tray of Scrabble letters. I peered at him in the flicker of the firelight, wishing I could see if he'd gone pale. He got up and went to the window, his back to us.

"Yes, she is," Mama replied. "But you will not mention that particular subject. They are guests in our home, and I will not have any unpleasantness."

Especially because we're cooped up here for the duration of the storm, I mentally added. In this weather, no one could leave in a huff. We would simply have to put up with each other.

"Sarah, come help me fix a supper tray for our guests," Mama said.

In the kitchen, we filled bowls with still-warm chili from the Crock-Pot and arranged them on a tray with the basket of corn bread, some sour cream, grated cheese, and the butter dish. I rolled silverware in a couple of napkins and added them to the tray. When we got back to the parlor, Camilla and Bentley were once more warming themselves by the fire, while Mr. Morris continued to stare out the front window.

Daddy cleared away the Scrabble game to make room for the chili. He even pulled out Camilla's chair for her, giving Mama a look that clearly said, *See, I'm behaving myself.*

Camilla, however, pointed to the chair on the other side of the table. "I'd rather sit there, closer to the fire."

My father dutifully held that one for her, while Bentley was relegated to a colder and more shadowed seat by a wave of his mother's hand.

"I don't think the weather will change any time soon, Fred. Why don't you have a seat?" Grandma Ruth said.

"I'm fine," he said.

"I'd like to see those samples again," my grandmother said.

The hope that Grandma Ruth really would upgrade her casket propelled Mr. Morris away from the window. He retrieved his samples from his briefcase and laid them once more in her lap.

"This really is beautiful." She held up the pale blue silk. "I'd rather have the color I've already picked out, though. Does it come in rose?"

Mr. Morris consulted the catalog he'd brought with him while Grandma Ruth studied his face by the light of the lantern on her bedside table. I saw her cut her eyes over at the card table, where Bentley was putting away chili and corn bread with a gusto that would warm any cook's heart. Then she looked at Mr. Morris again, her lips set in a grim line.

I stepped back so I could see both Bentley and Mr. Morris and tried to see what my grandmother was seeing. In the lantern light I could see Mr. Morris fairly clearly. He was the picture of the well-dressed undertaker, his dark suit tailored to fit his tall and lanky frame. His tie was subdued, and his polished wingtips glowed softly in the pool of light from the lantern. His face wore a look of concerned attentiveness as my grandmother dithered over the catalog. It really was uncanny the way Mr. Morris's eyes drooped, giving the impression that he was quite sad about the prospect of Grandma Ruth's demise while he tried to upsell her on a coffin.

It was harder to study Bentley, seated on the dark side of the card table as he was. I couldn't see much more than a profile as he crumbled corn bread into his bowl and eagerly spooned chili into his mouth. He, too, was tall and lanky. The cuffs of the sweatshirt Mama had commandeered from my father stopped several inches short of Bentley's wrists. Luckily, Daddy still had spare tube socks from the eighties, since the borrowed sweatpants didn't reach Bentley's ankles either. His hair was dark like Mr. Morris's, and he still needed a haircut. All in all, Bentley looked decidedly scruffy.

"Bentley," Grandma Ruth said. Her voice was firm, no-nonsense.

"Ma'am?" Bentley's Adam's apple bobbed as he hastened to swallow his latest bite of corn bread.

"Come here, please." My grandmother's voice brooked no argument.

"Yes, ma'am." Bentley wiped his mouth on his napkin and pushed back his chair.

"Finish your supper, Bentley," Camilla said sharply. "While it's still hot," she added, taking the sudden edge out of her voice.

Bentley looked back and forth between his mother and my grandmother. Grandma Ruth's powerful gaze prevailed. Bentley stood and approached the bed as though in a trance. At the sound of a gasp from his mother, he stopped short of the circle of lantern light. Grandma Ruth beckoned imperiously, as she cast a steely-eyed glance at Camilla.

Mr. Morris realized what was happening about three seconds too late.

"I shouldn't tire you, Miss Mary Ruth." He shoved his samples into his briefcase and rose to step into the shadows.

"Not at all," Grandma Ruth told him. "Bentley should be quite interested in the business, don't you think?"

Even in the flickering firelight, I saw the color drain from Camilla's face.

"I see what you mean, Mary Ruth," Mama said as she looked from Bentley's face to Mr. Morris's and back again. "I'm not sure what it is, but there's something about his face—it's so, well, so—" She hesitated.

"Mournful?" I offered, as Bentley stood, eyes drooping, next to Mr. Morris.

"I was going to say 'sympathetic,'" my mother said. "It's something around the eyes, don't you think? Why, Fred, you and Jeff have those same sympathetic eyes. Isn't that funny?"

"More like funny business," my grandmother snapped.

"Mama," my father said, "there is nothing funny about the funeral business."

"She doesn't mean funny, ha-ha," I said. I turned to my grandmother. "Do you, Grandma?"

"Indeed, I do not," Grandma Ruth said. "There is a reason Bentley has Morris eyes, isn't there, Fred?"

Mr. Morris swallowed hard. "I can explain."

"Please do," my grandmother said.

"Don't you dare," Camilla said.

Mr. Morris turned his sad eyes on Camilla and shook his head. "It's no use, Millie. I don't want the truth to come out any more than you do, but there's really no denying it. Look at him." He pulled Bentley into the circle of light next to Grandma Ruth's bed.

As they stood side by side, the resemblance between Bentley and Mr. Morris was both uncanny and clear. They were nearly the same height, thin, dark-haired. Granted, Mr. Morris carried his lanky limbs with professional grace, whereas Bentley was gangly and awkward. It was the eyes, though, that were unmistakable—droopy, sad, mournful, sympathetic. The way Jeff Morris had haunted me with those eyes at every funeral I'd attended since I'd finished college, I was surprised I hadn't put it together sooner. Bentley was the spitting image of his father all right, but only if that father was Fred Morris, not P. B. Harrington.

"No, no, no!" Camilla shrieked. "He's a Harrington. He has to be a Harrington."

"Oh, the Morrises aren't good enough for you, is that it?" Mr. Morris's face flushed a deep and angry red. "It was certainly good enough for you thirty-odd years ago."

"And just what is that supposed to mean?" Camilla shot back.

"Now, now," Mama said. "Let's all take a deep breath and calm down."

"I have a better idea," Daddy said. "Let's raid the pantry for some of your brownies, Lily. You come too, Bentley." He picked up his industrial-sized Maglite and led the way to the kitchen.

Bentley obeyed, but the worried look he cast over his shoulder went straight to my heart. He was probably wondering who the heck he really was.

CHAPTER 27

"As I was saying"—Camilla resumed once the kitchen door had swung shut—"just what do you mean by that?"

"The way you went after me back then, it was pretty clear I was quite a prize," Mr. Morris said.

"*I* went after *you*? You were the one who started it, never mind you were a married man."

"I didn't think you'd care about that," Mr. Morris said. "Hubert was married too."

"Practically divorced," Camilla said through gritted teeth. "Besides, how did you know about him?"

"Movie projectionists aren't blind, you know." Mr. Morris sneered. "Lester's my second cousin and he sure liked to talk about the goings-on at the theater. Made him feel important before he got a real job over at the feed store."

They seemed to have forgotten that Grandma Ruth and I were there, hanging on every word.

"So what if I'd rather Bentley was P. B.'s son? He was an honorable man. He wouldn't have left me high and dry when I got pregnant the way you did." Camilla lifted her chin in defiance.

"Yes, P. B. Harrington was an honorable man," Mr. Morris said. "He wouldn't have left you high and dry because he never would have fooled around with you or anyone else."

"But you did," Camilla said. "It was all fun and games until there were consequences."

"What was I supposed to do? Lurleen's father would have gotten out his shotgun again, and he wouldn't have just waved it around like he did when I got Lurleen in the family way."

"No, you would have told him it wasn't yours, that I'd been sleeping around like you tried to do to Lurleen. You know good and well you were the only one."

I couldn't be quite sure in the firelight, but I thought her lower lip trembled as she said it.

"I don't understand," I said, finally getting a word in edgewise. "How in the world did you expect to get away with passing Bentley off as P. B.'s son? The DNA test would show that he wasn't."

"Who said Bentley would take a DNA test?" Camilla scoffed.

I shook my head in confusion. "Then how did you plan on getting the inheritance? Mr. Nidden wouldn't let a penny of P. B.'s money go unless Bentley was entitled to it."

"I didn't necessarily need the inheritance," Camilla said. "I just needed money. And Bent offered me plenty of it, just to go away. I knew he would. He knows that money can solve just about anything." There was a note of bitterness in her voice.

"But at Bi-Lo, you sounded like you wouldn't take it," I said. "You said he wasn't offering you nearly enough."

"And he wasn't." Camilla tossed her head. "Not then, anyway. But I knew that if I held out long enough, he'd come around."

"That was something of a risk, wasn't it?" Grandma Ruth said. "The longer you and Bentley stayed in town, the more likely it was that someone would notice the resemblance. The Morris men do tend to favor one another in a distinctive way."

"We do, don't we?" Mr. Morris said, proudly treating us to his profile.

"It was a risk I was willing to take," Camilla said.

"It's not too late to do the right thing." My grandmother's voice was quiet, but firm.

Mr. Morris whirled around. "Just what do you mean by 'the right thing'? You cannot mean I ought to leave Lurleen and marry Millie. After Millie, I swore off other women. Lurleen and I have a good thing going now."

"Of course I don't expect you to leave Lurleen," Grandma Ruth said, with a dismissive wave of her hand. "That wasn't even the right thing back then." She fixed her gimlet eye on Camilla, who took a step back. "The right thing would have been to stay away from a married man, no matter how lightly he took his marriage vows."

"Then what?" Mr. Morris said. "What's this 'right thing' you keep talking about?"

"You both need to come clean," my grandmother told them. "As Father David says, confession is good for the soul."

"Are you crazy?" Mr. Morris burst out. "Things may be good between me and Lurleen now, but they sure won't be if I tell her about Millie and Bentley. Her daddy has passed, but he left her that shotgun in his will." He shuddered. Then his eyes narrowed as a crafty look crossed his face. "Tell you what, Miss Mary Ruth. I could see my way clear to upgrade your casket at no extra charge if you'll keep this just between us."

I cleared my throat to remind him that "us" included me.

He swallowed hard. I could almost see him adding up the figures in his head. His eyebrows shot up as he arrived at the total. Then he squared his shoulders and said, "You too, of course, Sarah Elizabeth."

"A mahogany casket?" I said. "How generous, Mr. Morris. I hardly know what to say."

"Well, maybe not mahogany," he said with a nervous tug at his shirt collar.

"Oh. Well," I said, "if you really want me to keep quiet—"

"Sarah!" Grandma Ruth said. "Nobody is accepting any bribes."

"I'm open to it," Camilla said, which earned her a quelling look from Grandma Ruth.

"You have to tell the truth," Grandma Ruth said again.

"Yeah," I said, finally getting my bearings in the moral morass. "You've hurt Mrs. Harrington and tried to cheat Mr. Bent. And I'm sure it's quite a shock to Bentley to find out P. B. isn't his father."

"Bentley already knows that," Camilla said. "I always let him think his father was Mr. Allen, who I married shortly before he was born. I let Mr. Allen think that too."

"You told your son to lie?" This boggled my mind, considering the firm and uncompromising hands that had raised me. Yes, I know I told Miss Charlotte she looked lovely when she really looked like something the cat dragged in, but that's different. Completely, bless-your-heart different.

"Well, of course," Camilla said. "I couldn't pass up an opportunity like that, especially since we were running low on funds. Mr. Kowalski's life insurance policy was not as generous as he had led me to believe."

As she said this, in my mind's eye I saw the words Gold Digger flash across her forehead. I felt sick at heart for Miss Charlotte, Bentley, Jimmy and Pearl Boudreaux, Malcolm Hartwell, and heck, maybe even Great-Uncle Hubert. Well, probably not G-Uncle, but definitely for all the people who had been hurt by Camilla Holtgrew's quest for someone rich to take care of her.

"Money isn't everything," Grandma Ruth said.

"That's easy for you to say," Camilla said. "You might be bedridden, but you've still got this nice house and people to take care of you. I'll bet you're leaving your son, his wife, and your granddaughter well-off when you go. Not only that, people listen to you in this town, because you have money."

My hands clenched and I could feel my face flush with anger. It was all I could do not to haul off and slap her, never mind her age. "We don't take care of Grandma Ruth because she's going to leave us anything!" I shouted. "I don't ever want her to leave us. I love her."

"Because she's rich." Camilla smirked.

"Because she loves me." I was close to tears. "All my life she's loved me. And people listen to her because . . . because . . ." The first thing that came to mind was "because she's bossy," but I caught myself in time to say, "Because she cares about people and she's usually right."

"Usually?" Grandma Ruth raised an eyebrow. "When have I been wrong?"

"I can't think of anything at the moment, Grandma, but nobody's perfect," I said as the tears spilled over.

Mama chose this moment to return to the parlor with dessert, Daddy and Bentley following in her wake. She took in the scene—me crying, Camilla red-faced, and Mr. Morris looking like he wished he was in a coffin somewhere—and handed everyone a brownie. Silence reigned as each of us savored my mother's rich and soothing remedy for pain and discord.

"The cat's out of the bag," Camilla informed Bentley as she reached for another brownie.

"Thank goodness," Bentley said with a sigh of relief. "Now I don't have to remember to answer to Bentley anymore."

"Your name's not Bentley?" I asked, even though my mouth was full.

"Nah," he said. "That was just to get the inheritance."

"What's your real name, then?" I asked after I swallowed.

"Duane. And I'd rather be plain old Duane than Bentley any day." He turned to his mother. "Being rich isn't all it's cracked up to be, Mama, no matter what you think."

I thought about the credit card debacle at Fontanelli's.

Mr. Morris, his third brownie halfway to his mouth, gave Bentley—I mean, Duane—a long and speculative look. "Duane, have you ever considered the funeral business?" He went so far as to sling a fatherly arm across Duane's shoulders.

"You mean, like drive the hearse and such?"

Mr. Morris flinched, as though remembering the present state of his vintage limousine. "Well, maybe not the hearse, not just yet anyway. We'll start you out at viewings and you can work your way up."

"Bentley—I mean Duane—has never had to work a day in his life." Camilla stepped between them. "And he's not going to start now, especially for you."

At that, the awkward, hangdog, stoop-shouldered man was transformed before my very eyes. Shoulders thrown back, Duane looked his father in the eye over his mother's head. "Not for lack of wanting to work, sir. I have dreamed of being a mechanic all my life, but Mama said no son of hers was going to get his hands dirty. I would be proud to someday dirty my hands in the engine of that limousine. Now I'm even sorrier I damaged it."

Camilla whirled around to confront her son. "Duane, I forbid you to work for that man."

Duane looked down at her with his mournful Morris eyes. "I'm sorry, Mama, but this is my chance to do what I really want to do, what maybe I was born to do. I'm going to take it."

Camilla blinked the way I do when Grandma Ruth gains the upper hand with me, then she stepped aside. "It's your funeral, Duane. But don't come crying to me when he lets you down."

"I won't let you down, son." Mr. Morris stuck out his hand. Father and son shook on it. "And don't you worry none about the limousine. We'll get it all taken care of, you and me."

It was such a touching moment that I didn't want to ruin it by asking him how Lurleen would take it. If he had any sense, he would hide the shotgun shells before he broke it to her. The main thing was, however, that Camilla and Bentley/Duane would no longer be able to torment Miss Charlotte. I could hardly wait to tell her.

I sidled up to Grandma Ruth's bed where she sat observing the effects of my mother's excellent baking skills.

"Let's call Miss Charlotte with the good news!" I said.

My grandmother glanced at the clock on her bedside table. "It's after ten p.m. It's too late to be calling anyone."

"But it's such good news," I said. "Surely she won't mind."

"People rarely call after nine p.m. with good news," Grandma Ruth reminded me. "What with this storm and the lights going out and all, she's liable to think someone's calling with news of an accident or something. No need to scare the daylights out of her. It'll keep till morning. Besides, it's time we were all in bed. All this excitement has worn me right out."

She didn't look worn out to me. In fact, she'd probably be up half the night gloating to herself over being right about P. B. Harrington all along and planning the phone call to Patti Sue Seiden that would send the truth zinging along the Raeburne's Ferry grapevine.

Mama took the hint, however, and we soon had our guests settled in the extra bedrooms upstairs with flashlights, towels, and toothbrushes.

"What a night," I said as I set a lantern on the counter in the bathroom as a nightlight.

"I'd do it all over again to get at the truth for Miss Charlotte," Mama said. "That Camilla Holtgrew really put her through it."

A few minutes later, I was in bed under several quilts, wide-eyed and staring at the ceiling. Unlike my grandmother, I was not gloating. I wasn't even rejoicing anymore. I was worrying. Although Camilla had certainly "put Miss Charlotte through it," it was P. B. who had started it all in the first place. Yes, we knew now that "Millie" was not Camilla Holtgrew, which would no doubt be a great relief to Miss Charlotte, but we still didn't know who Mr. Harrington's Millie really was. And I knew it wouldn't be long before Miss Charlotte's Phi Beta Kappa brain realized that.

CHAPTER 28

I AWOKE THE NEXT MORNING to the sound of water dripping. *More rain*, I thought, and burrowed deeper under the covers. When I opened my eyes a few minutes later, however, it was to a room flooded with sunshine. Outside my window, water dripped from the eaves and the tree limbs that had been encased in ice the night before. I could hear my mother singing in the kitchen and debated leaving the cozy warmth of my quilts to go downstairs to help her fix breakfast. With the power out, the best she could do was cold cereal, I reasoned. She didn't need me for that. As I drifted off again, the sweet strains of "Für Elise" floated from my cell phone. I groped for it on my nightstand and answered without even opening my eyes.

"'Lo?"

"It's time you were up, young lady," came my grandmother's voice over the phone. "Your mother is cooking breakfast for this crowd all by herself."

"She can't cook, Grandma. The power's out."

"The least you can do is set the table," she said. "Besides, I can't wait much longer to call Charlotte. I'm about to call her whether you're down here or not."

That wiped all thought of sleep or staying warm in a cold house right out of my brain. "All right, all right. I'll be down directly."

"Not too directly, dear," Grandma Ruth said. "Remember we have guests in the house."

I therefore took the time to dress (in as many layers as possible), fix my hair, and dab on a minimum of makeup. I set the table in record time and skidded across the front hall into the parlor in the warm woolly socks I almost never get to wear in Georgia.

As soon as I sat down in the wing chair by her bed, Grandma Ruth speed-dialed Miss Charlotte.

"Charlotte, dear, I have the most wonderful news," she began, then paused, listening.

"No, our power hasn't come back on yet. Dean heard on the radio that it will take a few days to repair all the power lines."

Another pause.

"Well, of course our radio isn't working, Charlotte. I'm talking about the one he has for emergencies. You wind it up with a crank, like in those World War II movies."

Daddy purely loves cranking up that radio—almost as much as he loves s'mores. I savored the memory of toasted marshmallows, chocolate, and graham crackers, then realized Grandma Ruth was talking again.

"That's neither here nor there, Charlotte. I have something much better to tell you."

At that moment, I heard the rumble of a truck in the street. I moved to the window, where I saw Duane and Mr. Morris waving down a tow truck. It pulled up to the curb in front of the limousine and backed carefully toward the front bumper.

Grandma Ruth put her hand over the mouthpiece of the phone. "What is it, Sarah?"

"Tow truck's here for the limousine."

Grandma Ruth nodded and said into the phone, "Charlotte, you'll never guess what happened last night. Fred Morris was over to show me casket samples—"

Grandma Ruth broke off again to listen. From where I stood at the window, I could faintly hear Miss Charlotte's soft voice, rising at the end of her question.

"Well, yes, I already have a funeral plan, but I was thinking of upgrading. Anyway, he got stranded here when the roads iced over. Then the power went out and a car crashed into his limousine, which was parked in front of the house."

Grandma Ruth listened a moment.

"Yes, it was that beautiful old one. He was fit to be tied. But you'll never guess who was in the car that rear-ended the limousine." She didn't wait for Miss Charlotte to guess, but simply plowed on. "Camilla Holtgrew and Bentley."

"Only his name's not really Bentley," I leaned forward and called into the phone.

"Hush. Let me tell it the way it happened." Grandma Ruth batted me away. "As I was saying," she continued, and didn't stop until the whole story had been told. "So now you can rest easy, Charlotte. I never believed it for a minute, as you may recall."

At the sound of shouting from in front of the house, I left Grandma Ruth and Miss Charlotte to their rejoicing and stepped over to the window. Roy from over at the gas station had the limousine attached to the winch, front wheels up in the air, back wheels on the street. I expected him to pull away to Mike's Auto Repair at any moment, but there seemed to be some trouble on the back end of things. Roy, Duane, and Mr. Morris were gathered around the back bumper. Mr. Morris was shouting and waving his arms.

On closer inspection, I could see what the problem was. Camilla's sedan had gotten more than cozy with the limousine's back bumper. The cars were locked together, like the first kiss of a couple of middle schoolers with braces. After a lot of pointing and shouting between Roy and Mr. Morris, Duane intervened, speaking earnestly. Mr. Morris subsided and stepped back. Roy secured the steering wheel on the sedan, climbed into his tow truck, and drove slowly and carefully down the street, towing both cars. I held my breath when he got to the corner, but he managed to make the turn.

When I turned back to Grandma Ruth, she had finished sharing the good news with Miss Charlotte and had moved on to call Patti Sue Seiden. Soon everyone in Raeburne's Ferry would have something else to think about besides the power outage and tree limbs that had fallen under the weight of the ice.

It didn't take long for the news to reach Malcolm Hartwell, which was surprising. I never took him for someone who listened to gossip. Nevertheless, not much more than an hour after Grandma Ruth let Patti Sue loose in the rumor mill, he appeared at our front door, looking decidedly spiffy in a well-cut wool coat and Burberry scarf. He tipped his hat to me when I answered the doorbell.

"Good morning, Sarah. I've come to see if I can be of service to Miss Camilla. I understand she's having car trouble."

I swallowed my surprise and remembered my manners. "Please come in, Mr. Hartwell. I'll see if she's—" I started to say "dressed," as Camilla had come down to breakfast wrapped in a quilt, but once again remembered my manners, finishing the sentence with, "receiving visitors." I ushered him into the parlor, where Grandma Ruth greeted him warmly.

I hurried off to the kitchen to inform "Miss Camilla" that she had a gentleman caller in the parlor.

"Who is it?" Camilla wanted to know.

"Mr. Hartwell," I said.

"The janitor?" I saw her lip start to curl.

"It's true that he still cleans right alongside his employees," my mother said. "Mainly in a supervisory capacity, though, wouldn't you say, Sarah?"

"Oh yes." I nodded. "And he has quite a lot of employees."

Camilla looked down in dismay at the quilt she was wrapped in, which, while quite lovely, was not the proper attire for the beginning of a relationship. Further on down the road it would be entirely appropriate . . . if Mr. Hartwell succeeded in making his dream come true.

"Come upstairs, Mrs. Kowalski, and we'll find you something nice to wear," Mama said, understanding the situation perfectly. "Sarah, please offer our guest some light refreshment while he waits."

Daddy had heated water over the fire in the parlor and poured it into every available thermos. I was able to offer Mr. Hartwell his choice of tea, hot chocolate, and even coffee. (Mama had dug her French press out of the back of a cupboard.) He and my grandmother were enjoying a lively conversation when I came back with a tray laden with hot chocolate, marshmallows, and oatmeal raisin cookies.

"There are so many lines down," Mr. Hartwell was saying as I set the tray down. "The city thinks it will be a couple of days before everyone gets their power back. Will y'all be all right here?"

"We have plenty of food and firewood," Grandma Ruth told him. "My son does love to rise to the occasion. He's actually in his element. But what about you? This can't be good for business. Your people can't clean without lights or power for the vacuum cleaners."

"I've already arranged for us to clean up the debris at all our offices. The trash company will come by with trucks for the fallen branches and such, but somebody has to pile them at the curb. We won't be losing any money, plus we'll be helping get things back to normal. I've already got a crew clearing the parking lot at Crawford's, Sarah. It's a good thing there were no cars parked there last night. You know that big tree over by the northwest corner of the lot?"

"I always try to get to work early in the summer so I can park in its shade," I said.

"Well, I'm glad you weren't parked there last night, working late. That tree toppled right over. It would have flattened your little Civic like a pancake. My people are cutting it up with chain saws."

I sighed. I would miss that tree come July. At least my car was undamaged, unlike Camilla's.

Speak of the devil, Camilla appeared in the doorway of the parlor at that very moment, a vision of loveliness.

As I'm sure you can imagine, my mother dresses more conservatively than Camilla. I'm not saying Mama is frumpy. She stopped wearing skirts and cardigans when she retired. Her style now is classic and elegant. Framed in the parlor doorway, Camilla Holtgrew Allen Smith Kowalski looked classic and elegant too. Mama's red silk blouse brought out the color in Camilla's cheeks better than any blusher. The slim black slacks did more for her legs than her short skirts or stilettos ever had, although her red heels now struck exactly the right note in the outfit.

At the sight of her, Mr. Hartwell hurried to set down his cup and rise from his chair. "Miss Camilla, you are even lovelier than I remember." He made her a courtly bow.

"Why, Mr. Hartwell, how you flatter me." Her eyelashes fluttered becomingly, unencumbered with mascara, I noted.

"It's no more than the truth. Please, sit down," he said as he offered her his chair.

I missed what came next because Grandma Ruth sent me for more tea and cookies.

"I wouldn't want to take you away from your work," Camilla was saying when I returned. "I understand you have a great many employees to supervise."

"They're well-trained," Mr. Hartwell said. "They can carry on without me while I take care of you."

"I could use a lift back to my home in Dewey Creek," Camilla said.

"Consider it done," Mr. Hartwell said. "And anything else you need. Do you have enough food until the power comes back on? Do you need me to bring in firewood, build a fire?"

"That won't be necessary," my father said as he came in with another log for our own fire. "They're just far enough south that they didn't get the ice in Dewey Creek."

Mr. Hartwell's face fell, but brightened considerably when Camilla reached over and squeezed his hand.

"It is so kind of you to offer to help. I accept." She turned wide, damsel-in-distress eyes on him. If he weren't already a goner, that look alone would have done him in.

"The offer extends to Bentley too, of course," Mr. Hartwell said as he glanced out the window at Duane and Mr. Morris, who were pouring rock salt on the front steps and the sidewalk.

Camilla had the grace to drop her eyes.

"You'll probably hear it sooner or later," she said so softly we all had to lean close enough to catch a whiff of my mother's Chanel No. 5. "His name's not Bentley, and he's not P. B.'s son."

Mr. Hartwell laid his hand over hers. "I know. I've always known."

She looked up then, her eyes wide and her mouth forming the word *How?*

I held my breath, willing Mr. Hartwell to forget that Grandma Ruth and I were listening.

"I was there that night," he said. "The night you told him you were pregnant with his child."

"What? How? I didn't see you." Camilla looked puzzled and confused.

"No, you didn't," Mr. Hartwell said, his tone a bit wistful. "Most people didn't see me in those days. I was in the background, just the janitor. I didn't mean to eavesdrop, but, as you may recall, you were both angry. I was clear across the funeral home, cleaning the men's restroom, but I heard the whole thing."

Camilla's eyes filled with tears. "You heard that?" she whispered.

"Every word," Mr. Hartwell said. "I wanted to punch Fred Morris in the nose, not that it would have done any good. He was a piece of work back then. I don't know what you saw in him."

I did, but nobody was asking me.

Camilla shrugged helplessly and let a tear trickle down her cheek.

"He didn't deserve you, anyway." Mr. Hartwell stood and offered Camilla his hand. "Now let's get you home."

Moments later, Camilla descended our front steps, her hand tucked securely into Mr. Hartwell's elbow as he took great care to steer her around the icy patches. Duane opted to stay, as he and Mr. Morris had plans to salt the sidewalks over at the funeral home.

"I'll run him home later," Mr. Morris told Camilla.

I watched from the parlor window as Mr. Hartwell settled Camilla Holtgrew in the front seat of his Mercedes.

"I'm glad to see the back of her," I said with relief. "Good riddance."

"I doubt that Raeburne's Ferry is rid of her," my grandmother said. "But I don't think she'll be any more trouble, at least not to Charlotte."

CHAPTER 29

THE WEEKS AFTER THE GREAT Ice Storm were full and busy for many of us in Raeburne's Ferry. For some, they were downright eventful.

Take Lurleen Morris, for example. Her husband presented her with a full-grown son—his son, but not hers. Rumor has it that her first inclination was to reach for the shotgun she'd kept lovingly oiled ever since her father's death. Rumor also has it that it was Duane who won her over. He made himself so useful over at the funeral home that Lurleen finally had time to join the garden club and have lunch with the gardening ladies once a week at the Magnolia. In addition, now that he had yet another son, Fred had left off pressuring Greg's wife to "try for a boy," when everyone but Fred was perfectly happy with the sweet and adorable little girls. Duane moved from Dewey Creek into an apartment a few blocks from the funeral home and set about working his way up to taking care of the Morris funeral fleet. Mike of Mike's Auto Repair agreed to teach him in exchange for free labor on the weekends.

Mr. Hartwell was busy, too, wooing his dream girl, Camilla Holtgrew. They were seen at Fontanelli's several times a week. The anticipation of a proposal was high among the staff. Every time Mr. Hartwell made a reservation, the pastry chef made sure there was a little cake ready for the occasion. The week that Mr. Hartwell bought the ring, he came by the homeplace to show it to Grandma Ruth and me.

"It's all because of you," he told us as he opened the little green box from Windsor's to reveal an exquisite ring. The diamond, however, was not as big as I'd thought it would be.

"She'll love it." Mr. Hartwell beamed.

"Um . . ." I stalled. "Did she pick it out?"

"Of course not," he said. "I want to surprise her."

"She'll be surprised all right," I couldn't help saying.

"Sarah!" Grandma Ruth said. "A lady does not notice or comment on the, er, the particulars of an engagement ring—her own or anyone else's. Sarah knows better, Malcolm. I do apologize. It's a beautiful ring. I'm sure she'll be quite pleased with it."

"No offense taken, I assure you." Mr. Hartwell turned to me. "I'm aware that the wagging tongues of Raeburne's Ferry are saying that Miss Camilla is a gold digger and I'm another fool in a long line of sugar daddies."

I nodded. There was no denying that. I'd heard it at the Blue Moon, Bi-Lo, and the coffee hour at St. Alban's.

"If that were true, I'd be buying Miss Camilla the biggest diamond I could afford. I'd do it, too, if that was what it took for her to marry me. That's not what she really wants, though."

You could have fooled me. She sure was fooling him, in my opinion.

"What does Camilla really want?" Grandma Ruth sent a quelling look my way.

"Way back in high school, I saw how hard she worked to get in with the snooty girls. They ignored her, no matter how hard she tried. They couldn't see her for who she really was, just because she lived in the trailer park and couldn't shop at Haviland's."

"What did you see that they didn't?" Grandma Ruth asked.

Mr. Hartwell gazed mistily at the top of Grandma Ruth's bookcase as he remembered. "A beautiful girl," he said. "She was so beautiful that those other girls knew they wouldn't look half as pretty next to her, so they kept her far away. Her heart was simple and pure then. I could see that she really believed that if she dressed like them, they'd let her in. She didn't start out as a gold digger. She simply thought money was the key to getting what she really wanted."

"What was it that she really wanted?" Mr. Hartwell had me wondering now.

"To belong. To her, belonging meant being a part of that group of pretty, happy, laughing girls. Instead, they ignored her to her face and laughed at her behind her back. It broke her sweet heart."

I shook my head. The man was a goner. Even so, there was a tiny flutter in my own heart at the thought of a man being so gone on me. A good man, that is, like Malcom Hartwell.

Or Preston Harrington.

I blinked and shook that idea right out of my head.

"There's something else, however, that she's always wanted more than money, more than being friends with the rich girls. She's tried so hard to fit into that world, when what she really wants, deep down, is to be loved for herself, never mind how she looks or what she has or doesn't have. And I love her that way," he said.

Like I said, he was a goner. I suppose only time will tell if his Miss Camilla wants Mr. Hartwell for his love and not his money. I hope he's right, for both their sakes.

The busiest people, though, were Grandma Ruth and Miss Charlotte. They plotted and schemed, prayed, and crunched numbers (actually, I crunched the numbers; Grandma Ruth grudgingly admitted a use for "that career of mine") to make the after-school program a reality. It was still tax season, and I was up to my eyeballs in work, but I didn't mind. The both of them were so tickled with their plans that laughter sparkled and splashed like a waterfall from the parlor out into the hall. Miss Charlotte was enjoying herself too much to bother about the question that had remained unanswered after we'd sorted out who the father of Camilla's son really was.

The question still rankled me on a regular basis. I believed Miss Charlotte when she said her husband had been "all there" for those few moments before he passed. I believed her when she said he had winked at her right after he said it too. I didn't think anyone would imagine something like that. So what was it all about? Who was Millie? Sometimes the question kept me awake at night. I would stare at the ceiling and picture that cranky old man looking into Miss Charlotte's eyes in the firelight, delivering his news with that wink. And once, I woke up with a start and a gasp, because I'd been dreaming about it, only the face had not been that of an old and grumpy man, but Preston, with those happy crinkles around his eyes.

One afternoon along toward the end of March, I served tea and snickerdoodles to Grandma Ruth and Miss Charlotte during one of their planning sessions.

"These would be lovely to have at the Bridge when it opens," Miss Charlotte commented as she nibbled on a cookie. "Preston is especially fond of them as well." She sent a significant look my way.

The plans to make Grandma Ruth and Miss Charlotte's brainchild a reality were well underway. Miss Charlotte had already bought an abandoned building downtown within walking distance of Hume Elementary and Prescott Middle School. Renovations would begin in a few weeks to turn it into a combination day-care center, after-school program, and senior center. They envisioned young and old enriching each other's lives, bridging the generation gap—hence the name. They were also building another kind of bridge to the younger generation—Grandma Ruth had recently acquired a laptop computer. It was surprising how quickly she caught on. Miss Charlotte bought herself a laptop too. With some help from Preston, Miss Charlotte was becoming adept at finding information.

I looked over Miss Charlotte's shoulder to see that the two friends were pricing fifteen-passenger vans for the center's use.

"We'll need at least two, don't you think, Mary Ruth?"

"So, are you just about broke yet, Miss Charlotte?" I said with a grin, mostly to distract her from trying to pair me up with Preston.

Miss Charlotte, is, however, a woman on a mission to better her town and the lives of the people in it whom she loves.

"Sarah Elizabeth, I've been thinking about how P. B. felt about Harvard going coed. He regretted not having a daughter to send, but I could send you! You scored so high on your CPA exam"—here she and my grandmother exchanged proud glances—"that I'm sure Harvard would jump at the chance to have you in their MBA program. And Preston would be there too, at law school, so you could keep seeing him," she said brightly.

I could feel my face flushing.

It had been one date, on the Friday after the ice storm. I'd almost forgotten that Preston had invited me to dinner at Fontanelli's, what with all the excitement. Preston, Grandma Ruth, and Miss Charlotte, however, had not. Miss Charlotte loaned me her sapphire earrings and Grandma Ruth insisted I wear the black peep-toe pumps. She advised against the Audrey Hepburn dress, as I'd worn that the last time I'd dined at Fontanelli's. She finally settled on a midnight-blue number with a sweetheart neckline. Daddy answered the door when Preston called for me and ushered him into the front parlor to visit with Grandma Ruth while he waited. After a suitable interval, Mama called from the top of the stairs, "Here she is!" (said as if I were Miss America).

I heard Preston excuse himself to Grandma Ruth, and then he appeared in the parlor doorway to watch me descend the staircase. The way he looked at me almost made my knees buckle. His eyes, those sunny blue eyes, shone like a day in June . . . with just a hint of July heat. I grabbed the banister to steady myself and managed to get down to the front hall, where Preston helped me into my wrap. And then we were off in the Rolls, with nothing more from Daddy than his blessing and Mama telling us to have a good time.

And we did have a good time. I'd been tongue-tied around handsome Preston Harrington when we were in high school, but he turned out to be easy to talk with. He wanted to know about my career and eagerly shared his dreams of practicing law. Before I knew it, it was time to order dessert.

"Are you sure you won't have the baked Alaska? I won't tell your mama," he said with a wink.

I shook my head. "She's trained me too well. I'll have the cannoli."

We lingered over coffee (caramel macchiato for me) and dessert, both of us unwilling to call it a night. The Fontanellis seemed in no hurry to free up the table either.

"I suppose we should go," Preston finally said. "I've heard about your daddy."

"I don't have a curfew anymore," I told him. "I'm twenty-four, for crying out loud."

"Still," he said. "They'll be waiting up for you. You mean a great deal to them."

It was too soon for him to say, "And you mean a great deal to me," but those words hung in the air, unspoken, nonetheless.

When he walked me to the door, I held out my hand.

"Rule number five," I said, feeling my face get hot. "No kiss on the first date."

He took my hand in both of his and looked down into my eyes. "Ah, something to look forward to."

I had gone straight upstairs, despite Grandma Ruth's summons from the parlor. I had kicked off my shoes and curled up in the window seat, troubled thoughts tumbling through my mind. Yes, I'd had a wonderful time, but I didn't dare give my heart to a Harrington until I knew who Millie was.

But while I was proceeding cautiously, it was clear that Miss Charlotte and Grandma Ruth were making plans to marry off their grandchildren as soon as possible. It was beyond embarrassing. Unchecked, these relentless matchmakers would soon be planning our wedding for us.

"As I said, Miss Charlotte"—I was desperate to distract her from her vision of Preston and me at Harvard together—"aren't you broke yet?"

Miss Charlotte laughed and her blue eyes shone. "Not yet, my dear. After all, P. B. left me much more than the million dollars he always promised me." Her chuckle was rich, delighted, throaty. I suddenly wished P. B. could have been there to hear it.

"Charlotte!" My grandmother gasped. "That's it!"

"What's it?" Miss Charlotte and I asked in unison.

"What P. B. said before he passed. It wasn't 'I loved you more than Millie.' There never was any Millie at all."

"No Millie? Are you sure?" Miss Charlotte asked.

"Yes." Grandma Ruth nodded. "By your own account, you were sleeping so soundly that P. B. had a hard time waking you up. You were still waking up when he spoke to you."

"Are you saying I dreamed it, Mary Ruth? I know what I saw, and I know what he said." Miss Charlotte set her jaw.

"Of course you weren't dreaming, but you were still waking up when he said it," Grandma Ruth said. "You misunderstood him, dear. He didn't say 'I loved you more than Millie.' And Camilla's version—'I left you more than Millie'—that wasn't right either, though she was closer to the truth than we ever dreamed."

I couldn't stand it anymore. My grandmother does like to string out a story so. "Then what *did* he say, for crying out loud!"

"No need to raise your voice, Sarah Elizabeth," she said, eyes flashing.

I mustered up my best how-to-speak-to-your-elders manners. "Please, Grandma Ruth, what did Mr. Harrington really say?"

She favored me with an approving glance before she turned to address her friend. "He didn't say 'loved,' Charlotte. He did say 'left.' But he didn't say 'more than Millie.' It was 'more than a million.' P. B.'s dying words to you were 'I left you more than a million.'"

A shocked silence filled the room as the truth sank in. It all made sense now. P. B. Harrington had loved his wife, well and truly, their whole married life and beyond. He had winked that broad, deliberate, delighted wink because he was happy to give her one last, loving surprise.

"'I left you more than a million,'" Miss Charlotte said. Her eyes grew large, and she swallowed hard. "'I left you more than a million.' Oh my goodness, Mary Ruth, I believe you're right."

She and Grandma Ruth began to laugh. They laughed until their faces were shiny with tears. They laughed deep belly laughs and high, hysterical giggles, completely overcome. I didn't join in the laughter, but I could feel the corners of my mouth turning up, as though something that had been weighing them down had melted away. And if the apple truly didn't fall far from the tree, then my mind and heart could rest easy about Preston too. Faithfulness ran in the family after all.

"Thank you, Mary Ruth," Miss Charlotte gasped when she finally caught her breath. "I don't know how I could ever have doubted that good man."

In that moment, I knew that much of the anguish of recent months had been erased. Not all of it, of course. Whenever my grandmother speaks of Grandpa Andy, I realize that mourning for a much-loved man doesn't ever really end. Now, however, Miss Charlotte knew she was mourning for the man who loved her, not the man who loved her and Millie. Her love story had been returned to her, untarnished and intact. And now, perhaps, mine could begin.

"I told you so," Grandma Ruth looked first at Miss Charlotte, and then, quite pointedly, at me. "God really is too big."

That night I curled up in the window seat once again, my hands wrapped around another calming mug of hot chocolate. As I gazed out over the rooftops of Raeburne's Ferry, I relived the hilarious joy of that afternoon. It had been like a gift straight from heaven. I hadn't laughed then, and I didn't laugh now. I felt a swelling in my chest, a joy so sharp and sudden that tears pricked my eyes and flowed unchecked down my face.

It was all too much—the death and resurrection of Miss Charlotte's love story, the final burial of my own with Jake, the fierce and loving circle of aunties telling me not to settle, Preston's eyes crinkling down at me, so blue and clear. Dreams had died with Jake's betrayal, but I caught my breath as I glimpsed the reality that was taking their place.

My tears fell faster. God was indeed too big—too big for me ever to have imagined what he had in store for me.

Acknowledgments

FIRST OF ALL, THANK YOU to Patricia Sprinkle. A busy novelist herself, she nevertheless took the time to read my early efforts at bringing Grandma Ruth and my love of the South to life—and encouraged me to keep at it.

And thank you to my agent, Ali Herring of Spencerhill Associates. I'm delighted that the book that moved her to offer me representation is going out into the world. I'm grateful she took a chance on Grandma Ruth and me. I'm beyond proud to be one of her Ali-ens!

To the team of editors (Rachel Overton, Rachel Kirsch, and Julie Davis) who took on the task of polishing this book so it glows like Miss Charlotte's wedding silver, thank you for your attention to detail.

Many, many thanks to all the people at Kregel Publications who work hard behind the scenes to make sure each book they publish is the best it can be.

I am thankful to all the Southerners who welcomed me with true Southern hospitality while I lived in Georgia. You refined my manners; taught me to slow down, pay attention, and chat in the checkout line; and introduced me to that divine sandwich filling, pimento cheese. I live in Texas now, but the soft, rounded edges of your voices still wrap around my heart like a humid summer morning in Georgia.

And thank you, Pam Stoker, for your influence on the mac and cheese recipe. Switching the milk to half-and-half was the tweak it needed.

As I wrote about love stories—Miss Charlotte and P. B.'s, Sarah and Jake's, and the one in the making for Sarah and Preston—my heart welled up in gratitude for my own story with my husband of forty-three years, Skip Mondragón. All my love for all my days, dear one.

The best for last—thanks be to God, Creator of all things visible and invisible, including the invisible ideas of stories, and the books they become. Thank you for letting me create with you.

Grandma Ruth's Signature
Funeral Macaroni and Cheese

Serves 8.

8 oz (2 c) elbow macaroni, uncooked
2 c half-and-half
2 T butter or margarine (butter is best!)
2 T all-purpose flour
½ t salt (scant)
¼ t black pepper
2 c shredded mild cheddar cheese, divided

Preheat oven to 400 degrees Fahrenheit.

Follow package directions to cook the macaroni. Drain and set aside.

Microwave half-and-half on High for 90 seconds.

Melt butter (or margarine) in a large skillet over medium-low heat, then whisk in flour until smooth. Cook, whisking constantly, for 1 minute.

Gradually whisk in the warm half-and-half and cook, whisking constantly, for 5 minutes or until thickened.

Whisk in the salt, black pepper, and 1 cup of the cheese until smooth, then stir in the macaroni.

Spoon into a lightly greased 2-quart baking dish (ours is a Corning-Ware French White casserole dish), top with remaining cheese, and bake uncovered for 20 minutes or until golden and bubbly.

Sharon Mondragón's Purls and Prayers duology is full of humor and heart!

Book 1

Book 2

Mondragón's debut first book is warm and delightful, full of real laughter, grief, and personality. It beautifully illustrates the women across generations caring for others and showing them God's lovehaving the power to reach people for Christ. Book two features characters who wrestle with the loneliness of being the forgotten spouse of a dementia patient. Moving past fear and into love and compassion a community who cares can make all the difference.

KREGEL
PUBLICATIONS